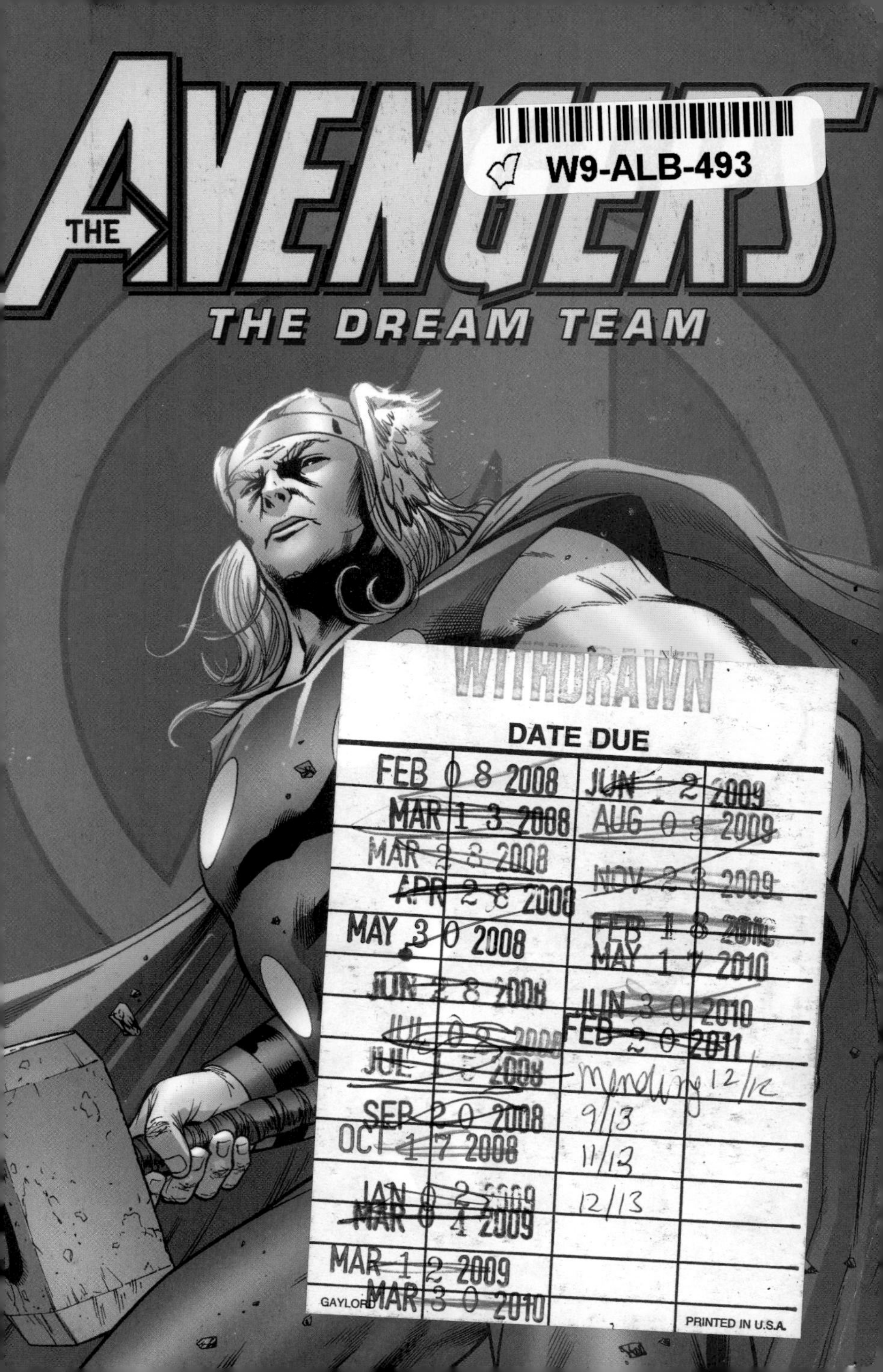
THE AVENGERS
THE DREAM TEAM

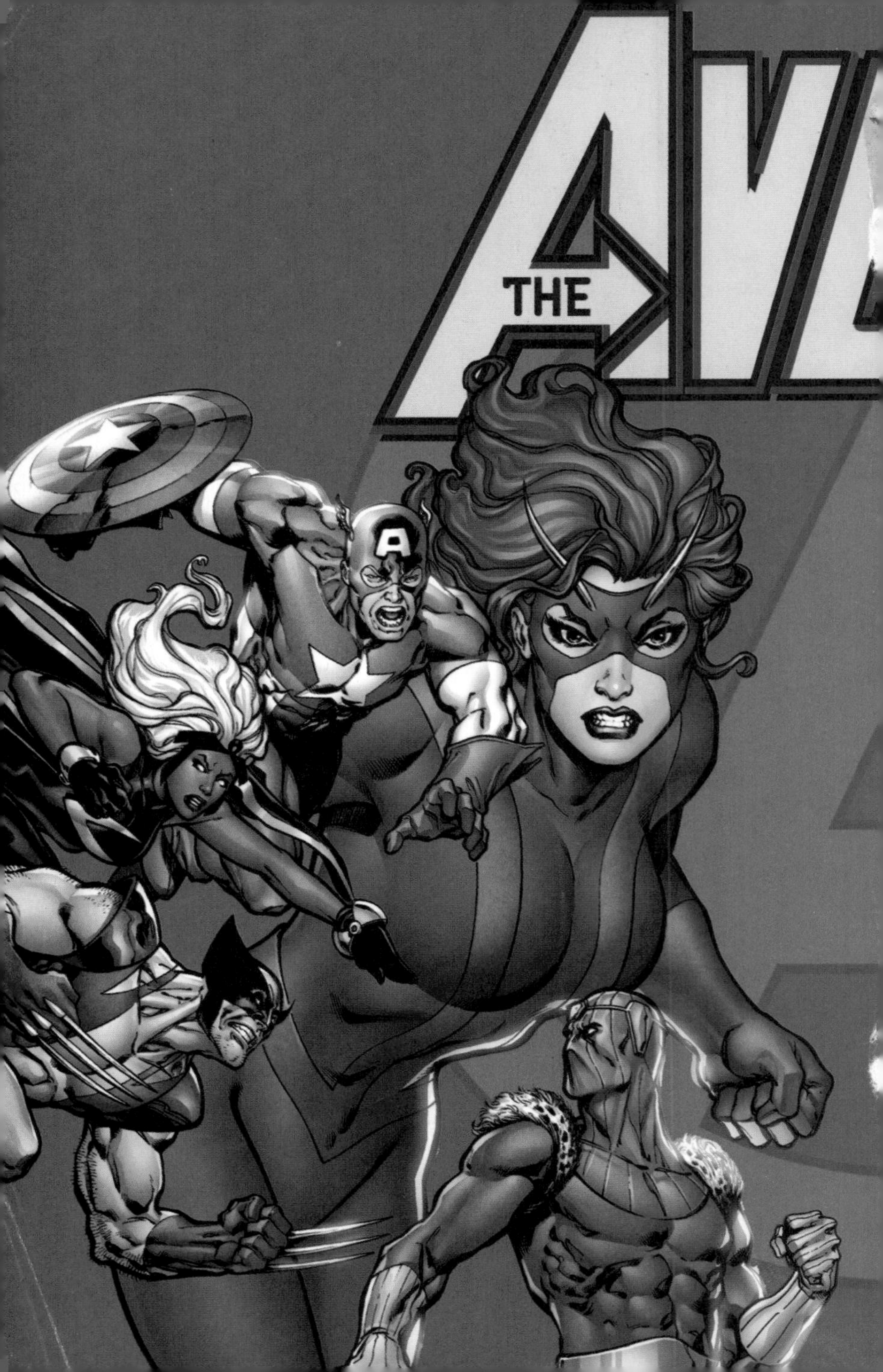
THE
AV

ENGERS

THE DREAM TEAM

Writer: **Jeff Parker**
Pencils: **Leonard Kirk**
with Cafu (Issue #15)

Inks: **Terry Pallot**
Colors: **Val Staples**
Letters: **Dave Sharpe**
Cover Art: **Kirk, Pallot, Sotomayor & Staples**
Assistant Editor: **Nathan Cosby**
Editor: **Mark Paniccia**

Captain America created by Joe Simon & Jack Kirby

Collection Editor: **Jennifer Grünwald**
Assistant Editors: **Cory Levine & John Denning**
Associate Editor: **Mark D. Beazley**
Senior Editor, Special Projects: **Jeff Youngquist**
Senior Vice President of Sales: **David Gabriel**
Vice President of Creative: **Tom Marvelli**

Editor in Chief: **Joe Quesada**
Publisher: **Dan Buckley**

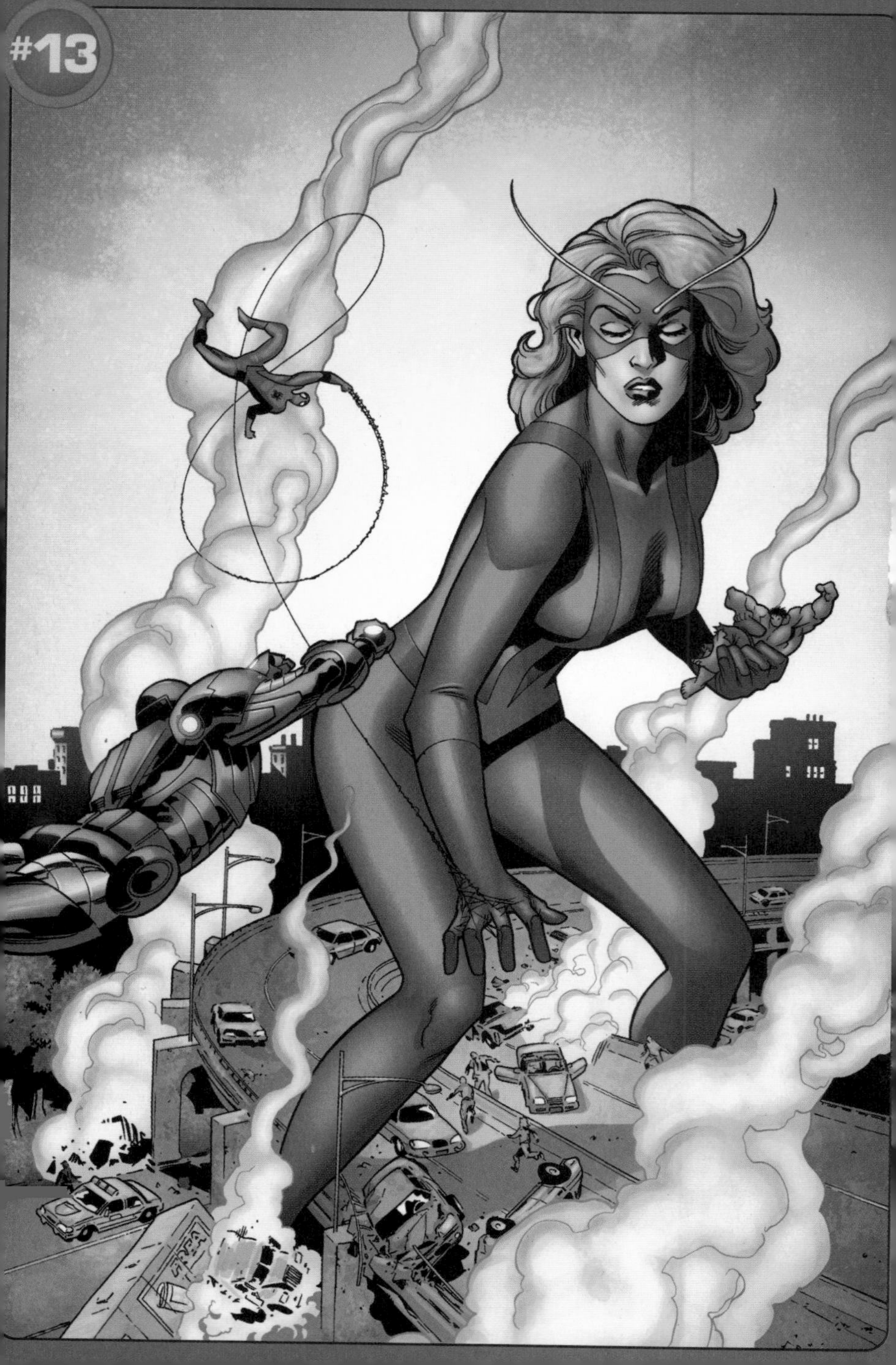
#13

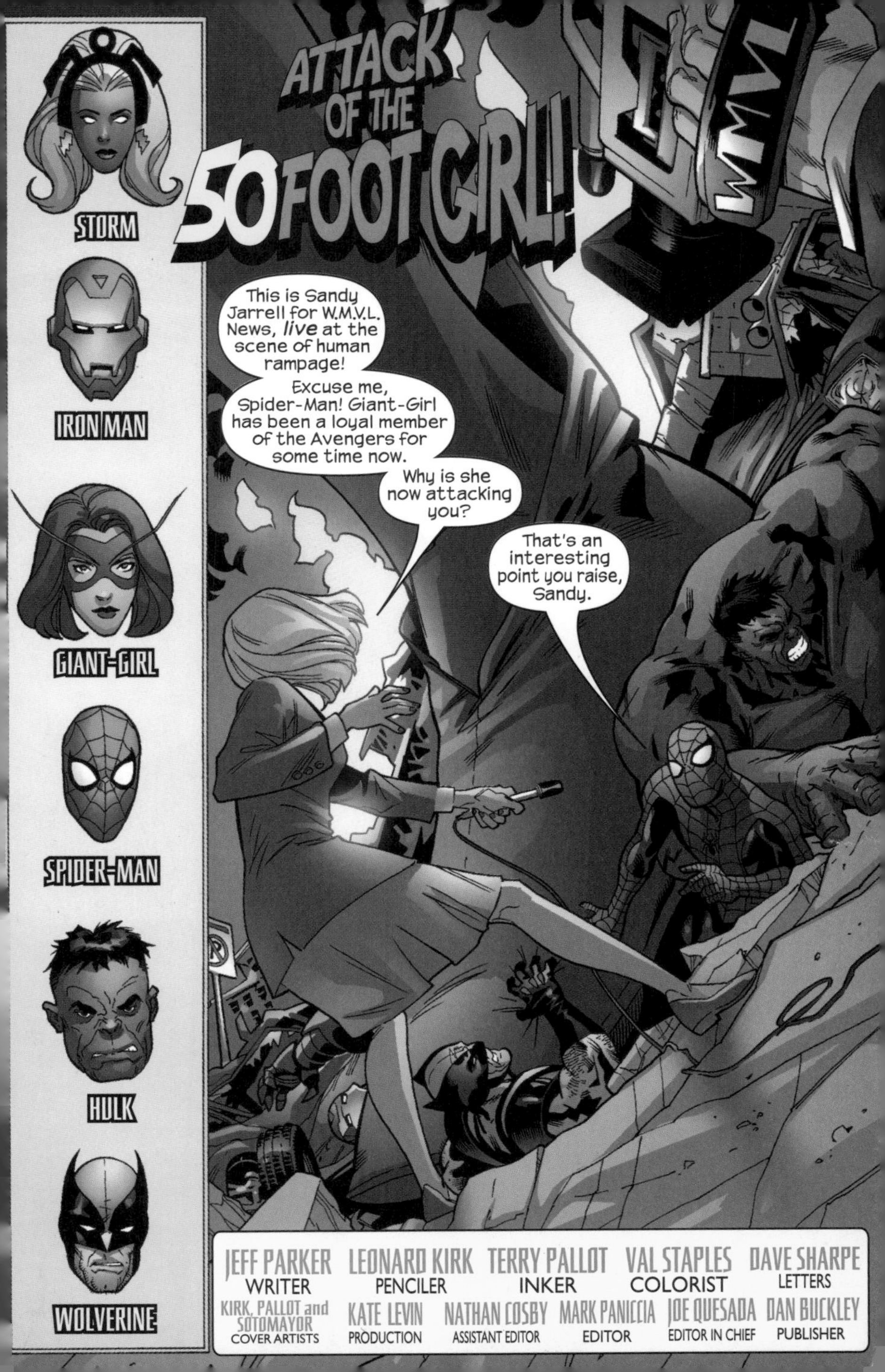
STORM
IRON MAN
GIANT-GIRL
SPIDER-MAN
HULK
WOLVERINE
ATTACK OF THE 50 FOOT GIRL!
WMVL
This is Sandy Jarrell for W.M.V.L. News, *live* at the scene of human rampage!
Excuse me, Spider-Man! Giant-Girl has been a loyal member of the Avengers for some time now.
Why is she now attacking you?
That's an interesting point you raise, Sandy.
JEFF PARKER WRITER
LEONARD KIRK PENCILER
TERRY PALLOT INKER
VAL STAPLES COLORIST
DAVE SHARPE LETTERS
KIRK, PALLOT and SOTOMAYOR COVER ARTISTS
KATE LEVIN PRODUCTION
NATHAN COSBY ASSISTANT EDITOR
MARK PANICCIA EDITOR
JOE QUESADA EDITOR IN CHIEF
DAN BUCKLEY PUBLISHER

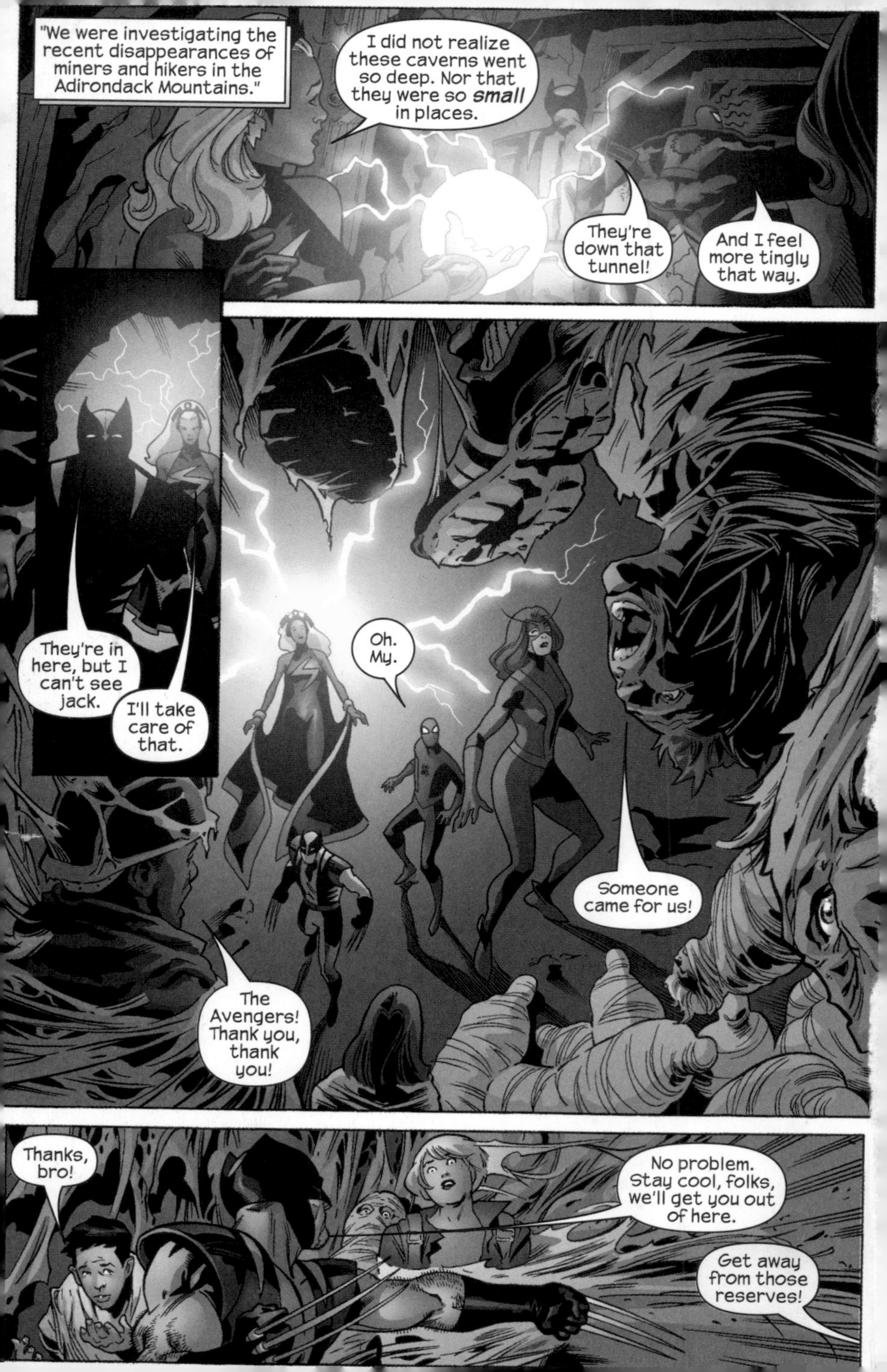

"We were investigating the recent disappearances of miners and hikers in the Adirondack Mountains."
I did not realize these caverns went so deep. Nor that they were so *small* in places.
They're down that tunnel!
And I feel more tingly that way.
They're in here, but I can't see jack.
I'll take care of that.
Oh. My.
Someone came for us!
The Avengers! Thank you, thank you!
Thanks, bro!
No problem. Stay cool, folks, we'll get you out of here.
Get away from those reserves!

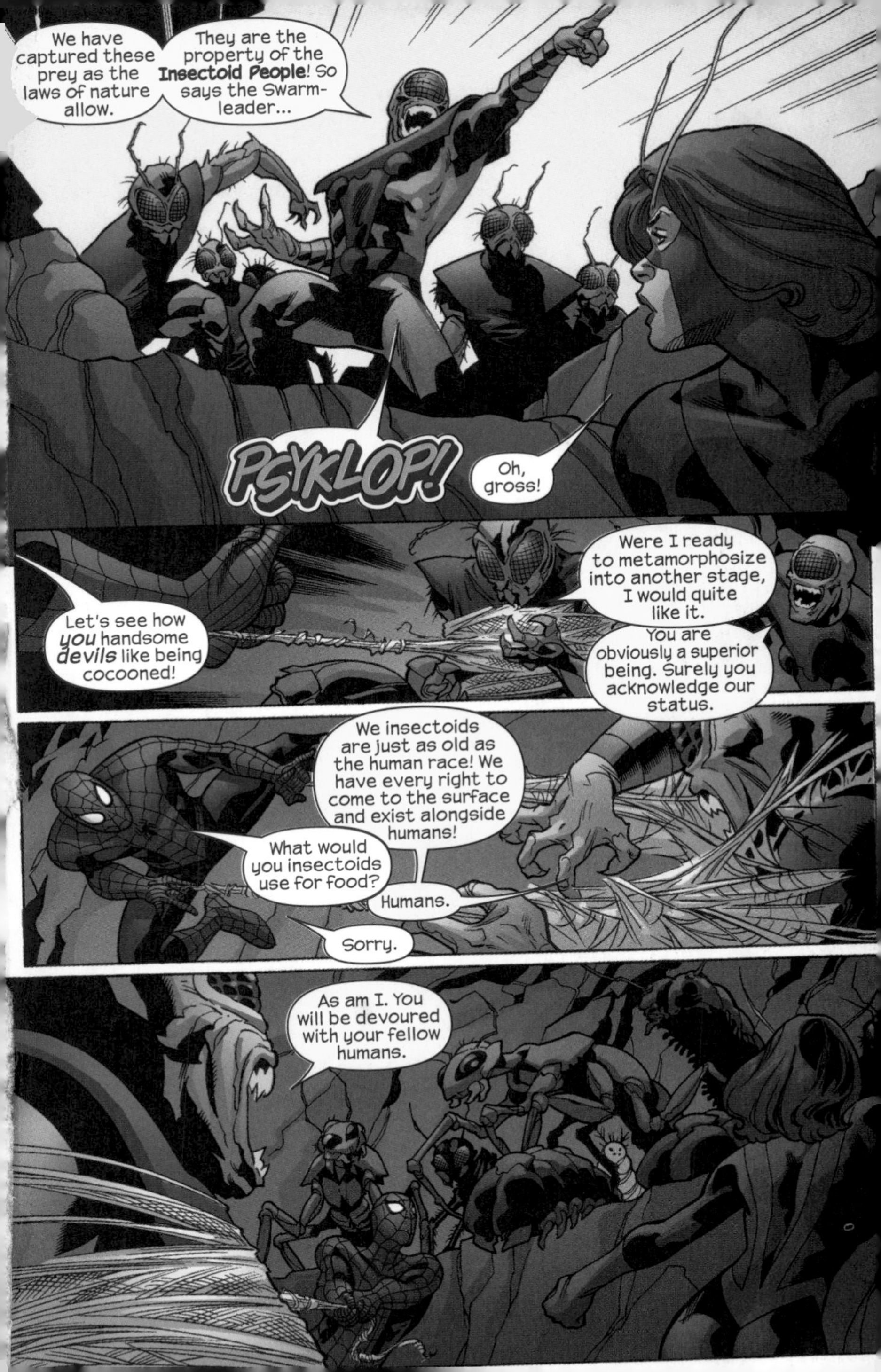
We have captured these prey as the laws of nature allow.
They are the property of the Insectoid People! So says the Swarm-leader...
PSYKLOP!
Oh, gross!
Let's see how you handsome devils like being cocooned!
Were I ready to metamorphosize into another stage, I would quite like it.
You are obviously a superior being. Surely you acknowledge our status.
We insectoids are just as old as the human race! We have every right to come to the surface and exist alongside humans!
What would you insectoids use for food?
Humans.
Sorry.
As am I. You will be devoured with your fellow humans.

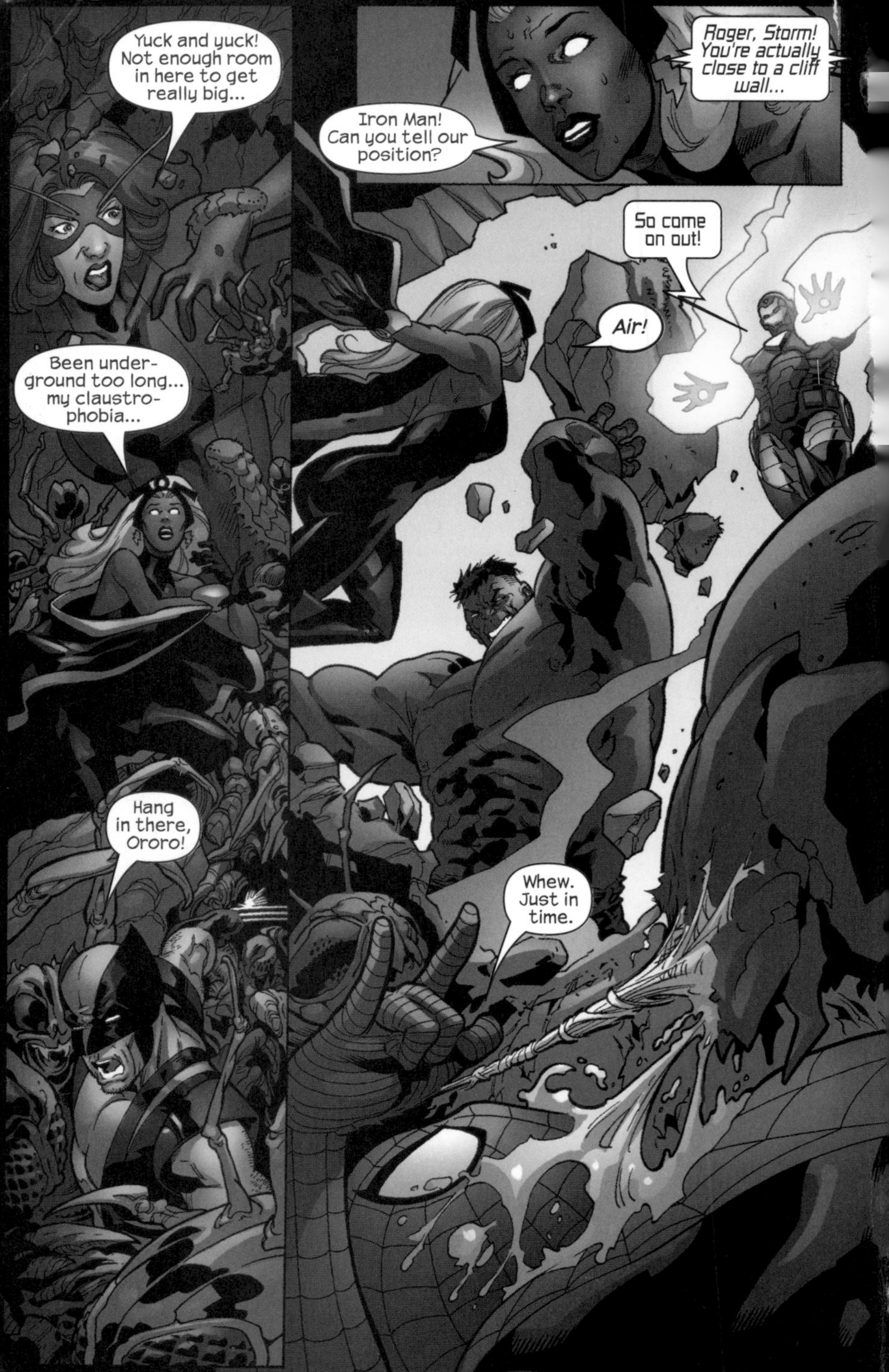
Yuck and yuck! Not enough room in here to get really big...
Been under-ground too long... my claustro-phobia...
Hang in there, Ororo!
Iron Man! Can you tell our position?
Roger, Storm! You're actually close to a cliff wall...
So come on out!
Air!
Whew. Just in time.

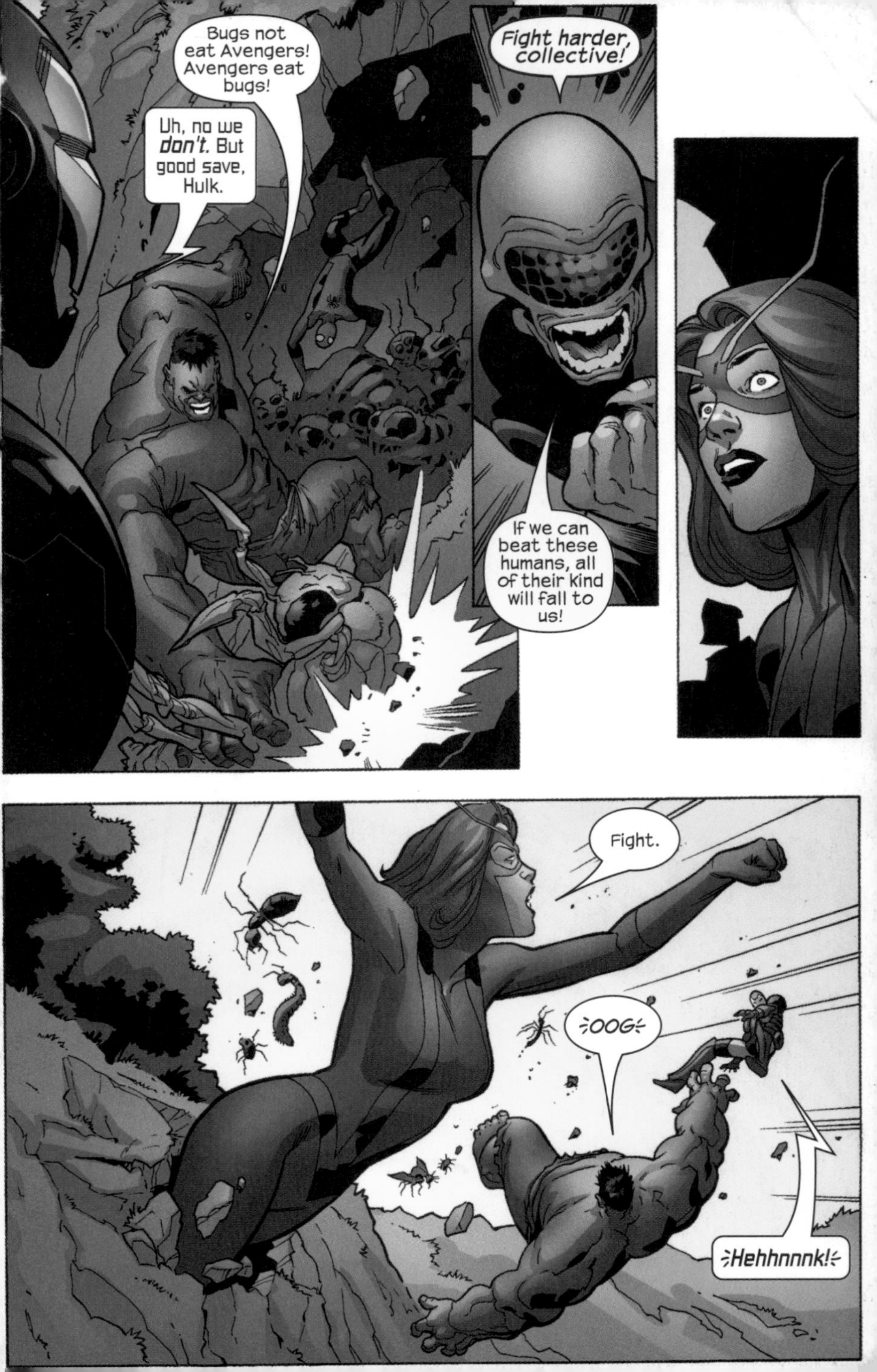
Bugs not eat Avengers! Avengers eat bugs!
Uh, no we *don't.* But good save, Hulk.
Fight harder, collective!
If we can beat these humans, all of their kind will fall to us!
Fight.
OOG
Hehhnnnk!

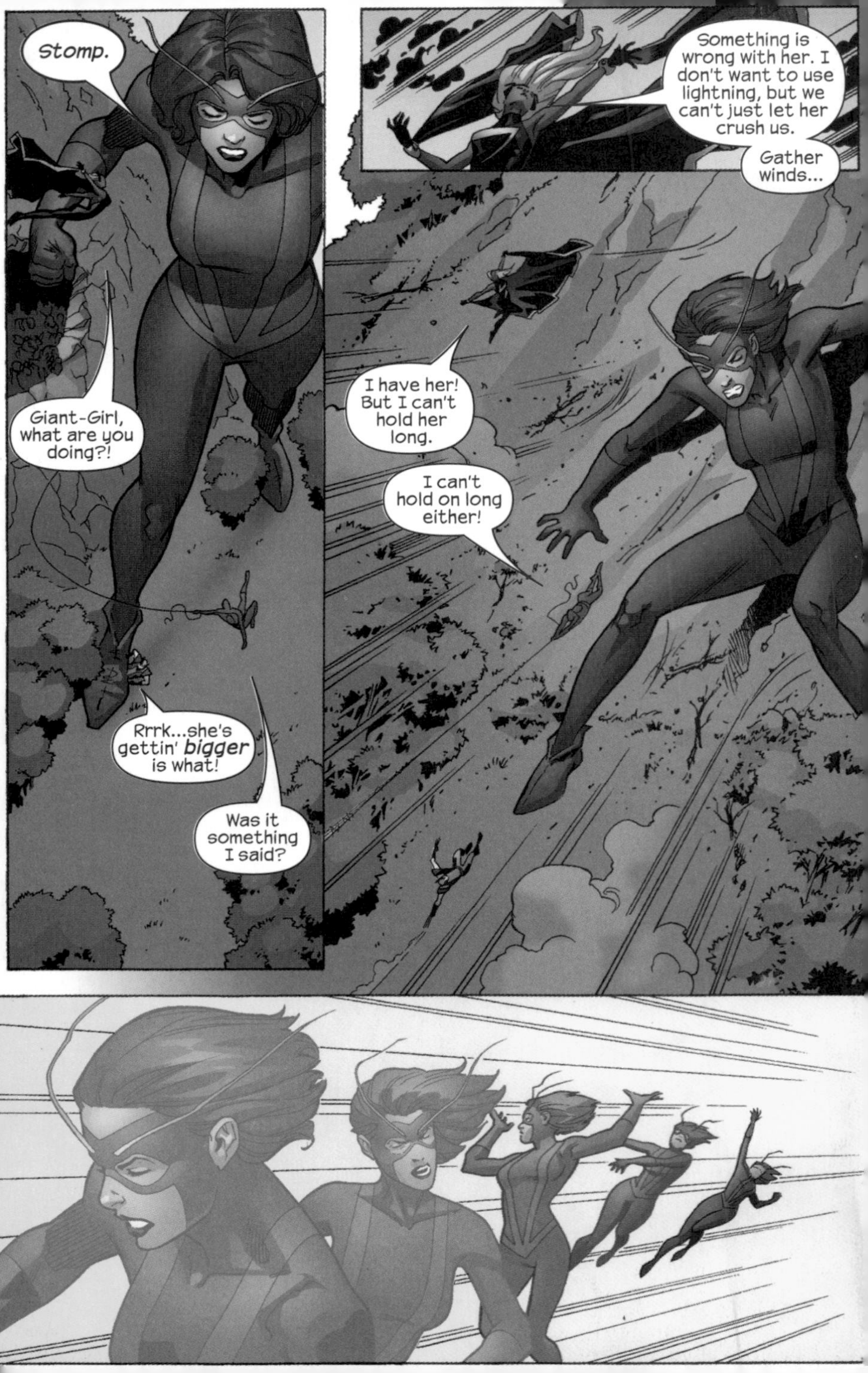

Stomp.
Giant-Girl, what are you doing?!
Rrrk...she's gettin' **bigger** is what!
Was it something I said?
Something is wrong with her. I don't want to use lightning, but we can't just let her crush us.
Gather winds...
I have her! But I can't hold her long.
I can't hold on long either!

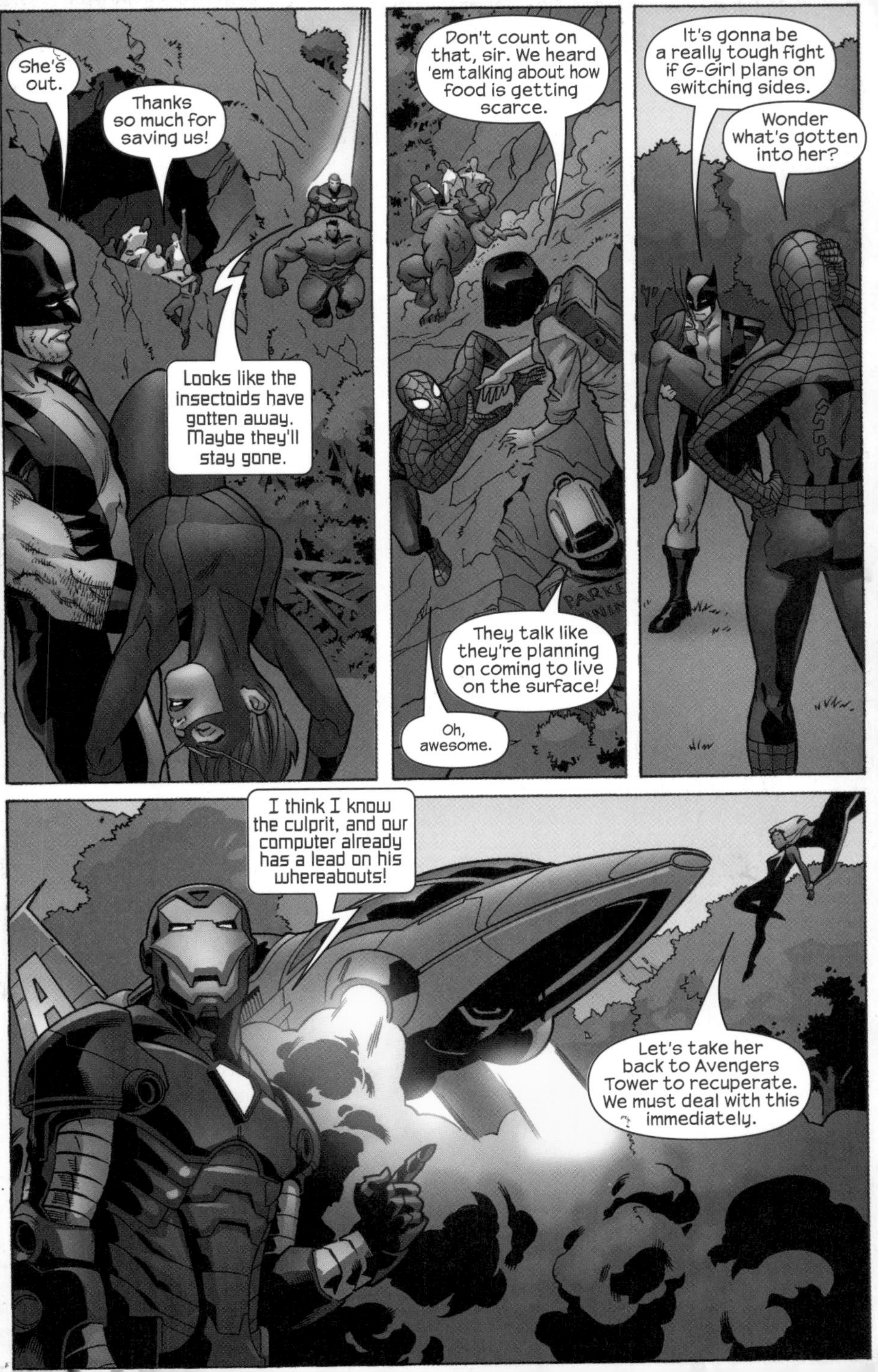
She's out.
Thanks so much for saving us!
Looks like the insectoids have gotten away. Maybe they'll stay gone.
Don't count on that, sir. We heard 'em talking about how food is getting scarce.
They talk like they're planning on coming to live on the surface!
Oh, awesome.
It's gonna be a really tough fight if G-Girl plans on switching sides.
Wonder what's gotten into her?
I think I know the culprit, and our computer already has a lead on his whereabouts!
Let's take her back to Avengers Tower to recuperate. We must deal with this immediately.

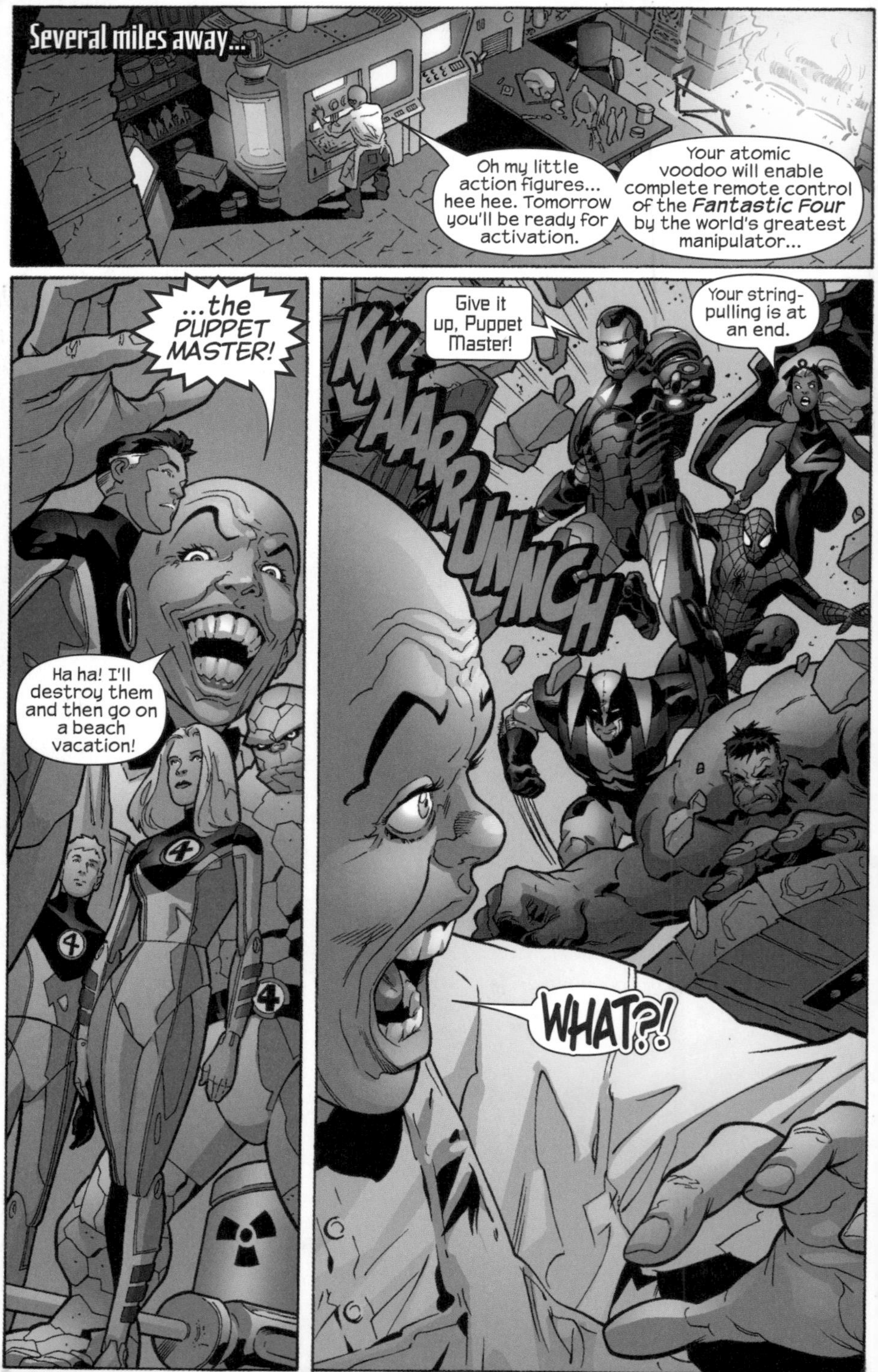
Several miles away...
Oh my little action figures... hee hee. Tomorrow you'll be ready for activation.
Your atomic voodoo will enable complete remote control of the Fantastic Four by the world's greatest manipulator...
...the PUPPET MASTER!
Ha ha! I'll destroy them and then go on a beach vacation!
KKLAARRUNNCH
Give it up, Puppet Master!
Your string-pulling is at an end.
WHAT?!

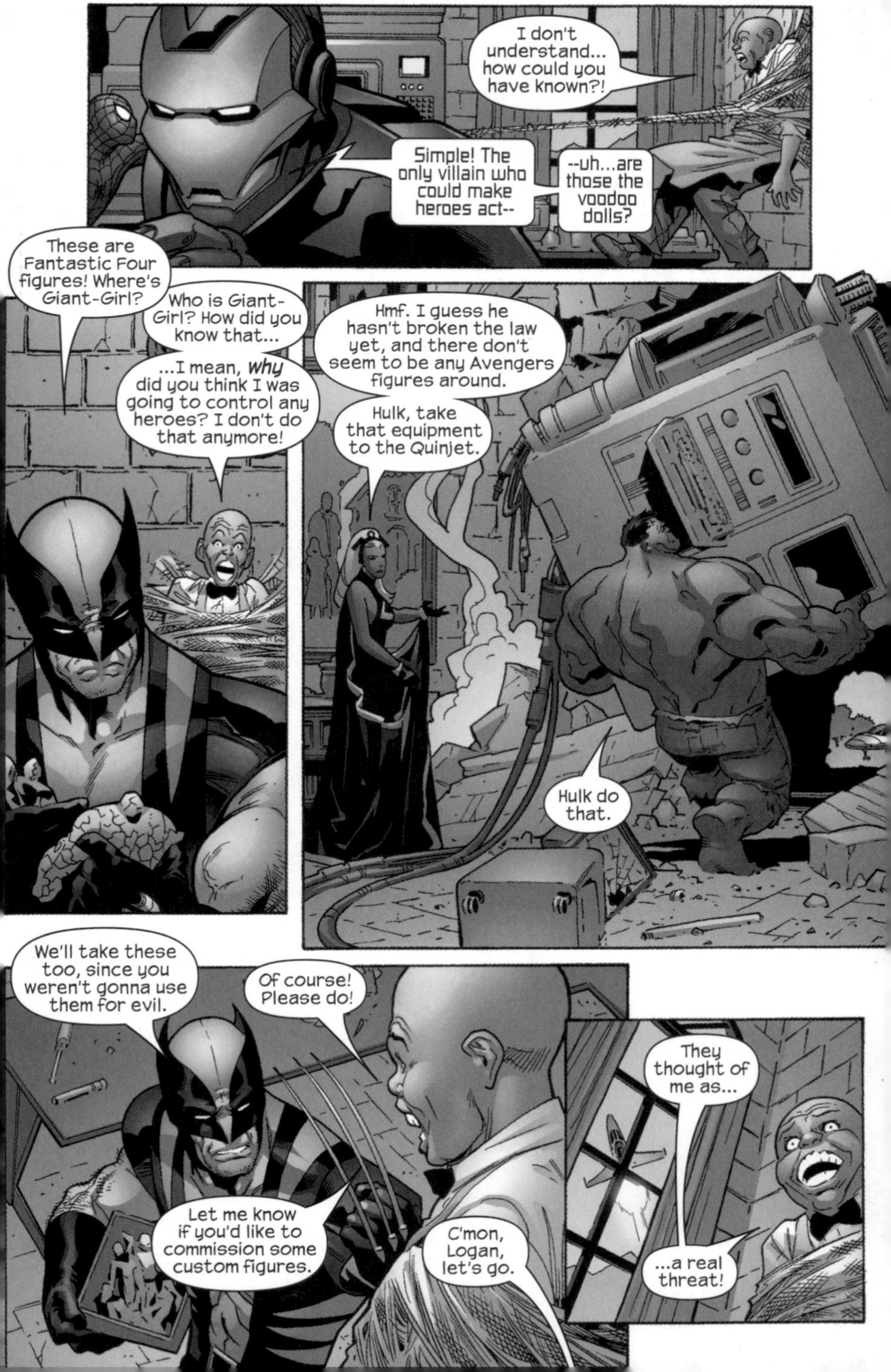
I don't understand... how could you have known?!
Simple! The only villain who could make heroes act--
--uh...are those the voodoo dolls?
These are Fantastic Four figures! Where's Giant-Girl?
Who is Giant-Girl? How did you know that...
...I mean, *why* did you think I was going to control any heroes? I don't do that anymore!
Hmf. I guess he hasn't broken the law yet, and there don't seem to be any Avengers figures around.
Hulk, take that equipment to the Quinjet.
Hulk do that.
We'll take these too, since you weren't gonna use them for evil.
Of course! Please do!
Let me know if you'd like to commission some custom figures.
C'mon, Logan, let's go.
They thought of me as...
...a real threat!

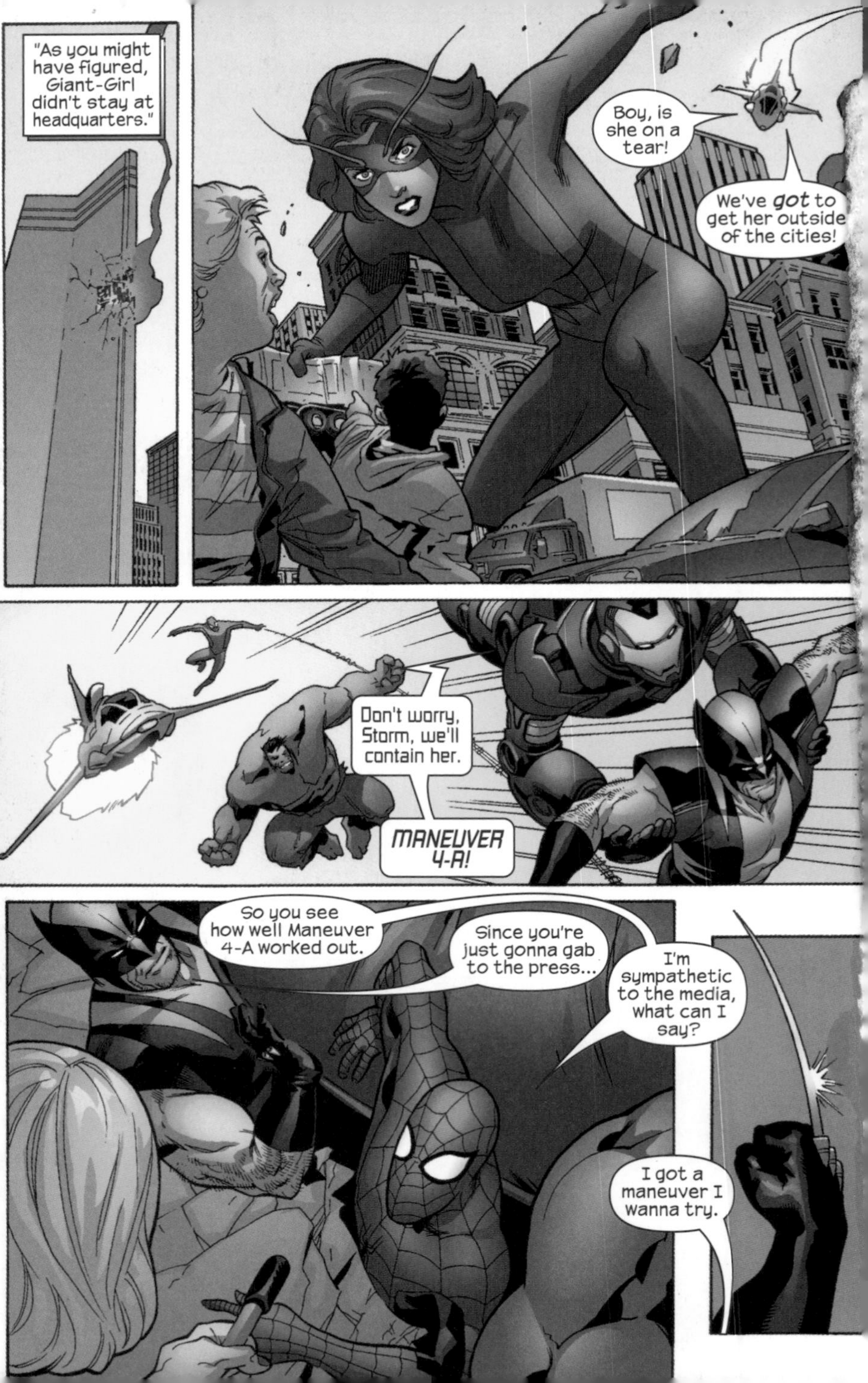
"As you might have figured, Giant-Girl didn't stay at headquarters."
Boy, is she on a tear!
We've *got* to get her outside of the cities!
Don't worry, Storm, we'll contain her.
MANEUVER 4-A!
So you see how well Maneuver 4-A worked out.
Since you're just gonna gab to the press...
I'm sympathetic to the media, what can I say?
I got a maneuver I wanna try.

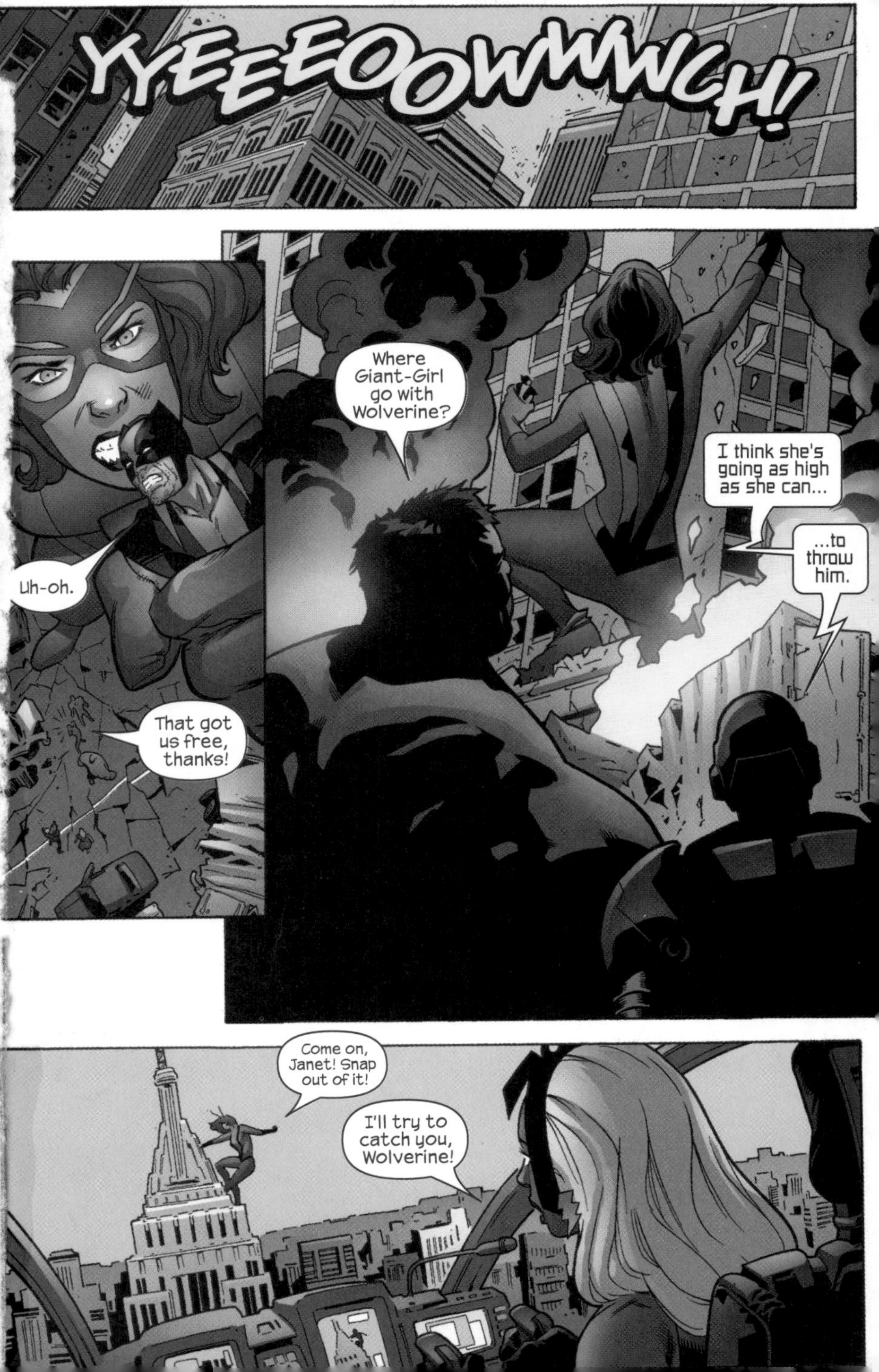
YYEEEOOWWWCH!
Uh-oh.
That got us free, thanks!
Where Giant-Girl go with Wolverine?
I think she's going as high as she can...
...to throw him.
Come on, Janet! Snap out of it!
I'll try to catch you, Wolverine!

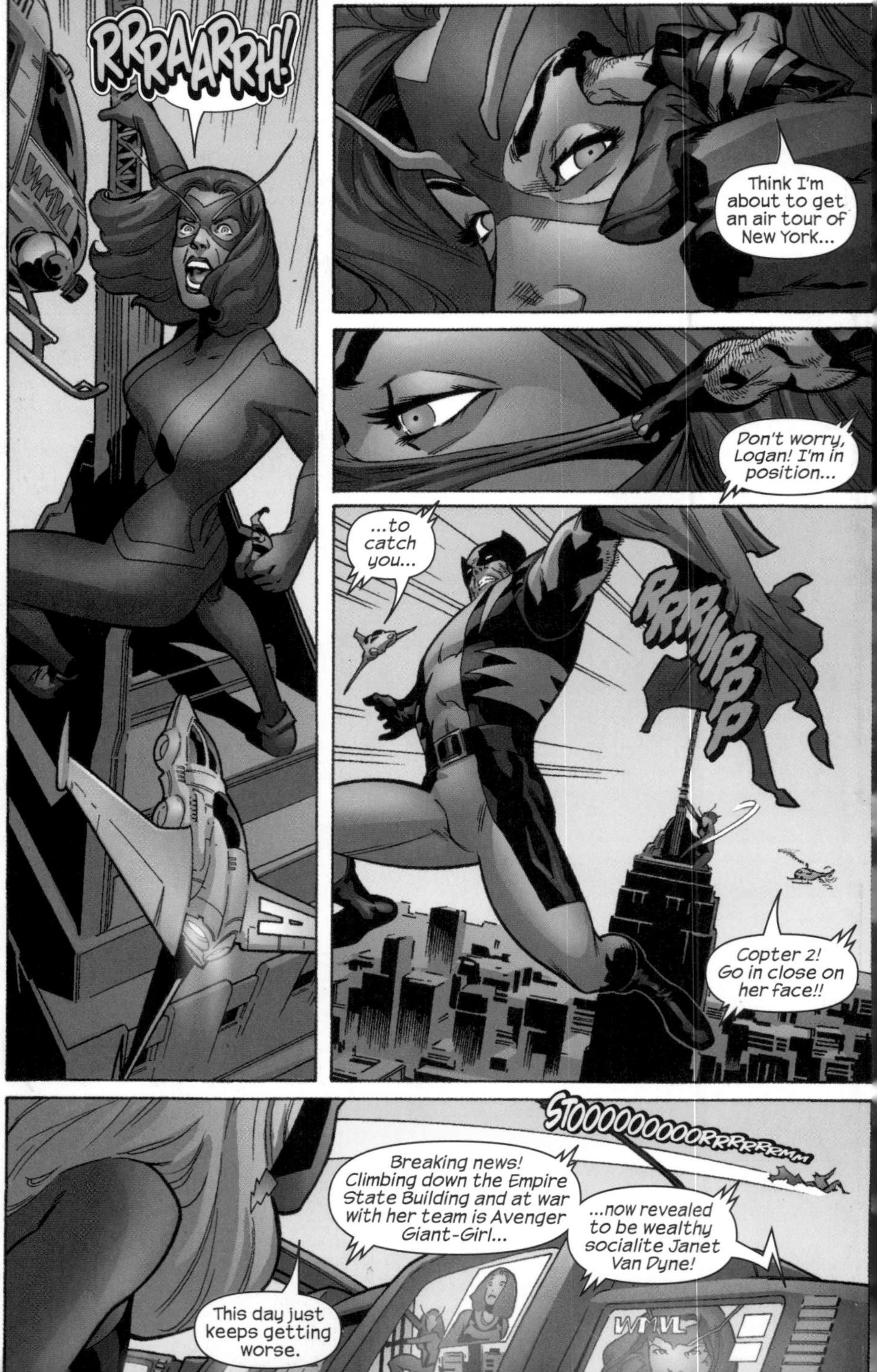
RRRAARRH!
Think I'm about to get an air tour of New York...
Don't worry, Logan! I'm in position...
...to catch you...
RRRIIPPP
Copter 2! Go in close on her face!!
STOOOOOOOOORRRRRRMM
This day just keeps getting worse.
Breaking news! Climbing down the Empire State Building and at war with her team is Avenger Giant-Girl...
...now revealed to be wealthy socialite Janet Van Dyne!

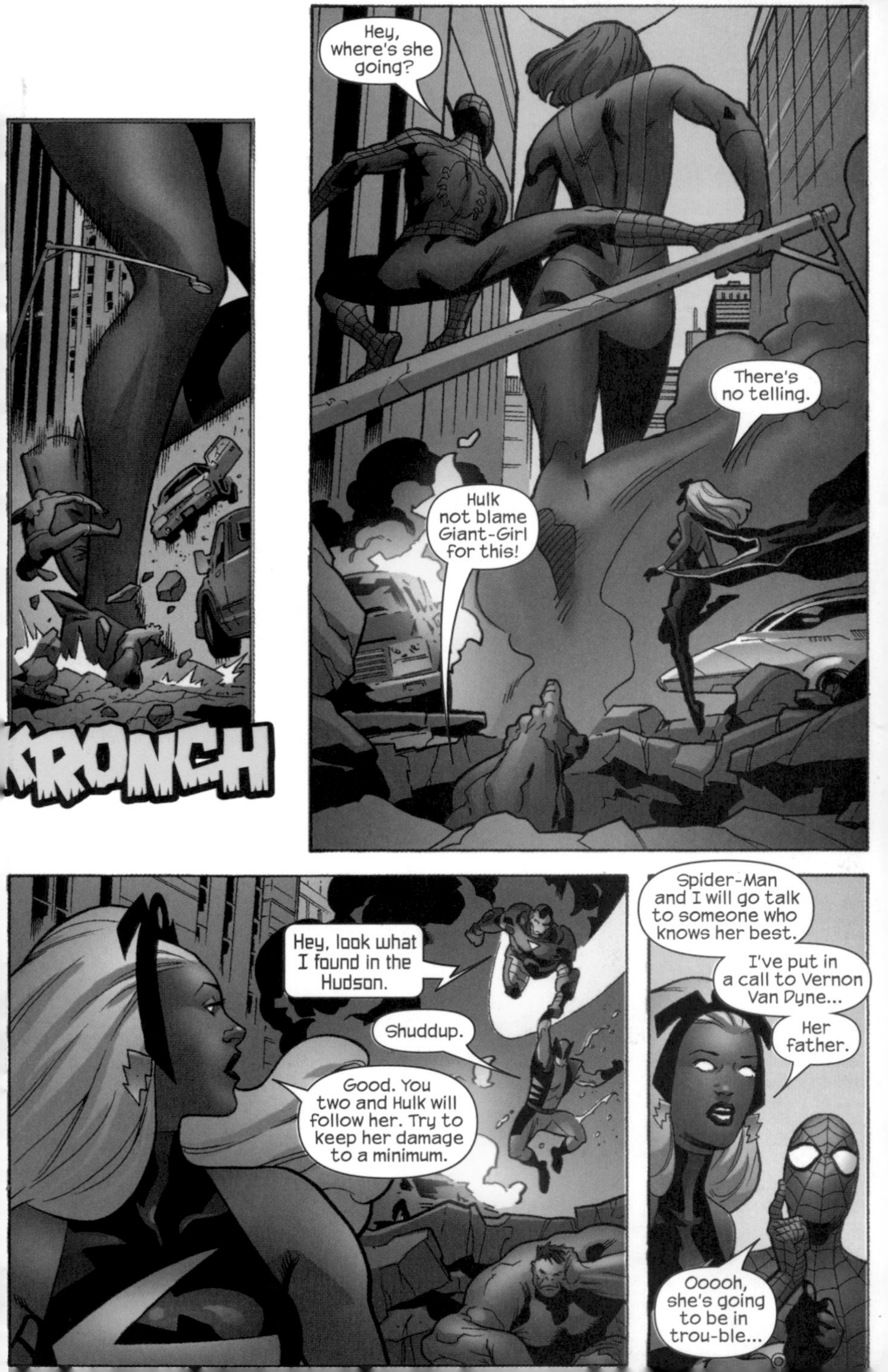
KRONCH
Hey, where's she going?
There's no telling.
Hulk not blame Giant-Girl for this!
Hey, look what I found in the Hudson.
Shuddup.
Good. You two and Hulk will follow her. Try to keep her damage to a minimum.
Spider-Man and I will go talk to someone who knows her best.
I've put in a call to Vernon Van Dyne...
Her father.
Ooooh, she's going to be in trou-ble...

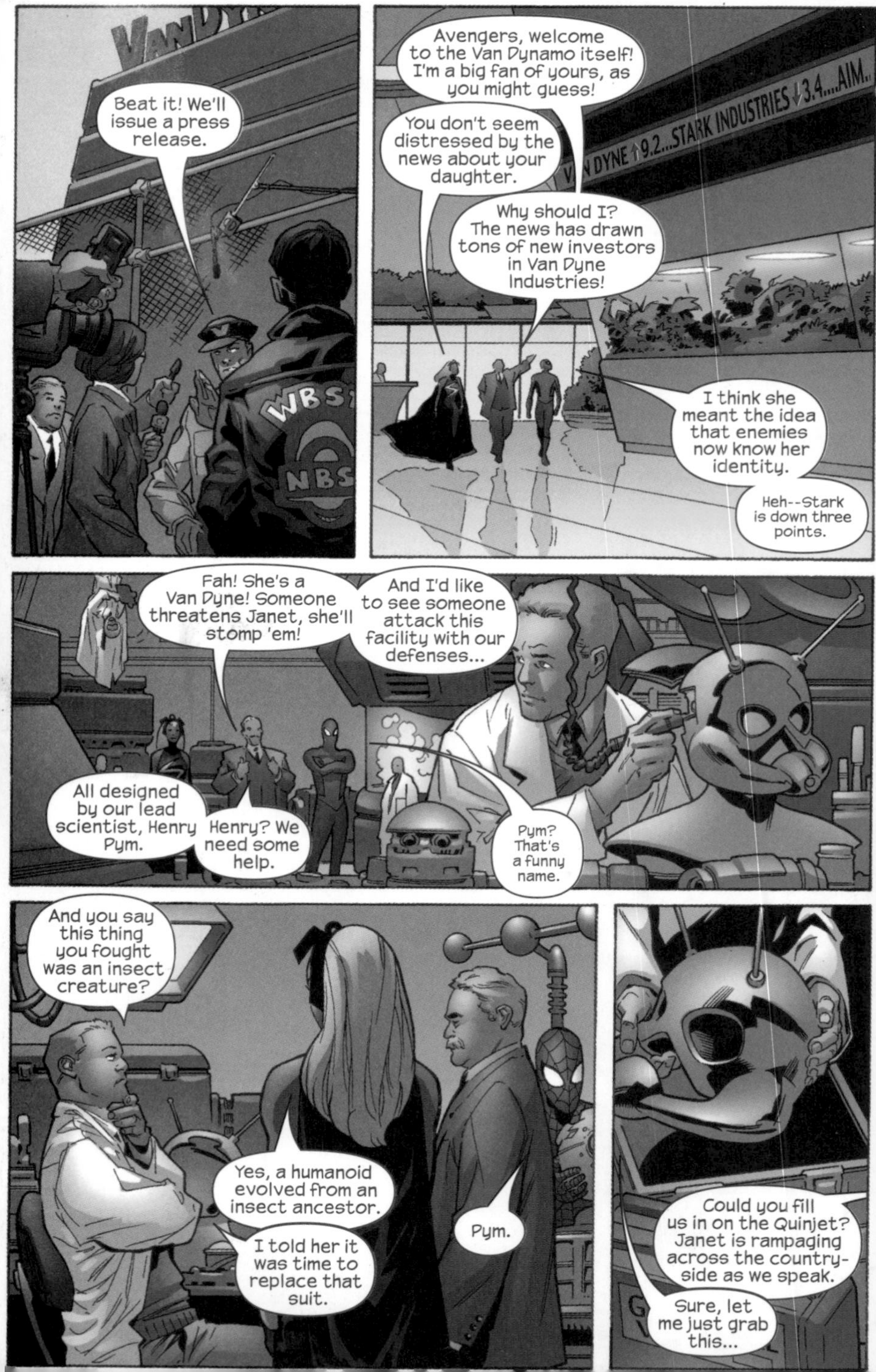
VanDyne
Beat it! We'll issue a press release.
WBS
NBS
Avengers, welcome to the Van Dynamo itself! I'm a big fan of yours, as you might guess!
You don't seem distressed by the news about your daughter.
Why should I? The news has drawn tons of new investors in Van Dyne Industries!
VAN DYNE 9.2...STARK INDUSTRIES 3.4....AIM...
I think she meant the idea that enemies now know her identity.
Heh--Stark is down three points.
Fah! She's a Van Dyne! Someone threatens Janet, she'll stomp 'em!
And I'd like to see someone attack this facility with our defenses...
All designed by our lead scientist, Henry Pym.
Henry? We need some help.
Pym? That's a funny name.
And you say this thing you fought was an insect creature?
Yes, a humanoid evolved from an insect ancestor.
I told her it was time to replace that suit.
Pym.
Could you fill us in on the Quinjet? Janet is rampaging across the country-side as we speak.
Sure, let me just grab this...

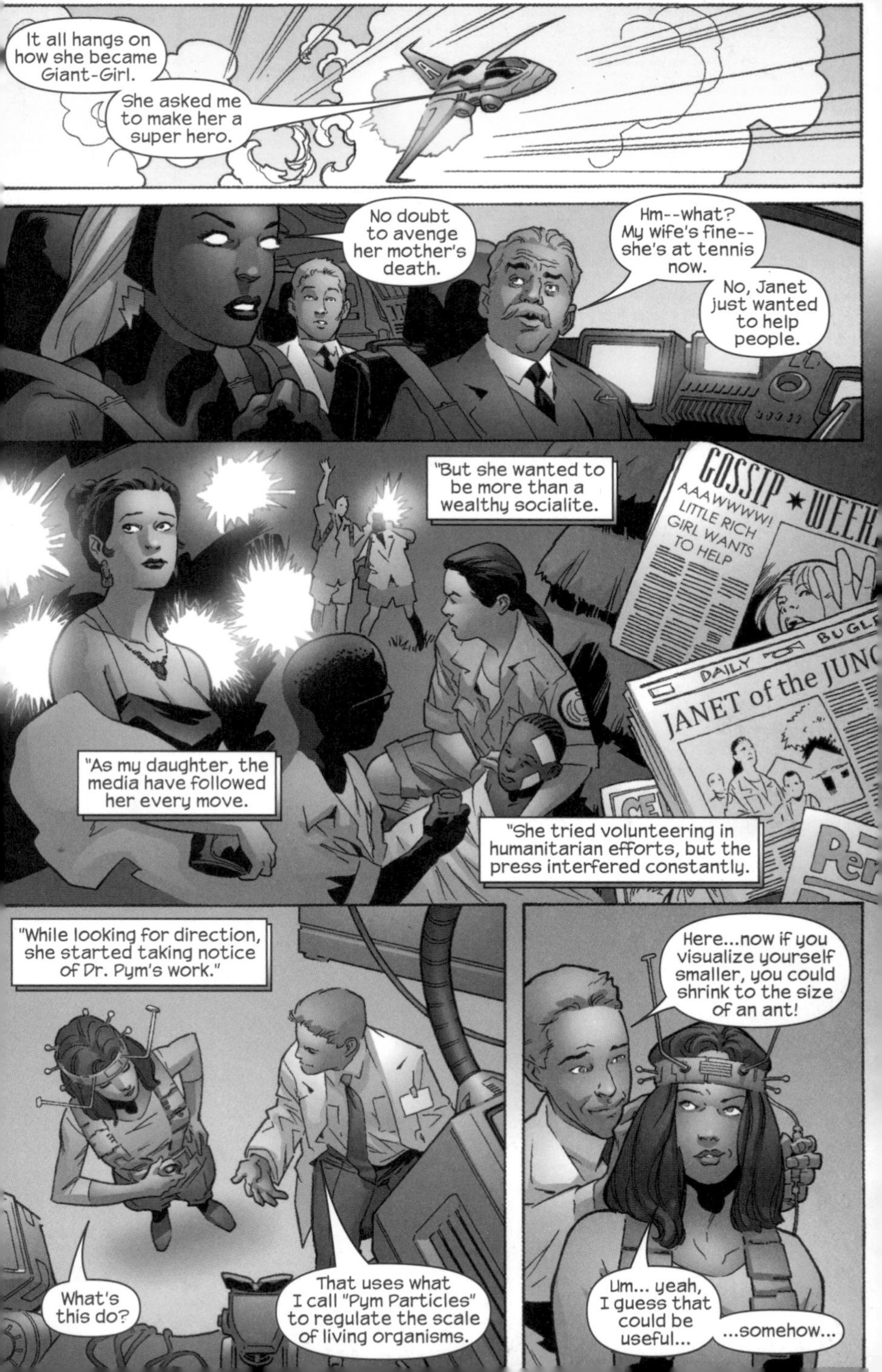

It all hangs on how she became Giant-Girl.
She asked me to make her a super hero.
No doubt to avenge her mother's death.
Hm--what? My wife's fine-- she's at tennis now.
No, Janet just wanted to help people.
"But she wanted to be more than a wealthy socialite.
GOSSIP ★ WEEK
AAAWWWW! LITTLE RICH GIRL WANTS TO HELP
DAILY BUGL
JANET of the JUNG
"As my daughter, the media have followed her every move.
"She tried volunteering in humanitarian efforts, but the press interfered constantly.
"While looking for direction, she started taking notice of Dr. Pym's work."
What's this do?
That uses what I call "Pym Particles" to regulate the scale of living organisms.
Here...now if you visualize yourself smaller, you could shrink to the size of an ant!
Um... yeah, I guess that could be useful...
...somehow...

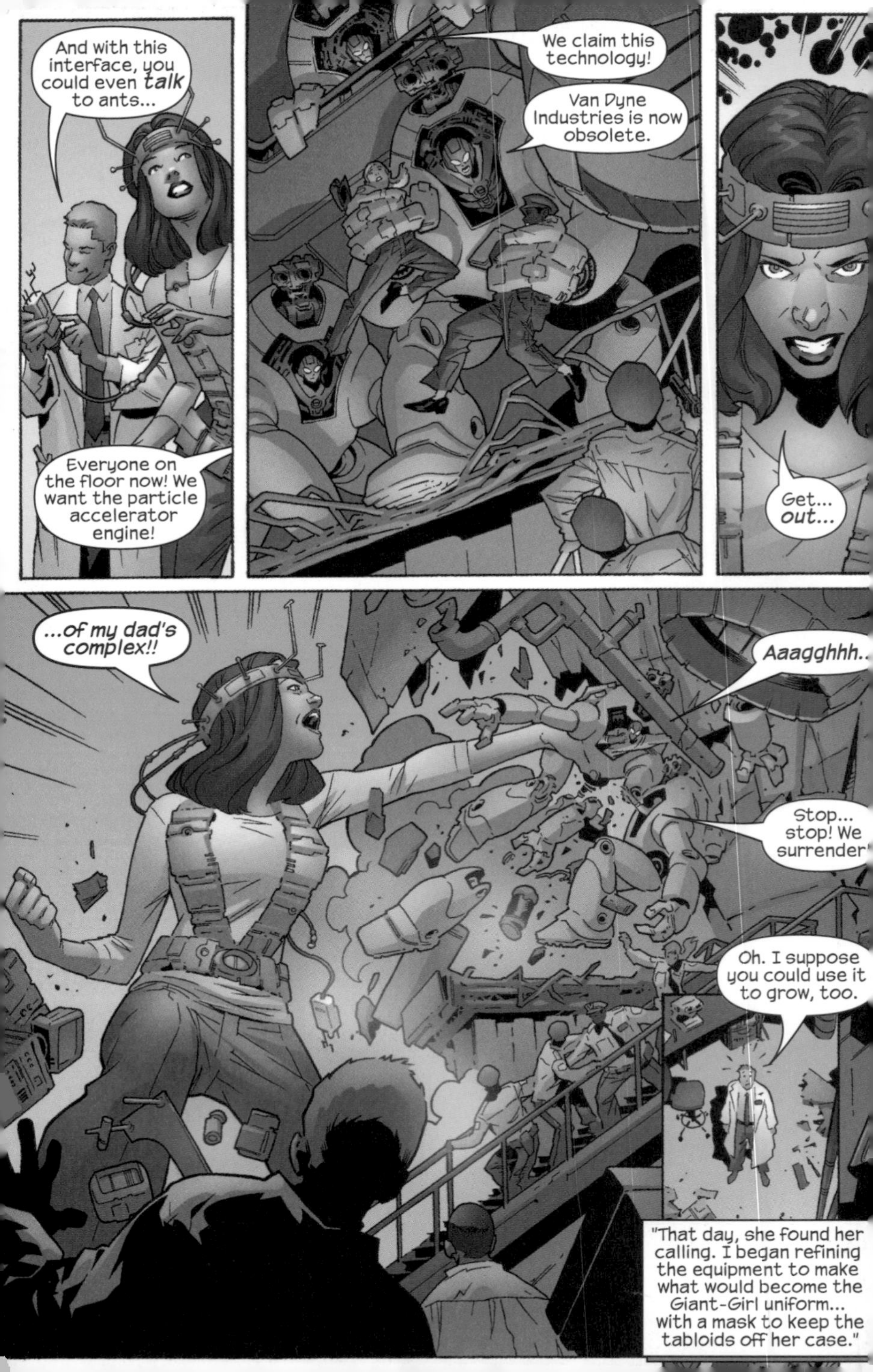
And with this interface, you could even *talk* to ants...
Everyone on the floor now! We want the particle accelerator engine!
We claim this technology!
Van Dyne Industries is now obsolete.
Get... *out...*
...of my dad's complex!!
Aaagghhh..
Stop... stop! We surrender
Oh. I suppose you could use it to grow, too.
"That day, she found her calling. I began refining the equipment to make what would become the Giant-Girl uniform... with a mask to keep the tabloids off her case."

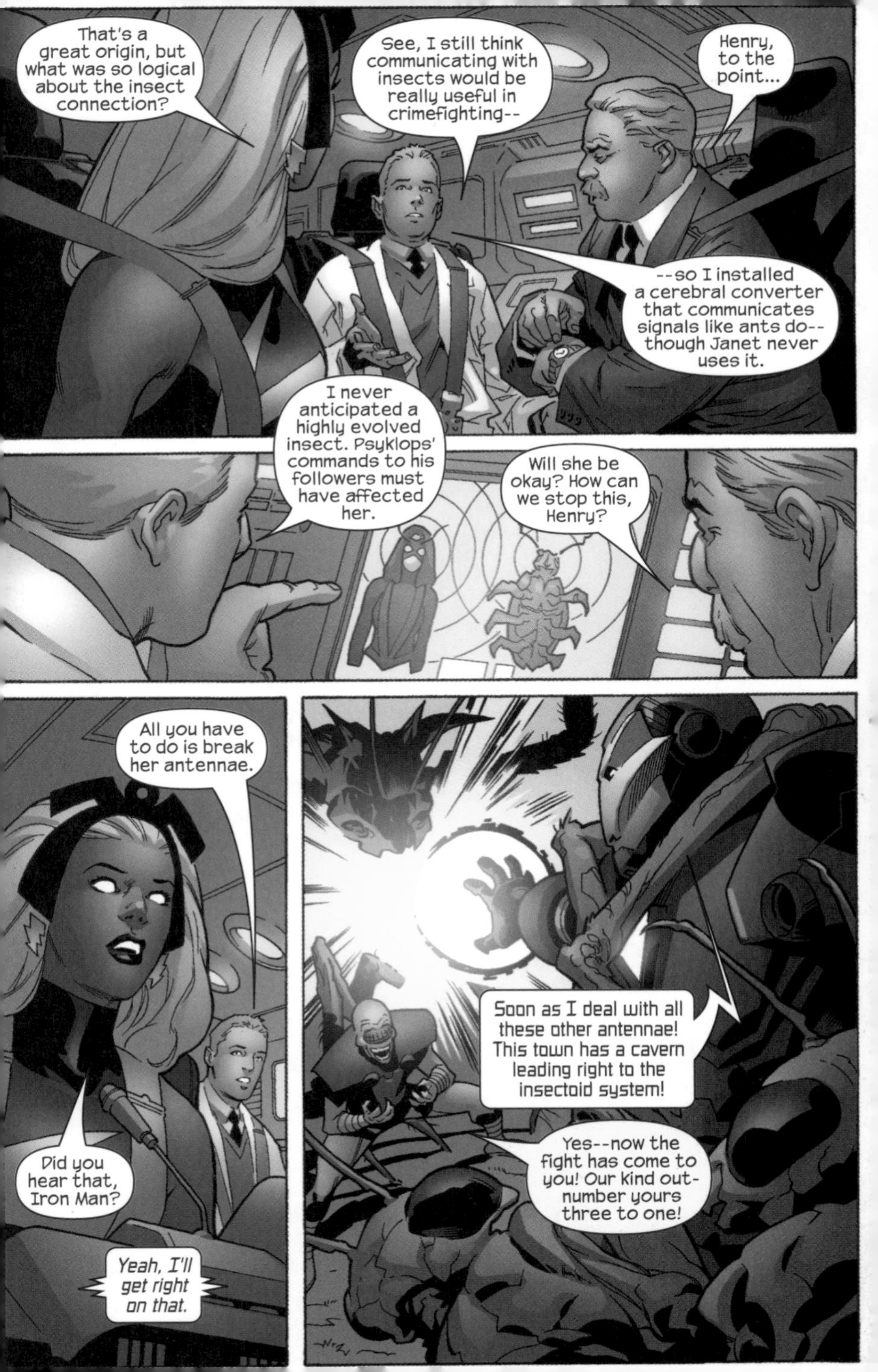
That's a great origin, but what was so logical about the insect connection?
See, I still think communicating with insects would be really useful in crimefighting--
Henry, to the point...
--so I installed a cerebral converter that communicates signals like ants do--though Janet never uses it.
I never anticipated a highly evolved insect. Psyklops' commands to his followers must have affected her.
Will she be okay? How can we stop this, Henry?
All you have to do is break her antennae.
Did you hear that, Iron Man?
Yeah, I'll get right on that.
Soon as I deal with all these other antennae! This town has a cavern leading right to the insectoid system!
Yes--now the fight has come to you! Our kind out-number yours three to one!

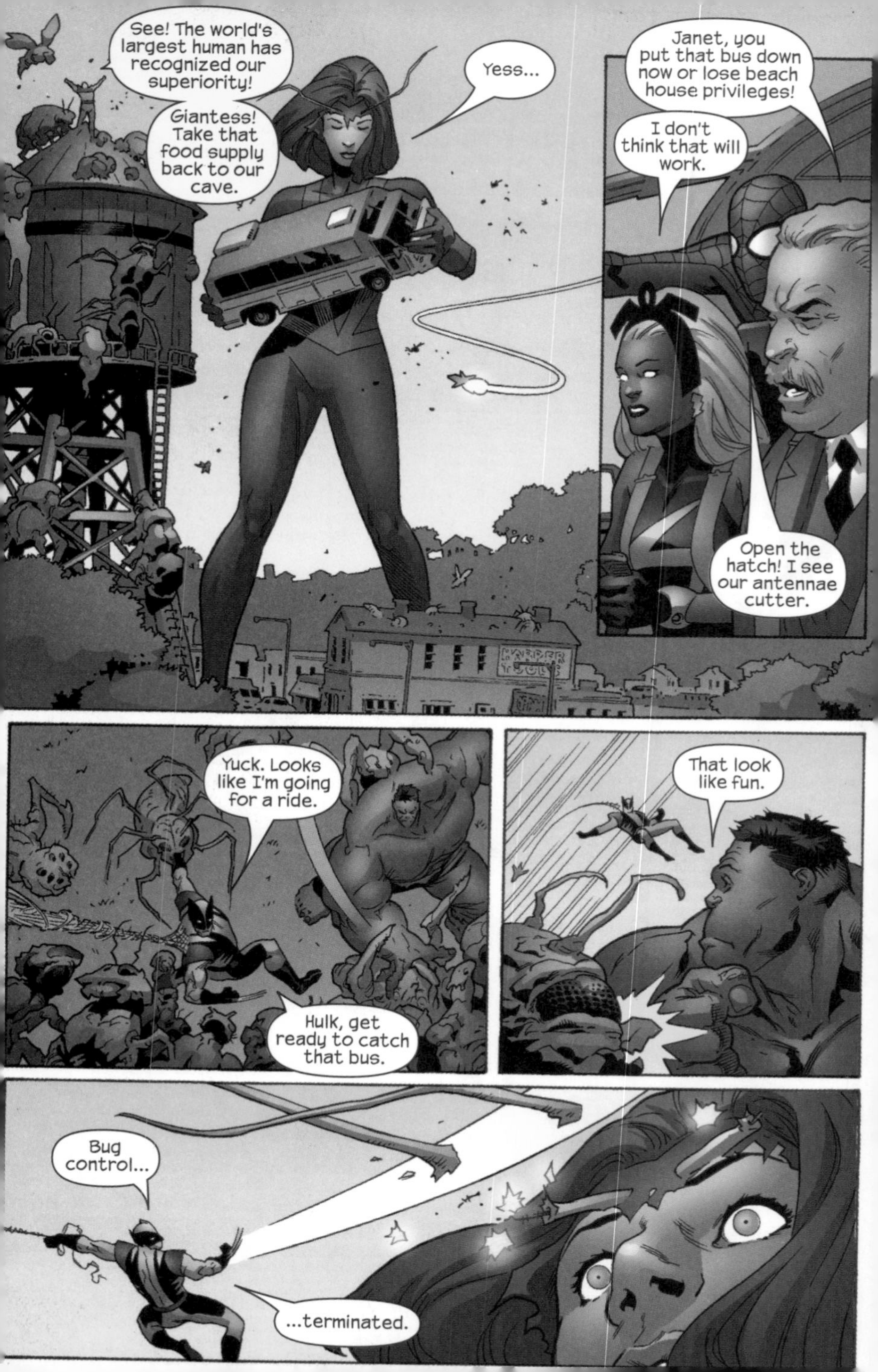
See! The world's largest human has recognized our superiority!
Giantess! Take that food supply back to our cave.
Yess...
Janet, you put that bus down now or lose beach house privileges!
I don't think that will work.
Open the hatch! I see our antennae cutter.
Yuck. Looks like I'm going for a ride.
Hulk, get ready to catch that bus.
That look like fun.
Bug control...
...terminated.

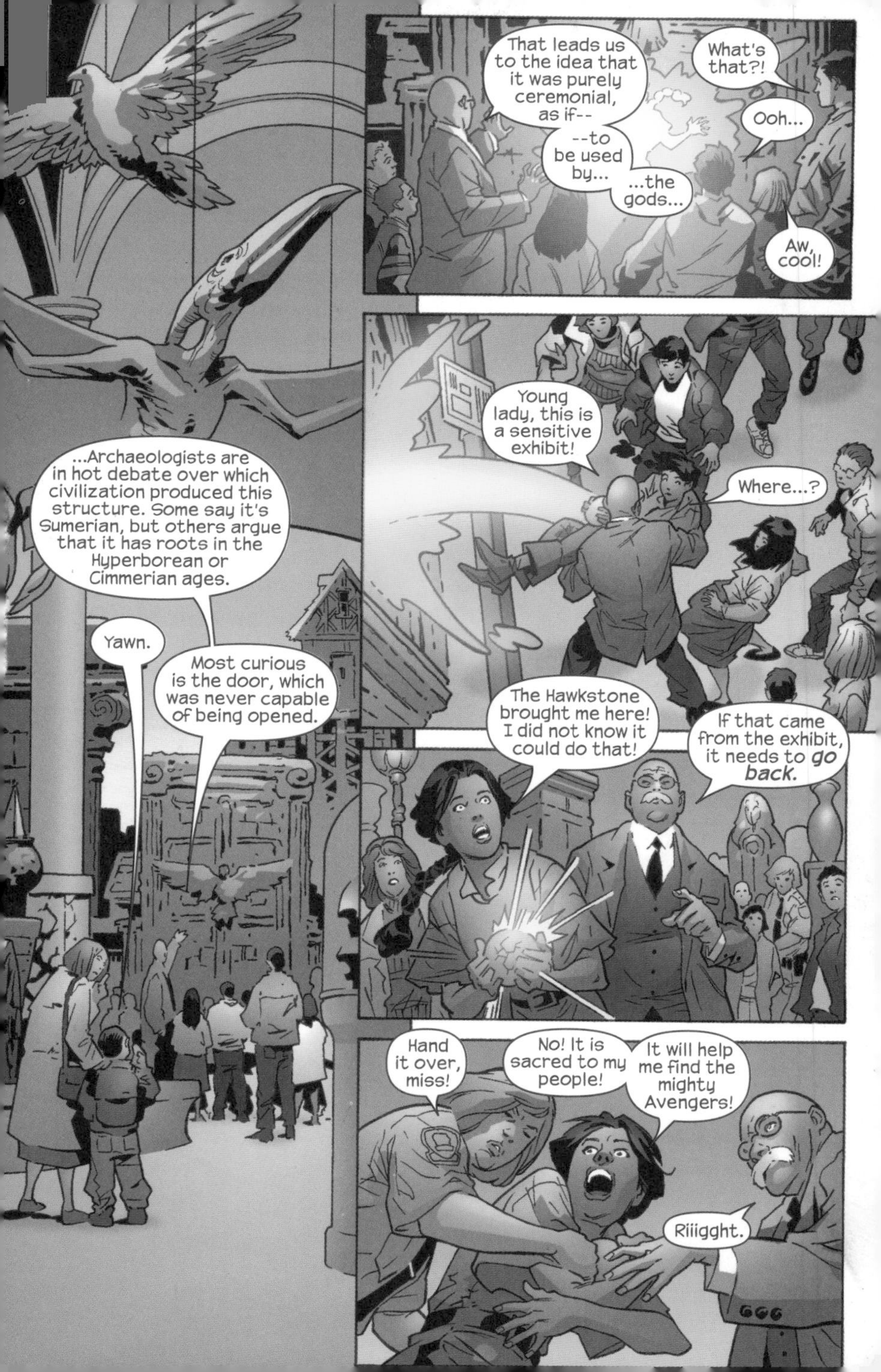
...Archaeologists are in hot debate over which civilization produced this structure. Some say it's Sumerian, but others argue that it has roots in the Hyperborean or Cimmerian ages.
Yawn.
Most curious is the door, which was never capable of being opened.
That leads us to the idea that it was purely ceremonial, as if--
--to be used by...
...the gods...
What's that?!
Ooh...
Aw, cool!
Young lady, this is a sensitive exhibit!
Where...?
The Hawkstone brought me here! I did not know it could do that!
If that came from the exhibit, it needs to *go back.*
Hand it over, miss!
No! It is sacred to my people!
It will help me find the mighty Avengers!
Riiigght.

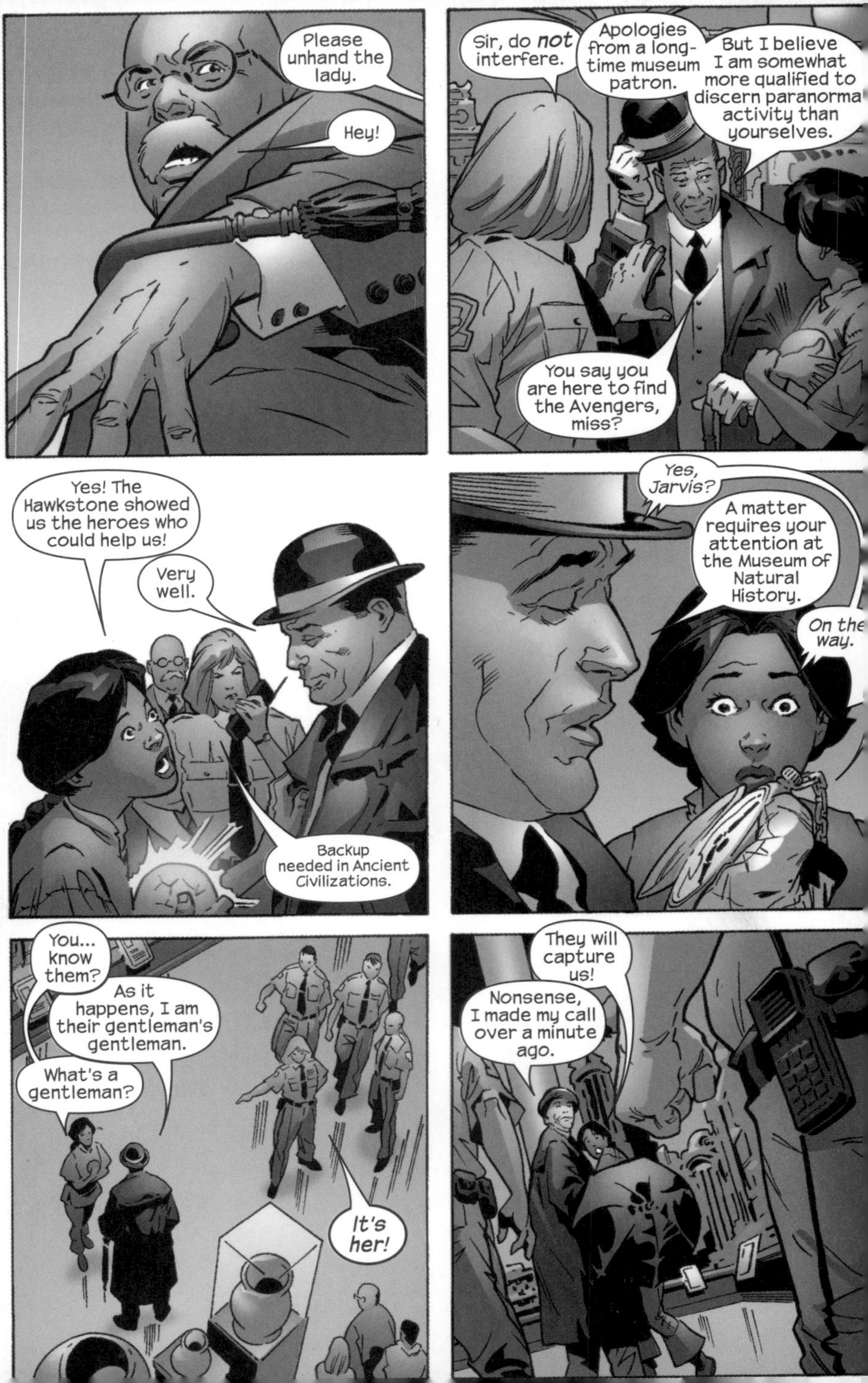

Please unhand the lady.
Hey!
Sir, do *not* interfere.
Apologies from a long-time museum patron.
But I believe I am somewhat more qualified to discern paranorma activity than yourselves.
You say you are here to find the Avengers, miss?
Yes! The Hawkstone showed us the heroes who could help us!
Very well.
Backup needed in Ancient Civilizations.
Yes, Jarvis?
A matter requires your attention at the Museum of Natural History.
On the way.
You... know them?
As it happens, I am their gentleman's gentleman.
What's a gentleman?
It's her!
They will capture us!
Nonsense, I made my call over a minute ago.

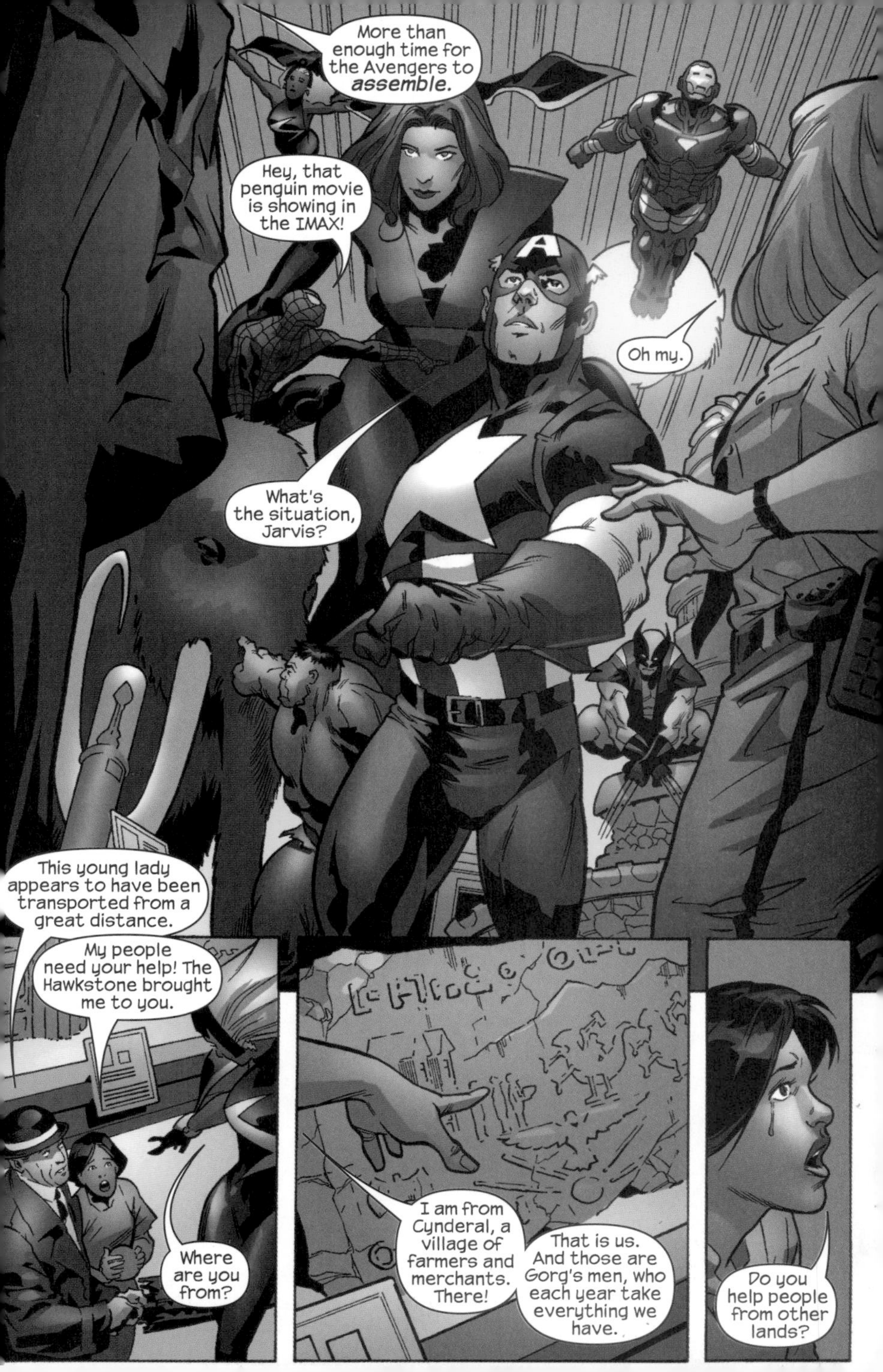

More than enough time for the Avengers to *assemble.*
Hey, that penguin movie is showing in the IMAX!
Oh my.
What's the situation, Jarvis?
This young lady appears to have been transported from a great distance.
My people need your help! The Hawkstone brought me to you.
Where are you from?
I am from Cynderal, a village of farmers and merchants. There!
That is us. And those are Gorg's men, who each year take everything we have.
Do you help people from other lands?

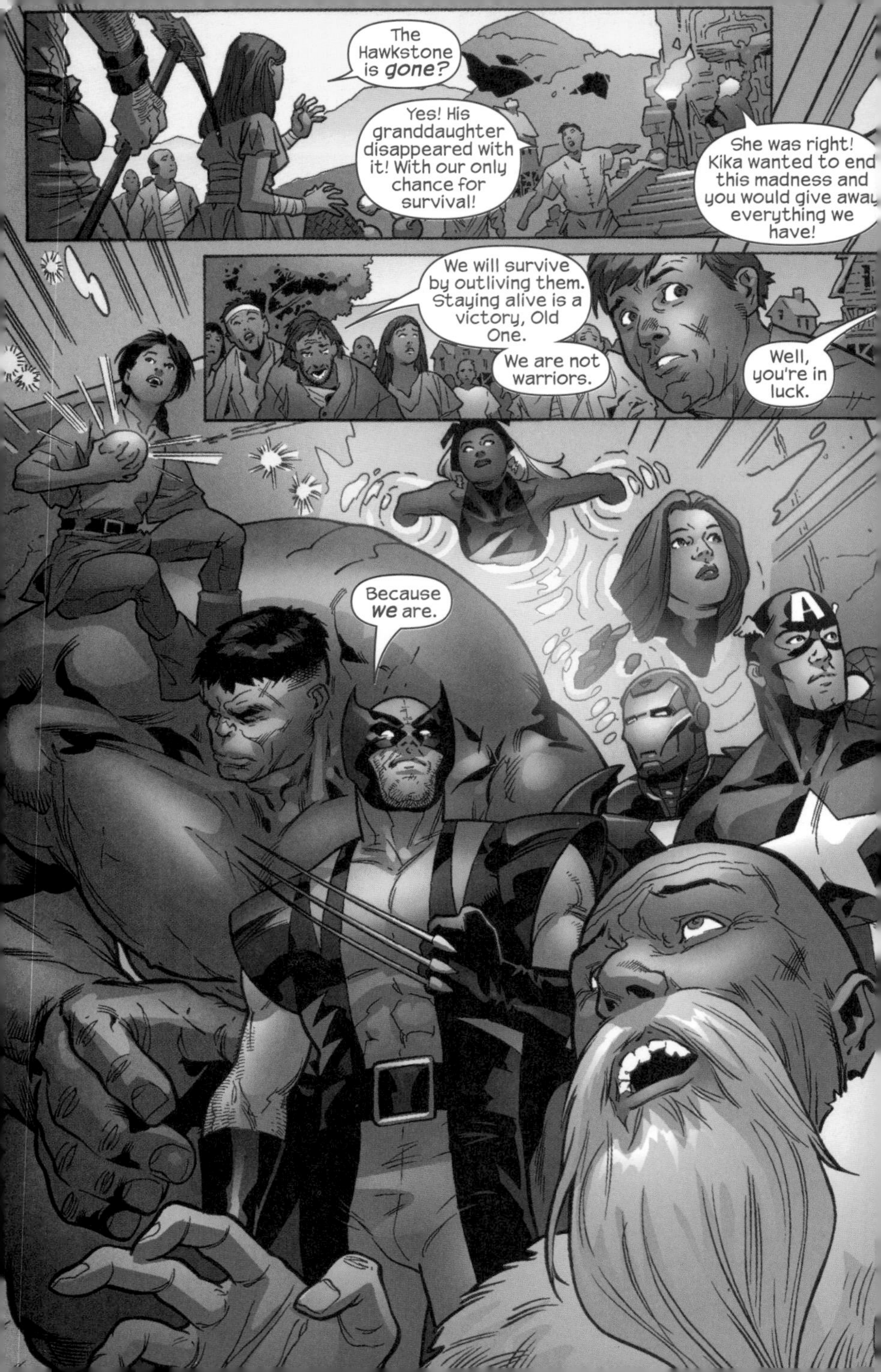
The Hawkstone is gone?
Yes! His granddaughter disappeared with it! With our only chance for survival!
She was right! Kika wanted to end this madness and you would give away everything we have!
We will survive by outliving them. Staying alive is a victory, Old One.
We are not warriors.
Well, you're in luck.
Because we are.

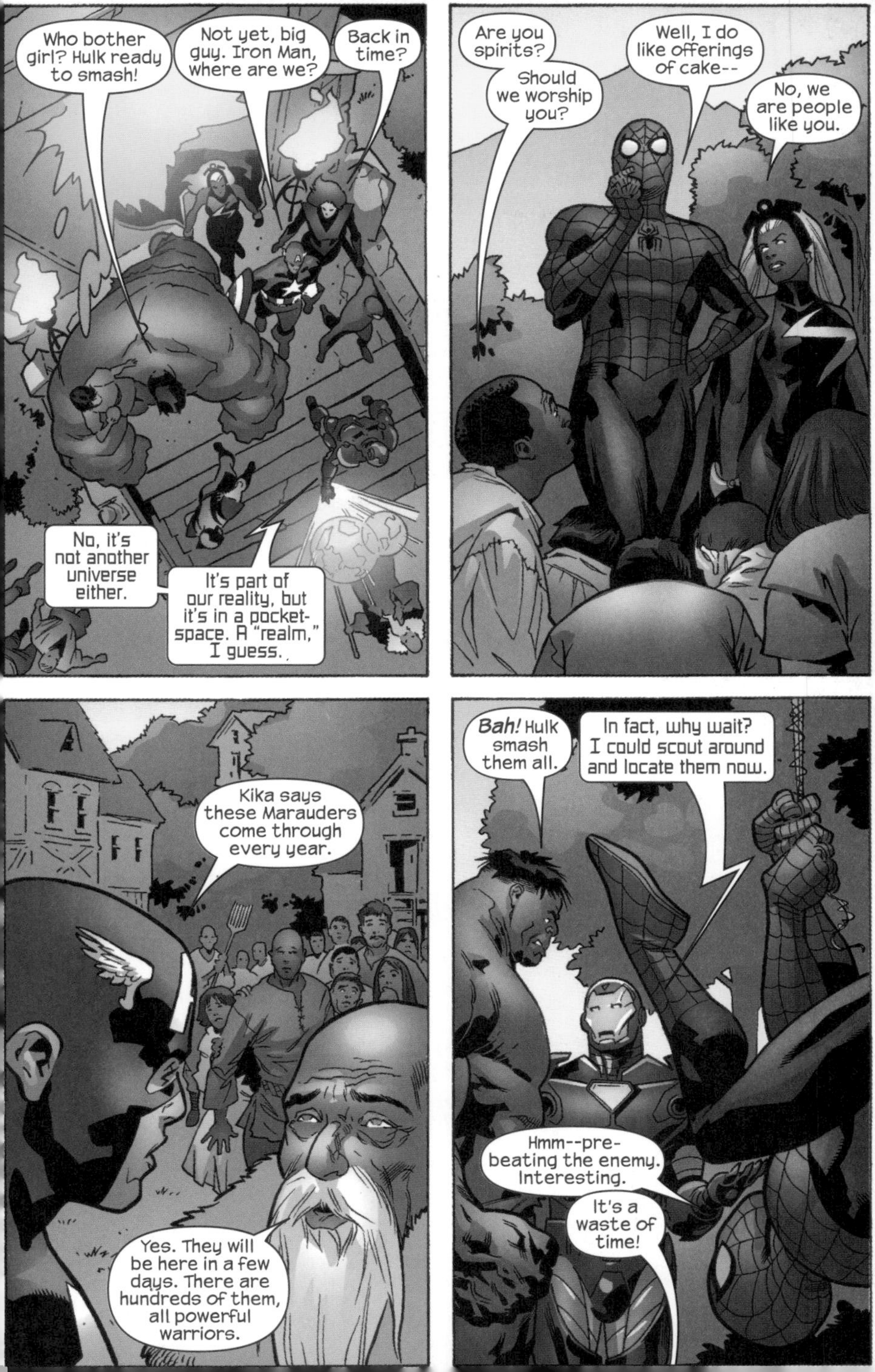
Who bother girl? Hulk ready to smash!
Not yet, big guy. Iron Man, where are we?
Back in time?
No, it's not another universe either.
It's part of our reality, but it's in a pocket-space. A "realm," I guess.
Are you spirits?
Should we worship you?
Well, I do like offerings of cake--
No, we are people like you.
Kika says these Marauders come through every year.
Yes. They will be here in a few days. There are hundreds of them, all powerful warriors.
Bah! Hulk smash them all.
In fact, why wait? I could scout around and locate them now.
Hmm--pre-beating the enemy. Interesting.
It's a waste of time!

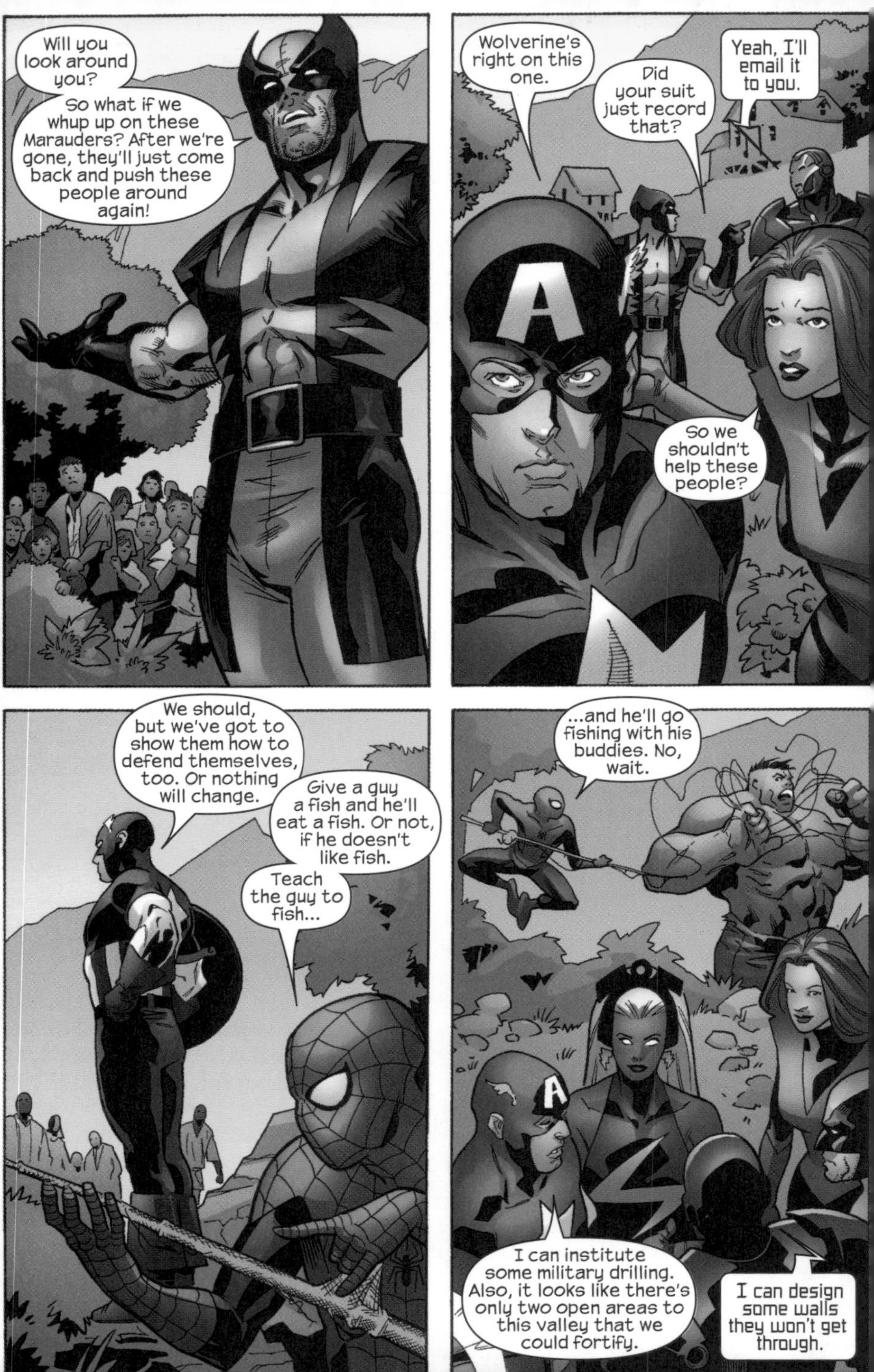
Will you look around you?
So what if we whup up on these Marauders? After we're gone, they'll just come back and push these people around again!
Wolverine's right on this one.
Did your suit just record that?
Yeah, I'll email it to you.
So we shouldn't help these people?
We should, but we've got to show them how to defend themselves, too. Or nothing will change.
Give a guy a fish and he'll eat a fish. Or not, if he doesn't like fish.
Teach the guy to fish...
...and he'll go fishing with his buddies. No, wait.
I can institute some military drilling. Also, it looks like there's only two open areas to this valley that we could fortify.
I can design some walls they won't get through.

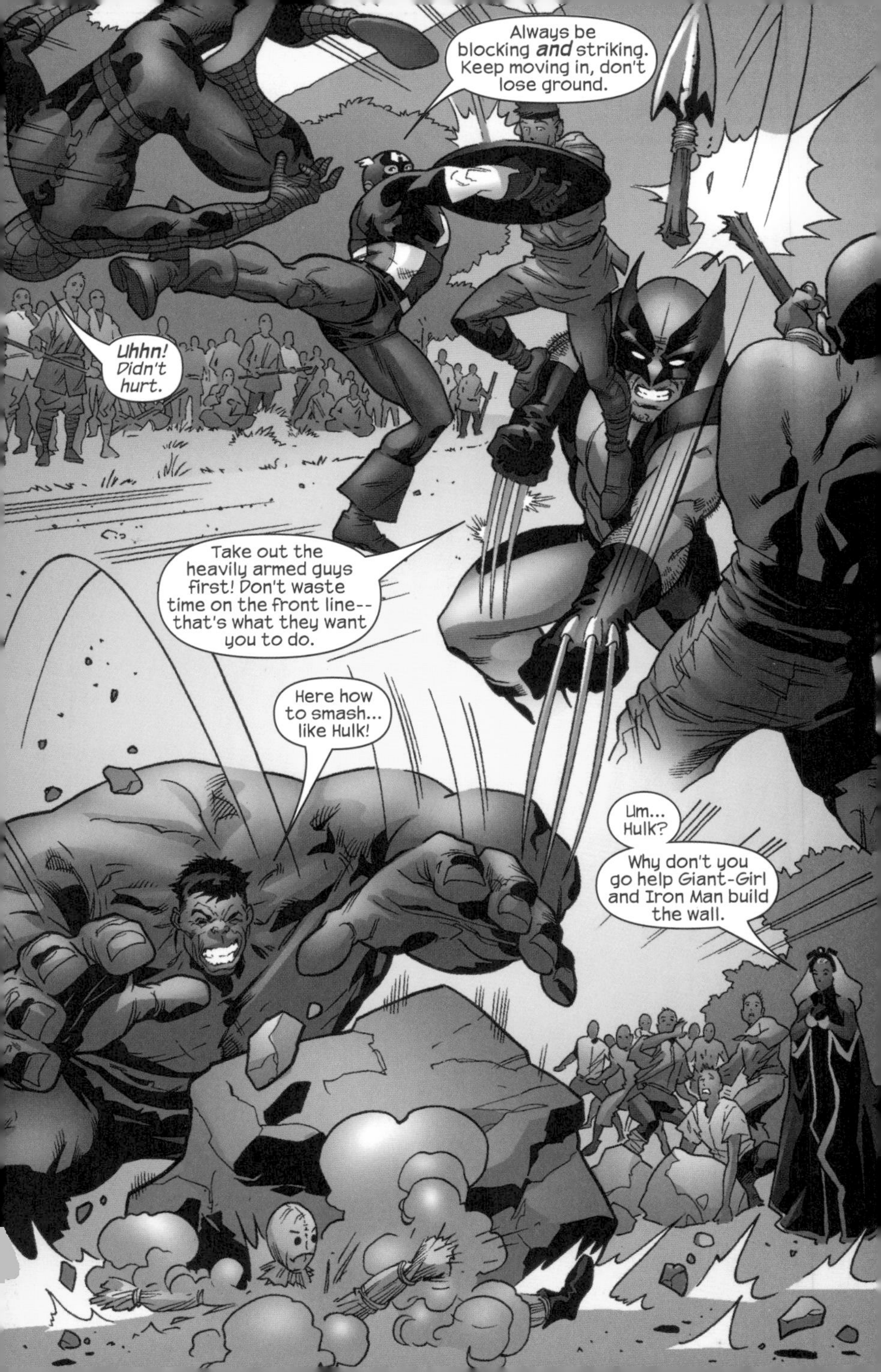
Always be blocking *and* striking. Keep moving in, don't lose ground.
Uhhn! Didn't hurt.
Take out the heavily armed guys first! Don't waste time on the front line-- that's what they want you to do.
Here how to smash... like Hulk!
Um... Hulk?
Why don't you go help Giant-Girl and Iron Man build the wall.

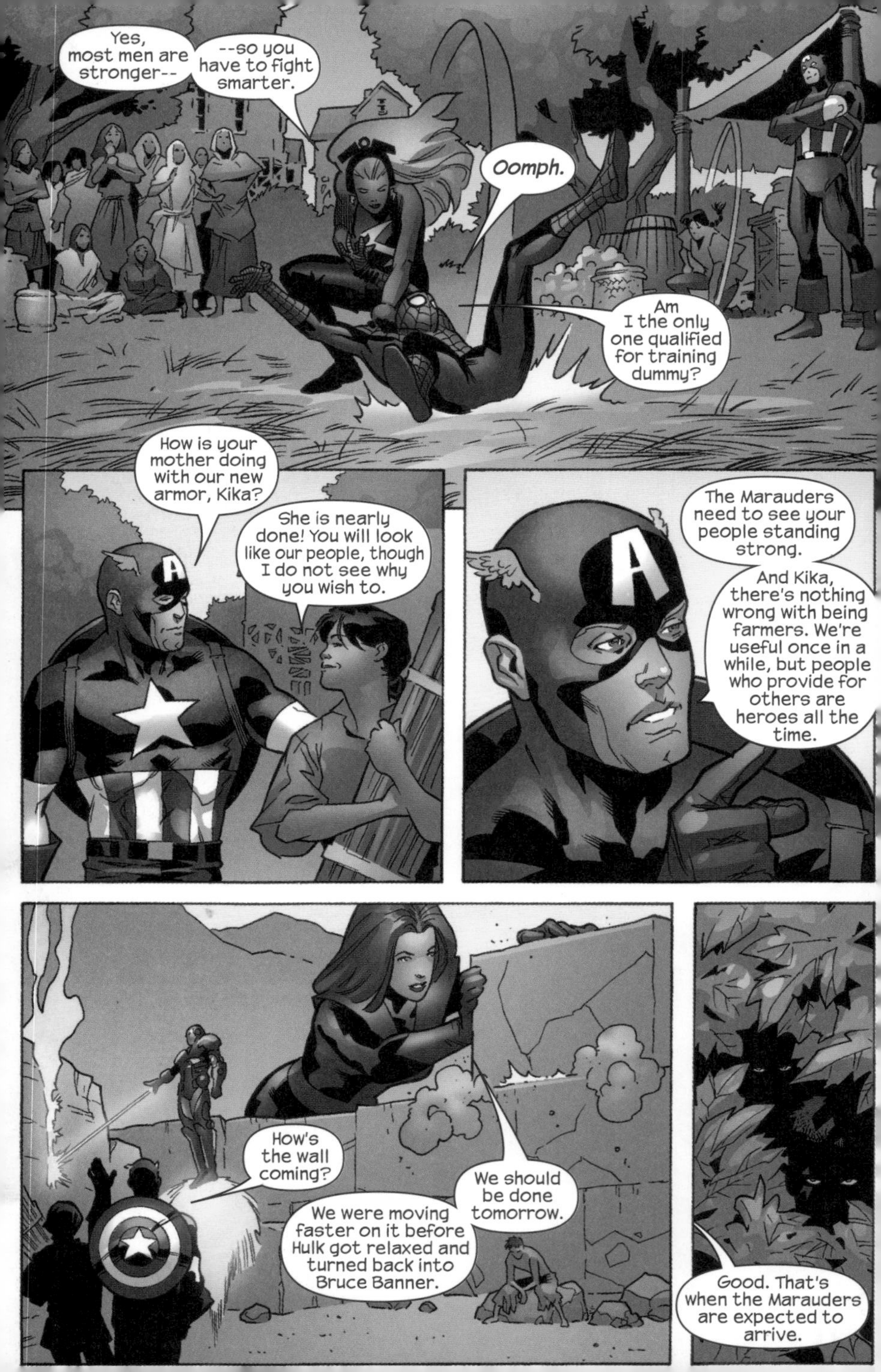

Yes, most men are stronger--
--so you have to fight smarter.
Oomph.
Am I the only one qualified for training dummy?
How is your mother doing with our new armor, Kika?
She is nearly done! You will look like our people, though I do not see why you wish to.
The Marauders need to see your people standing strong.
And Kika, there's nothing wrong with being farmers. We're useful once in a while, but people who provide for others are heroes all the time.
How's the wall coming?
We should be done tomorrow.
We were moving faster on it before Hulk got relaxed and turned back into Bruce Banner.
Good. That's when the Marauders are expected to arrive.

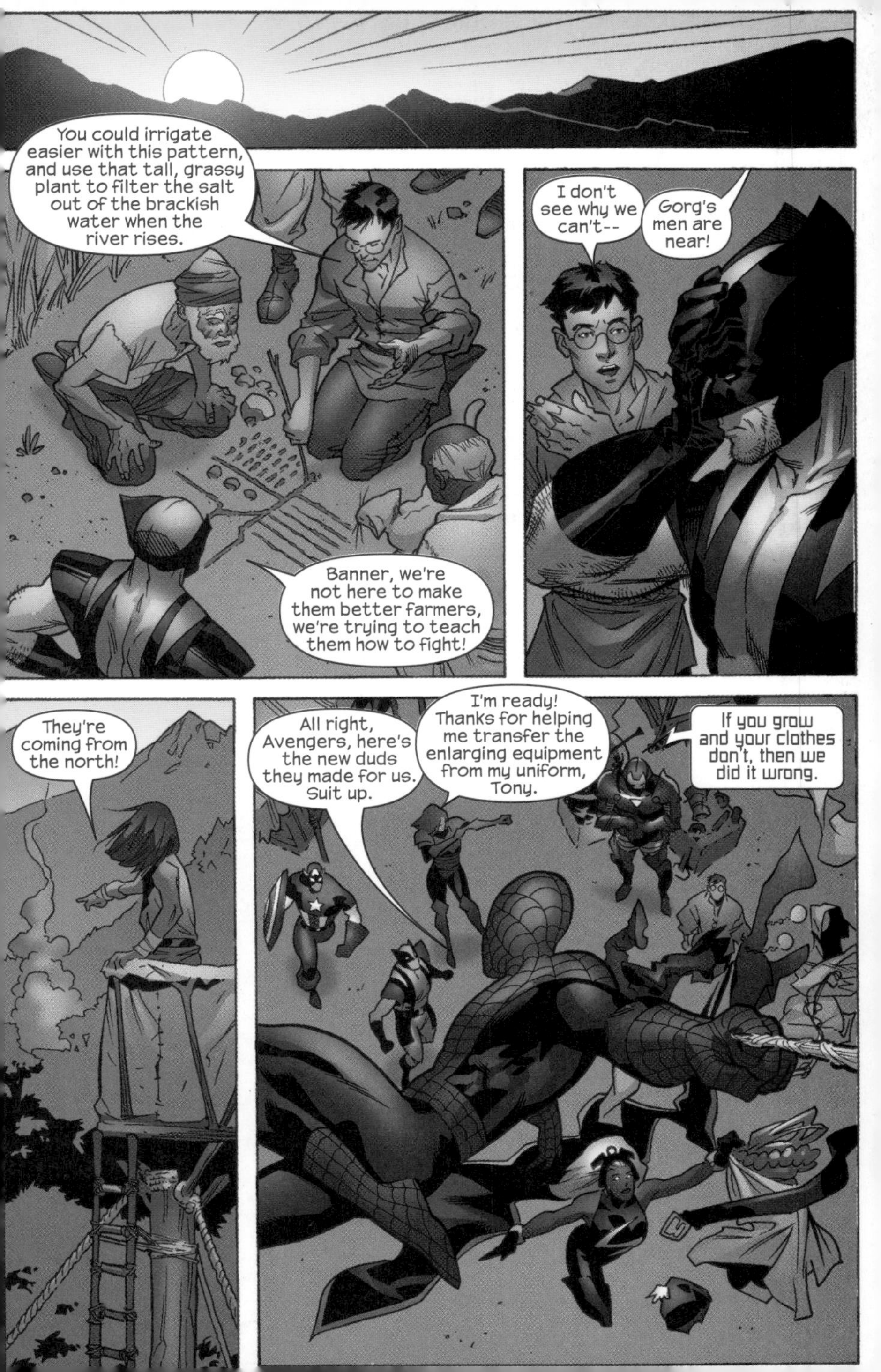
You could irrigate easier with this pattern, and use that tall, grassy plant to filter the salt out of the brackish water when the river rises.
Banner, we're not here to make them better farmers, we're trying to teach them how to fight!
I don't see why we can't--
Gorg's men are near!
They're coming from the north!
All right, Avengers, here's the new duds they made for us. Suit up.
I'm ready! Thanks for helping me transfer the enlarging equipment from my uniform, Tony.
If you grow and your clothes don't, then we did it wrong.

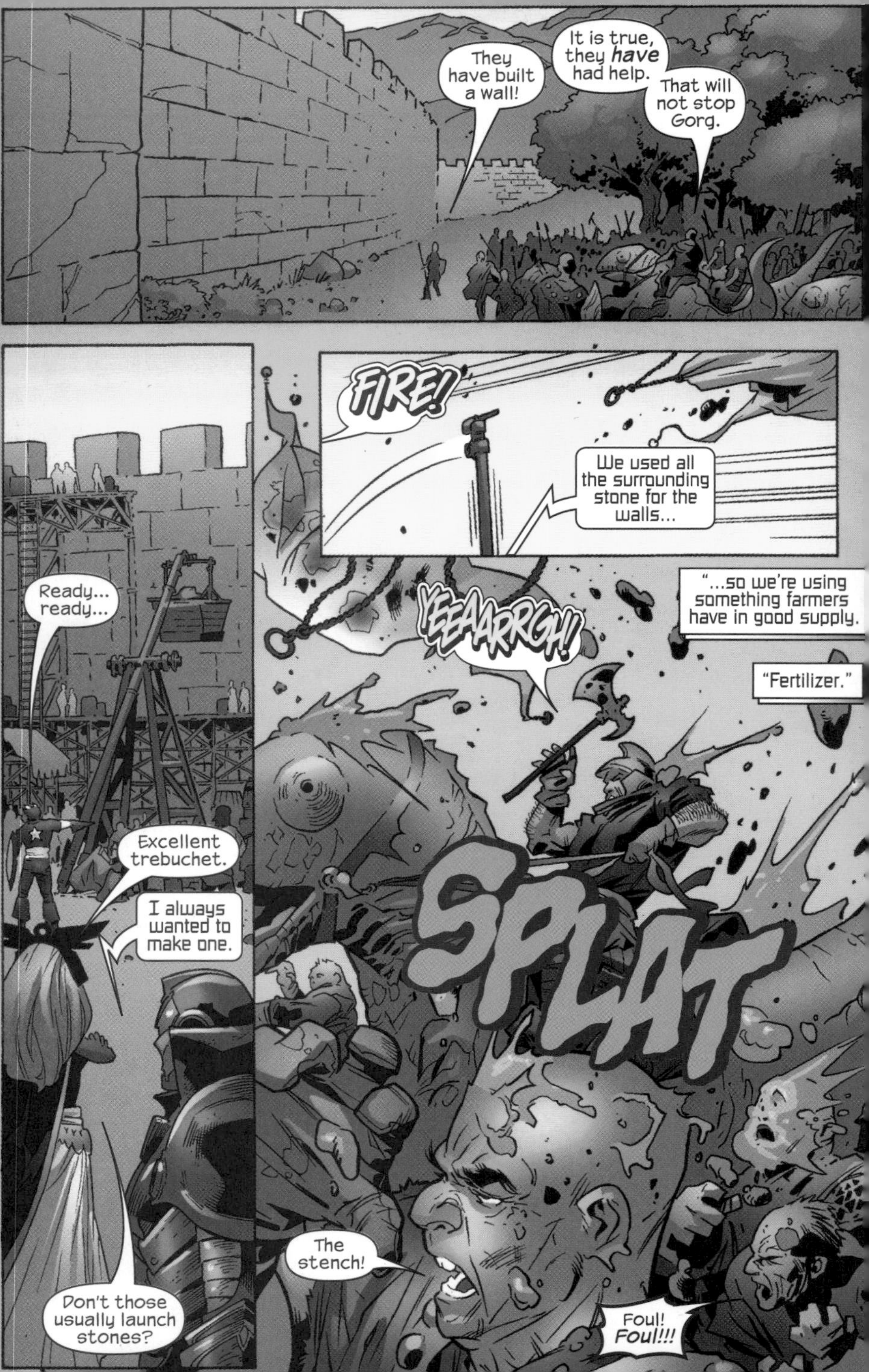
They have built a wall!
It is true, they *have* had help.
That will not stop Gorg.
Ready... ready...
Excellent trebuchet.
I always wanted to make one.
Don't those usually launch stones?
FIRE!
We used all the surrounding stone for the walls...
"...so we're using something farmers have in good supply.
"Fertilizer."
YEEAARRGH!
SPLAT
The stench!
Foul! *Foul!!!*

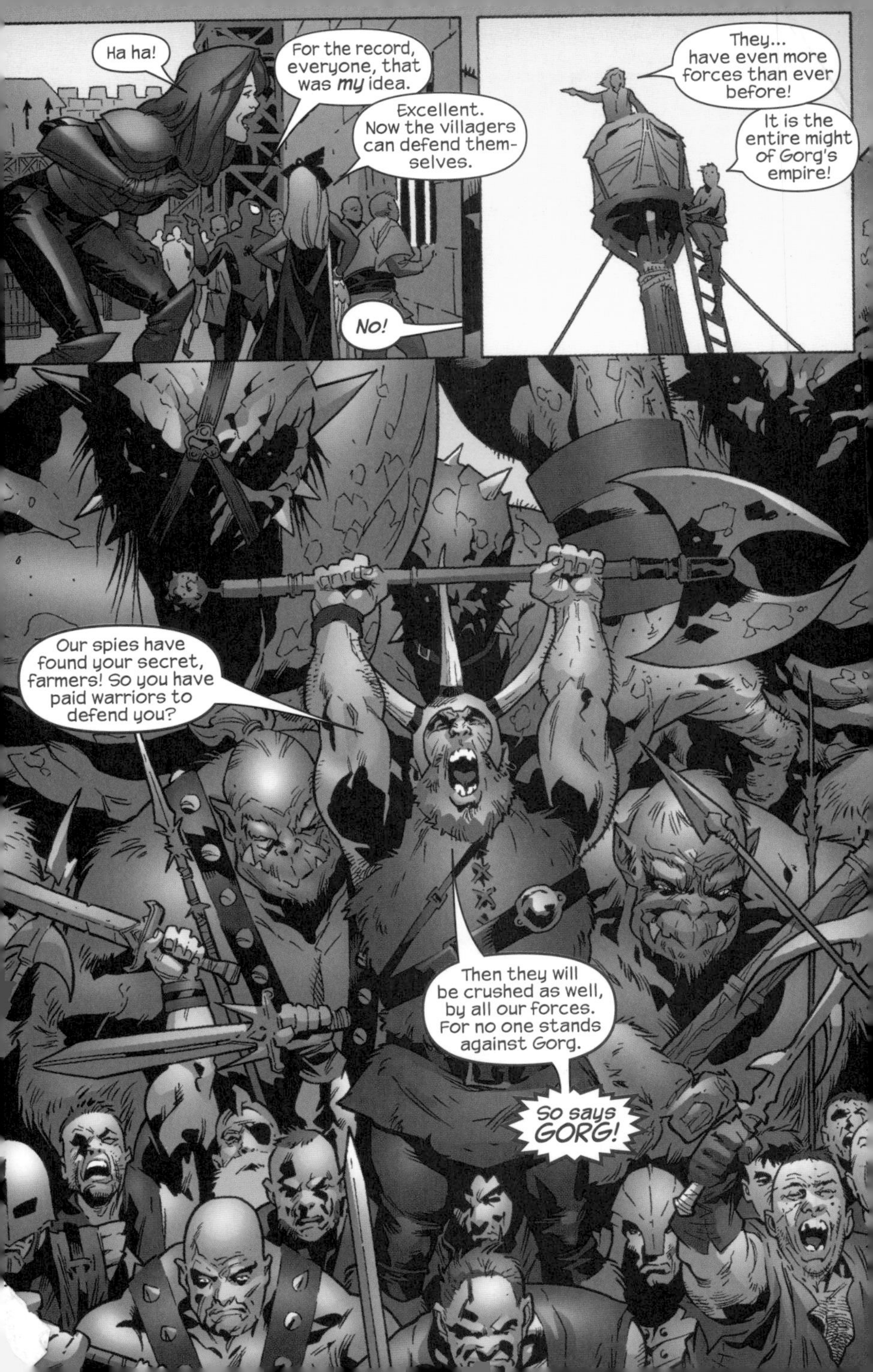
Ha ha!
For the record, everyone, that was *my* idea.
Excellent. Now the villagers can defend them-selves.
No!
They... have even more forces than ever before!
It is the entire might of Gorg's empire!
Our spies have found your secret, farmers! So you have paid warriors to defend you?
Then they will be crushed as well, by all our forces. For no one stands against Gorg.
So says GORG!

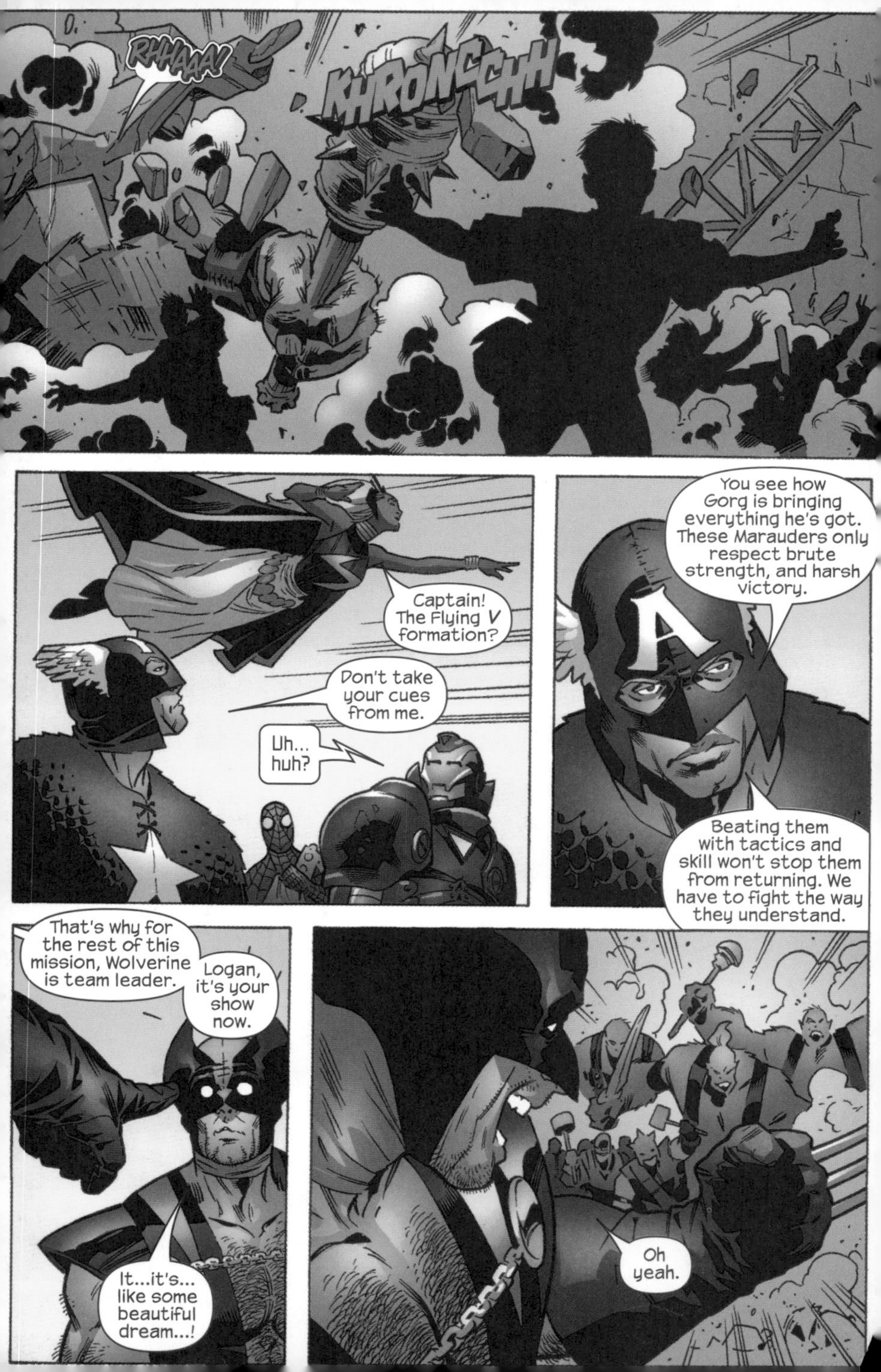
RHHAAA!
KHRONCHH
Captain! The Flying V formation?
Don't take your cues from me.
Uh... huh?
You see how Gorg is bringing everything he's got. These Marauders only respect brute strength, and harsh victory.
Beating them with tactics and skill won't stop them from returning. We have to fight the way they understand.
That's why for the rest of this mission, Wolverine is team leader.
Logan, it's your show now.
It...it's... like some beautiful dream...!
Oh yeah.

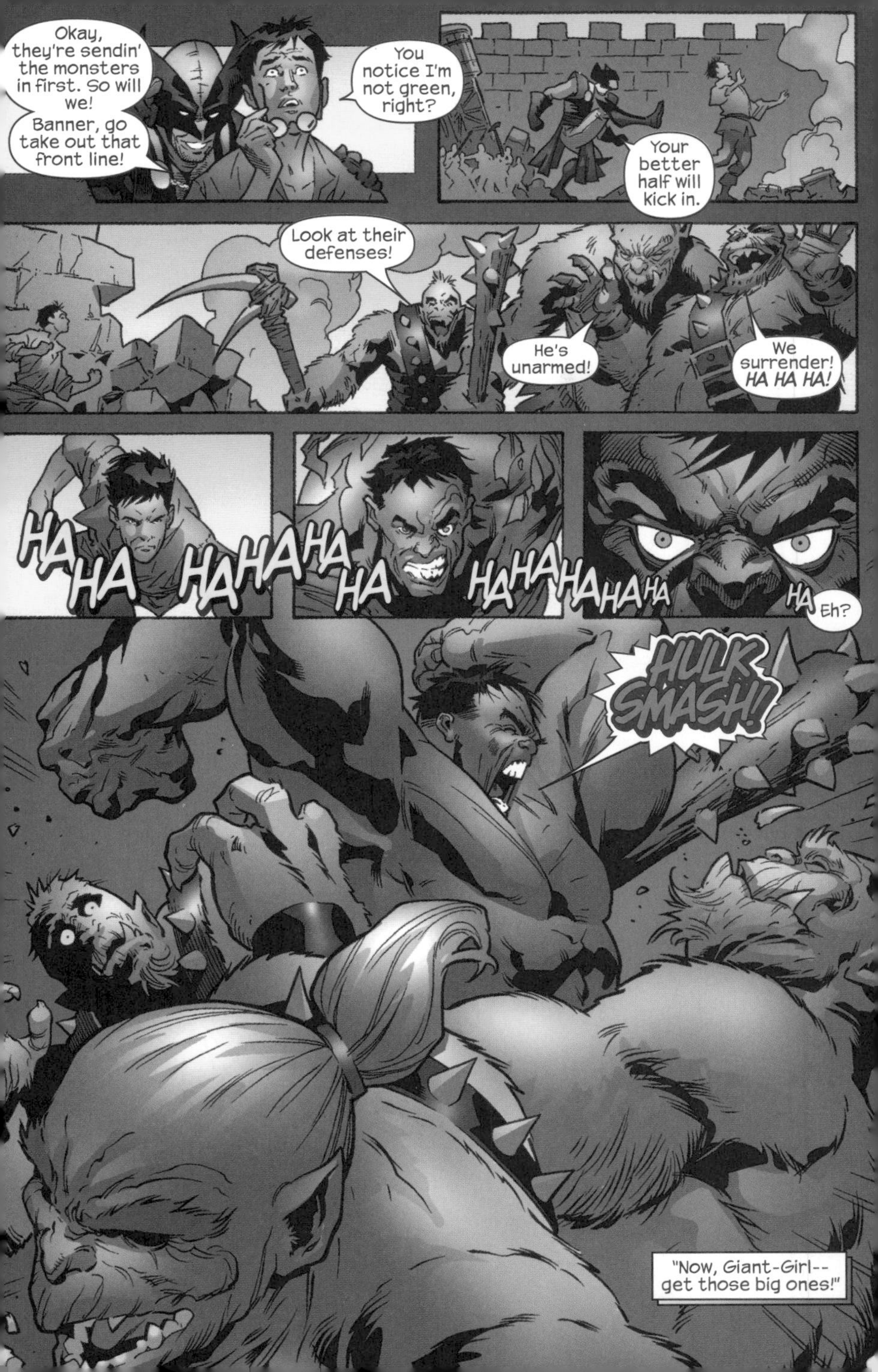

Okay, they're sendin' the monsters in first. So will we!
Banner, go take out that front line!
You notice I'm not green, right?
Your better half will kick in.
Look at their defenses!
He's unarmed!
We surrender! HA HA HA!
HA HA
HA HA HA HA HA
HA HA HA HA HA HA
HA
Eh?
HULK SMASH!
"Now, Giant-Girl-- get those big ones!"

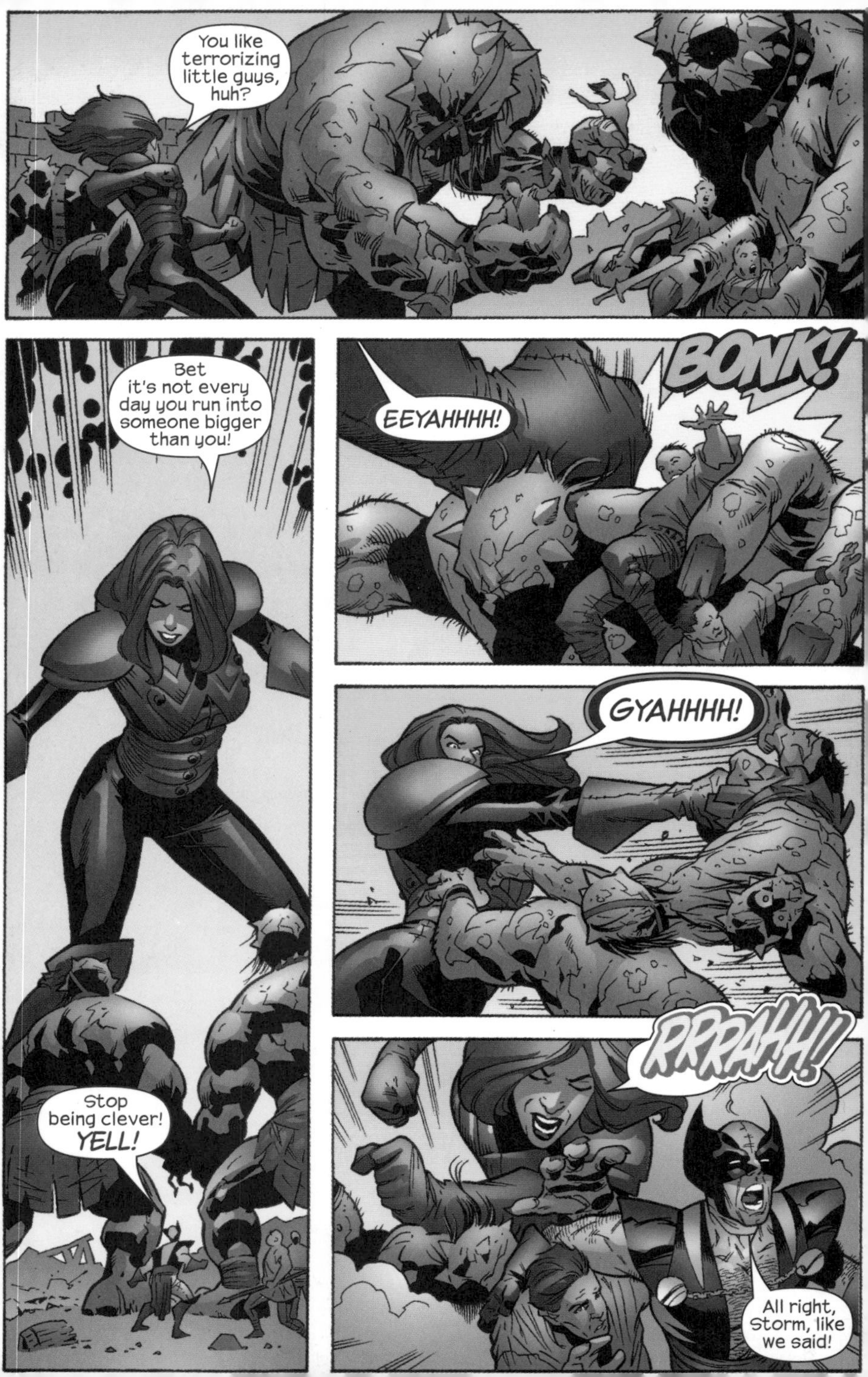
You like terrorizing little guys, huh?
Bet it's not every day you run into someone bigger than you!
Stop being clever! YELL!
EEYAHHHH!
BONK!
GYAHHHH!
RRRAHH!
All right, Storm, like we said!

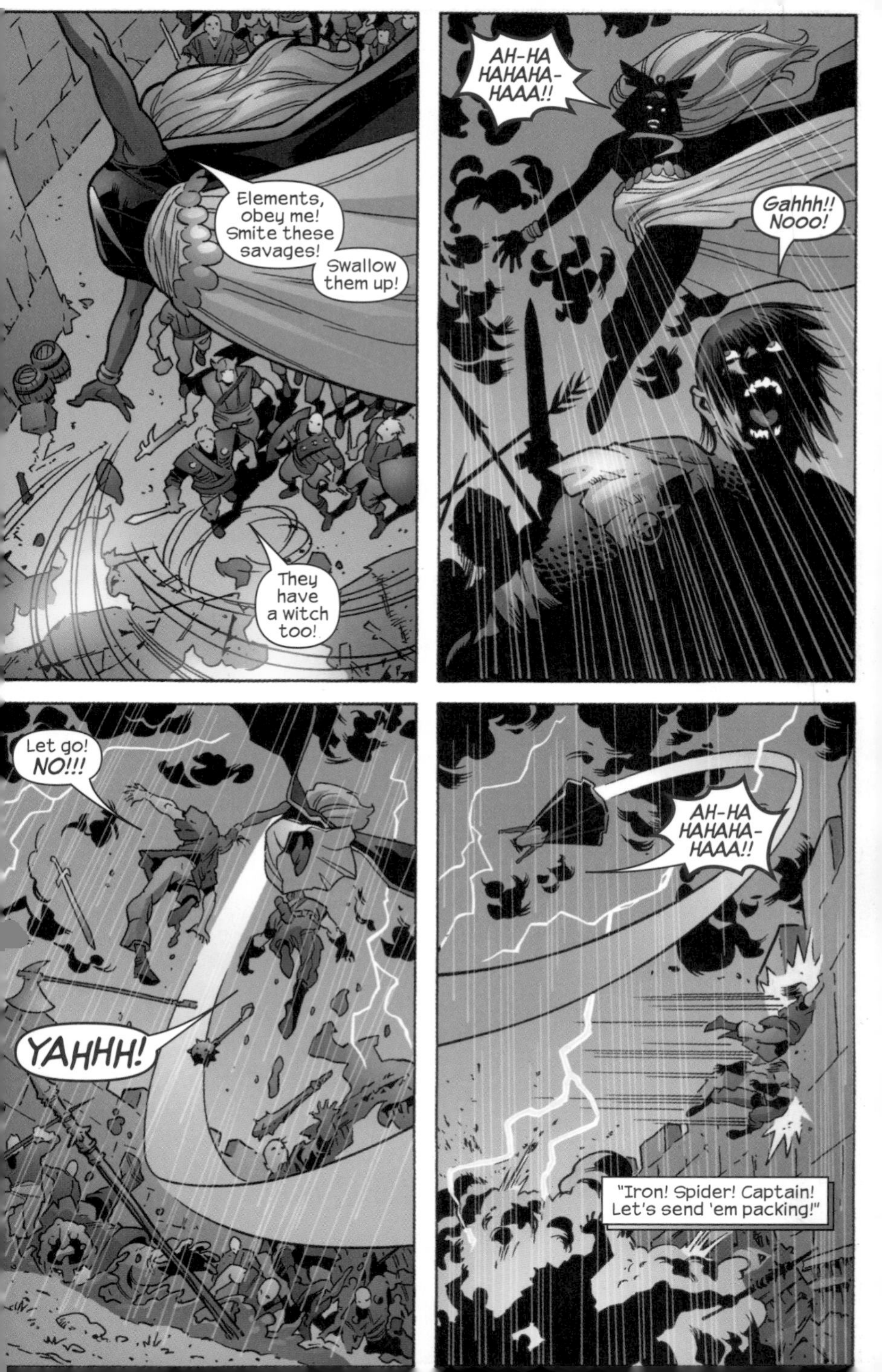

Elements, obey me! Smite these savages!
Swallow them up!
They have a witch too!
AH-HA HAHAHA-HAAA!!
Gahhh!! Nooo!
Let go! NO!!!
YAHHH!
AH-HA HAHAHA-HAAA!!
"Iron! Spider! Captain! Let's send 'em packing!"

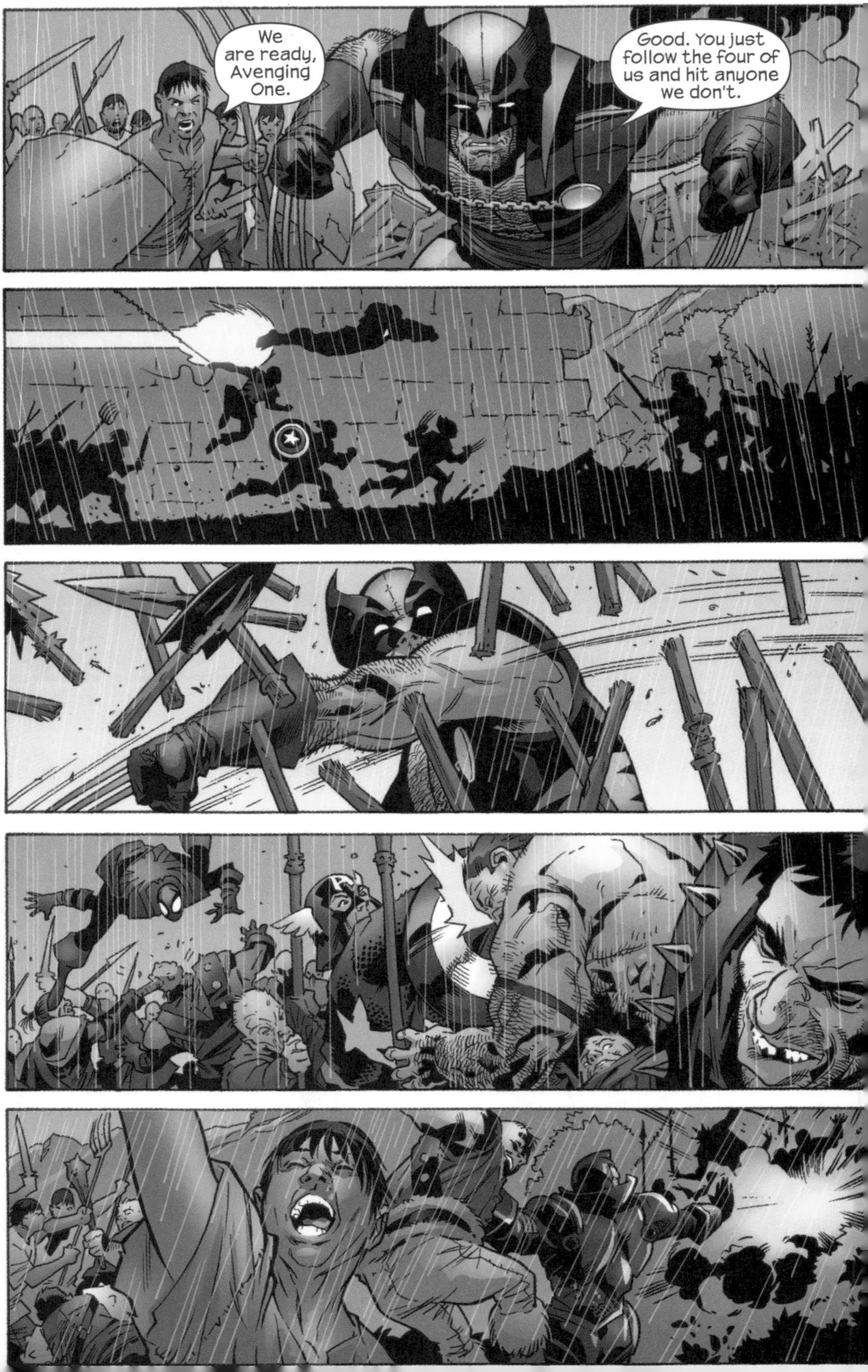
We are ready, Avenging One.
Good. You just follow the four of us and hit anyone we don't.

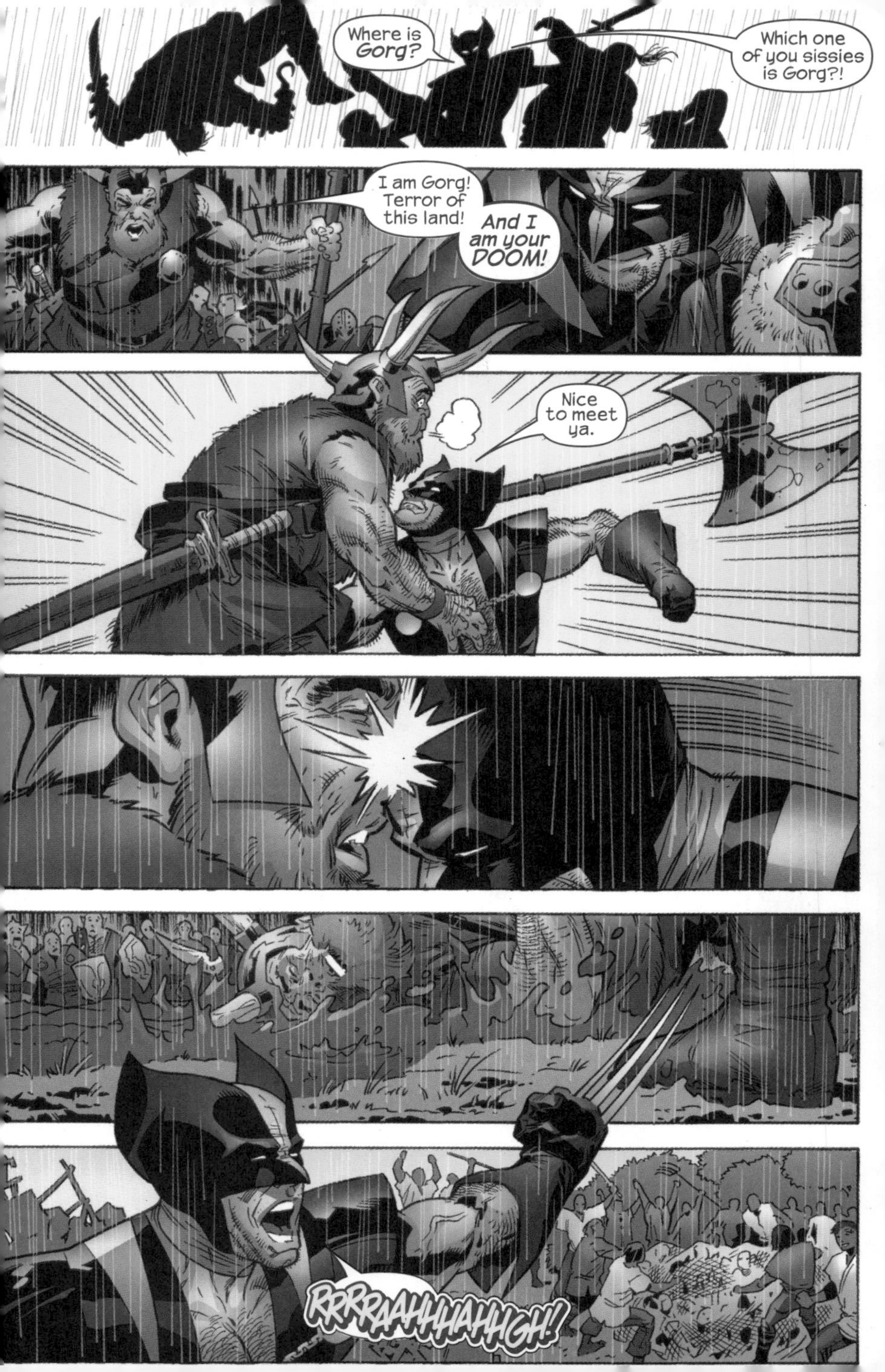
Where is Gorg?
Which one of you sissies is Gorg?!
I am Gorg! Terror of this land!
And I am your DOOM!
Nice to meet ya.
RRRRAAHHHAHHGH!

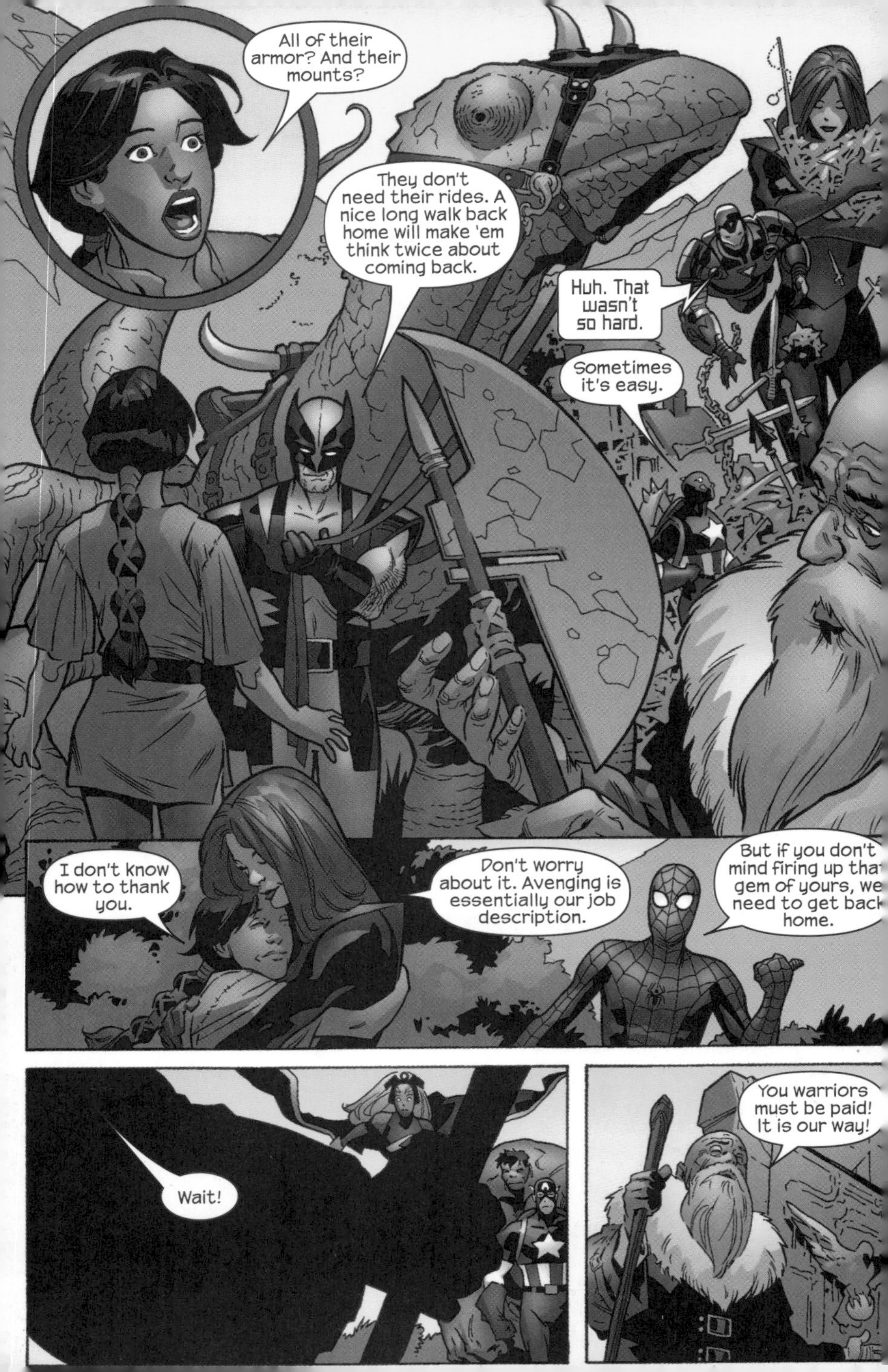
All of their armor? And their mounts?
They don't need their rides. A nice long walk back home will make 'em think twice about coming back.
Huh. That wasn't so hard.
Sometimes it's easy.
I don't know how to thank you.
Don't worry about it. Avenging is essentially our job description.
But if you don't mind firing up that gem of yours, we need to get back home.
Wait!
You warriors must be paid! It is our way!

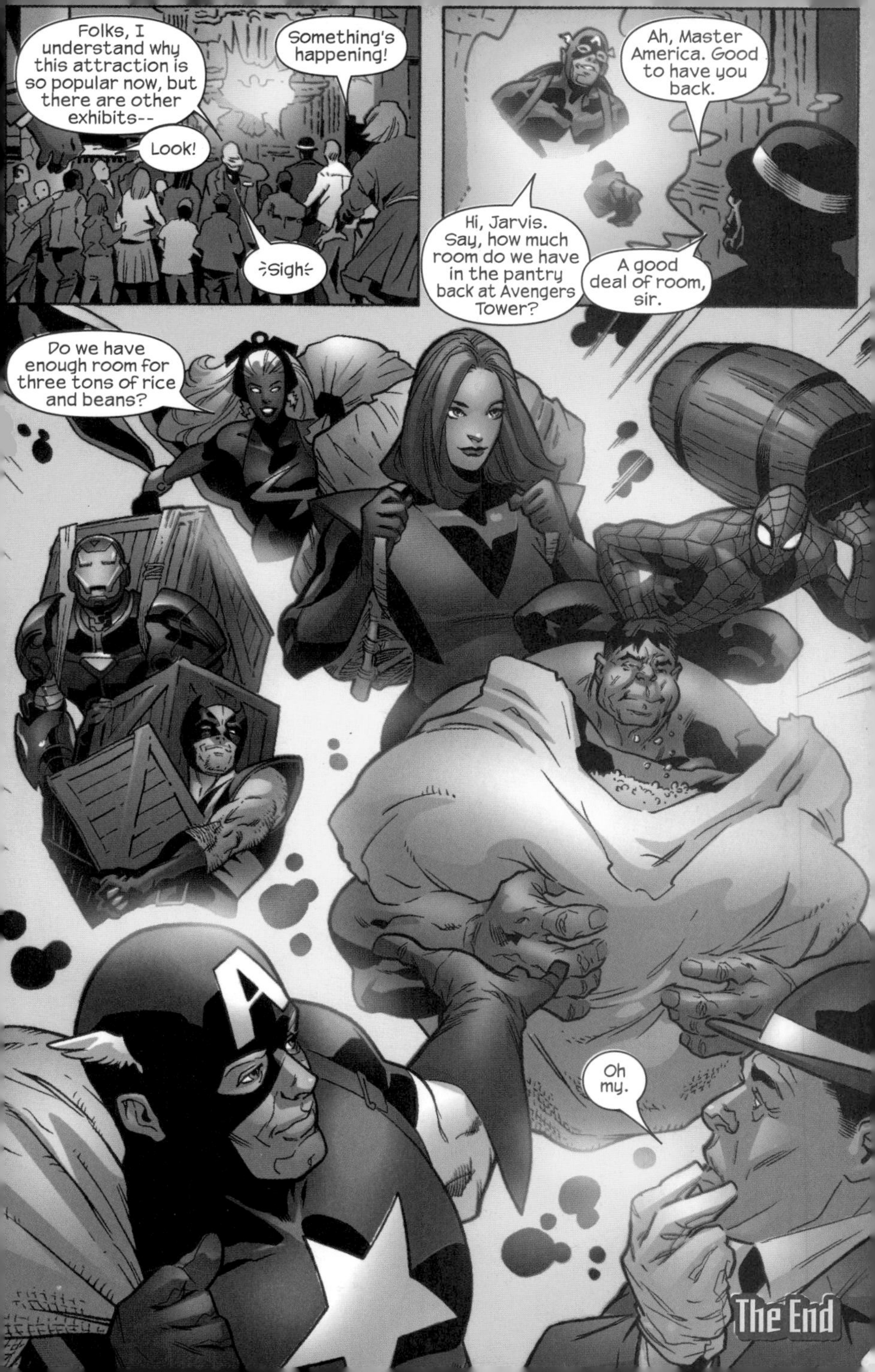

Folks, I understand why this attraction is so popular now, but there are other exhibits--
Something's happening!
Look!
Sigh
Ah, Master America. Good to have you back.
Hi, Jarvis. Say, how much room do we have in the pantry back at Avengers Tower?
A good deal of room, sir.
Do we have enough room for three tons of rice and beans?
Oh my.
The End

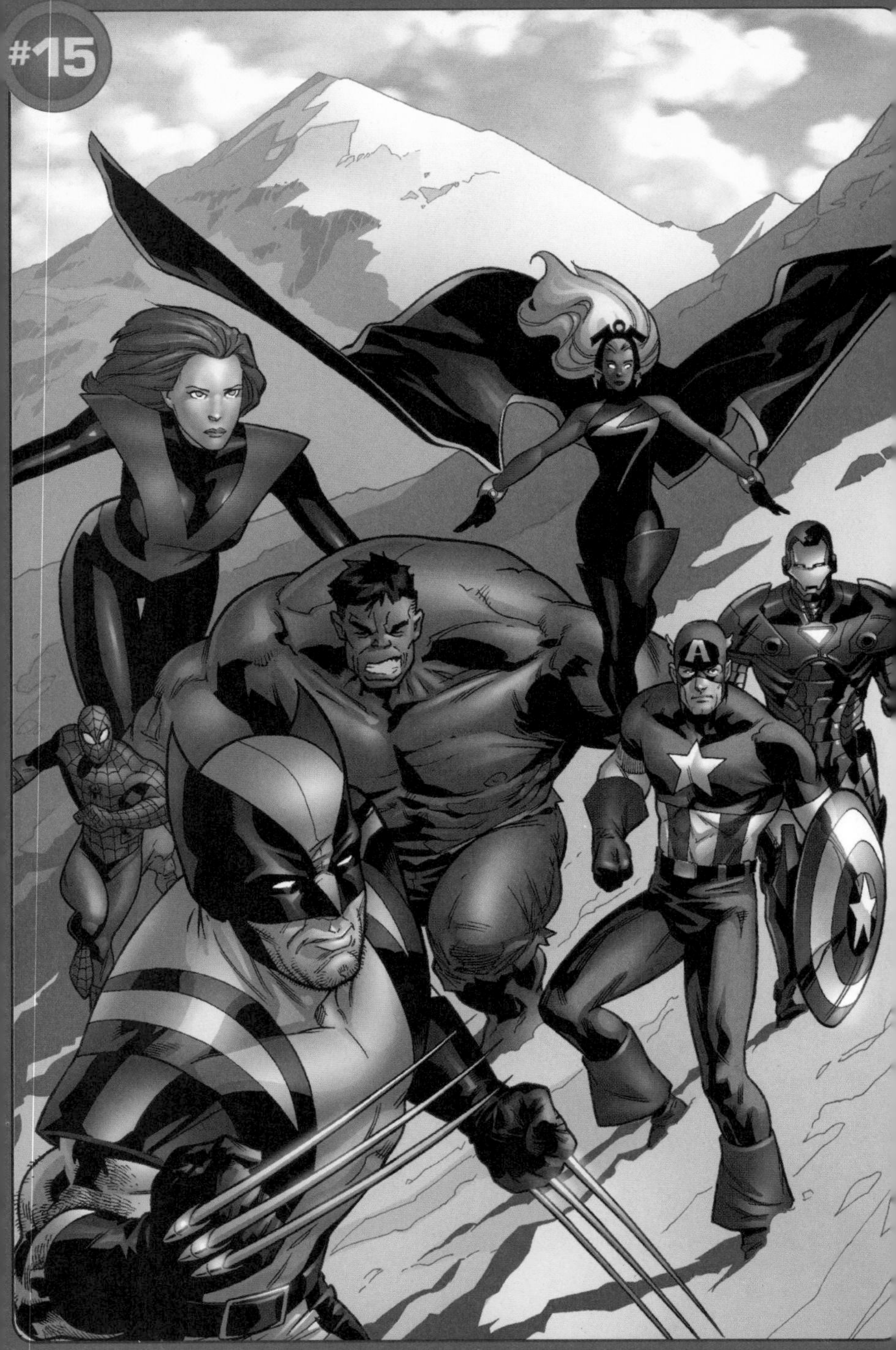
#15

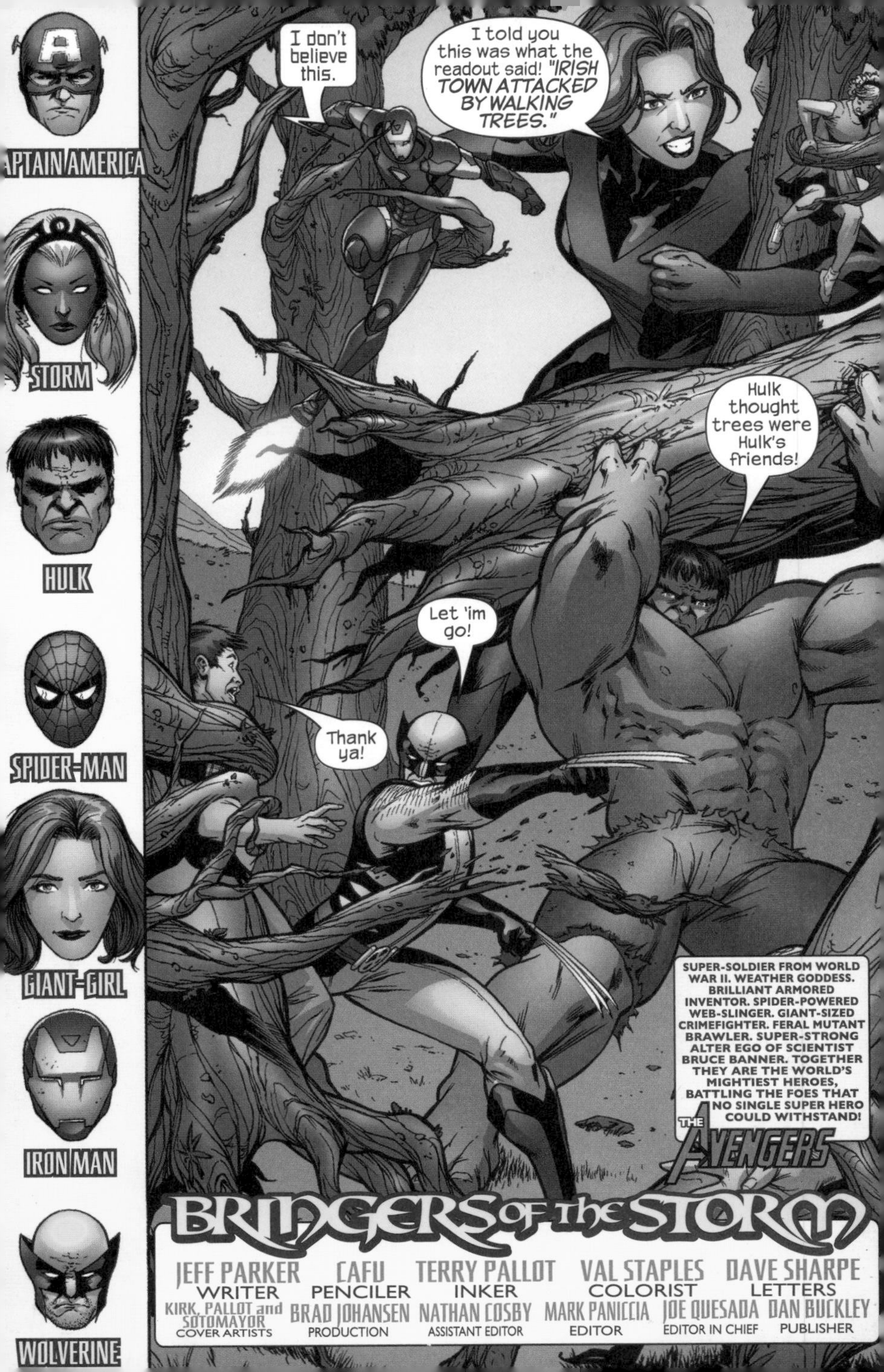

APTAIN AMERICA
STORM
HULK
SPIDER-MAN
GIANT-GIRL
IRON MAN
WOLVERINE
I don't believe this.
I told you this was what the readout said! "IRISH TOWN ATTACKED BY WALKING TREES."
Hulk thought trees were Hulk's friends!
Let 'im go!
Thank ya!
SUPER-SOLDIER FROM WORLD WAR II. WEATHER GODDESS. BRILLIANT ARMORED INVENTOR. SPIDER-POWERED WEB-SLINGER. GIANT-SIZED CRIMEFIGHTER. FERAL MUTANT BRAWLER. SUPER-STRONG ALTER EGO OF SCIENTIST BRUCE BANNER. TOGETHER THEY ARE THE WORLD'S MIGHTIEST HEROES, BATTLING THE FOES THAT NO SINGLE SUPER HERO COULD WITHSTAND!
THE AVENGERS
BRINGERS OF THE STORM
JEFF PARKER WRITER
CAFU PENCILER
TERRY PALLOT INKER
VAL STAPLES COLORIST
DAVE SHARPE LETTERS
KIRK, PALLOT and SOTOMAYOR COVER ARTISTS
BRAD JOHANSEN PRODUCTION
NATHAN COSBY ASSISTANT EDITOR
MARK PANICCIA EDITOR
JOE QUESADA EDITOR IN CHIEF
DAN BUCKLEY PUBLISHER

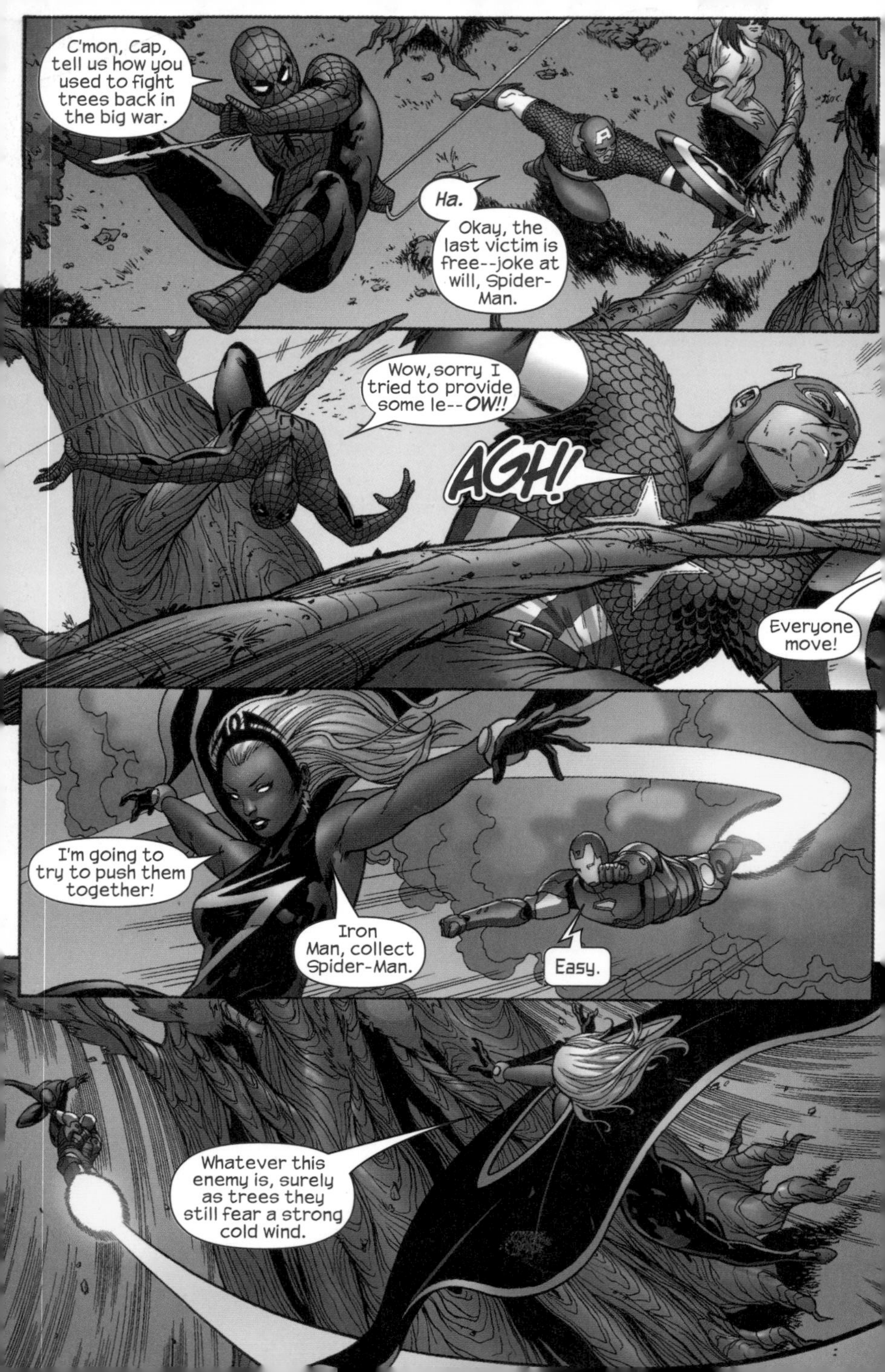
C'mon, Cap, tell us how you used to fight trees back in the big war.
Ha.
Okay, the last victim is free--joke at will, Spider-Man.
Wow, sorry I tried to provide some le--OW!!
AGH!
Everyone move!
I'm going to try to push them together!
Iron Man, collect Spider-Man.
Easy.
Whatever this enemy is, surely as trees they still fear a strong cold wind.

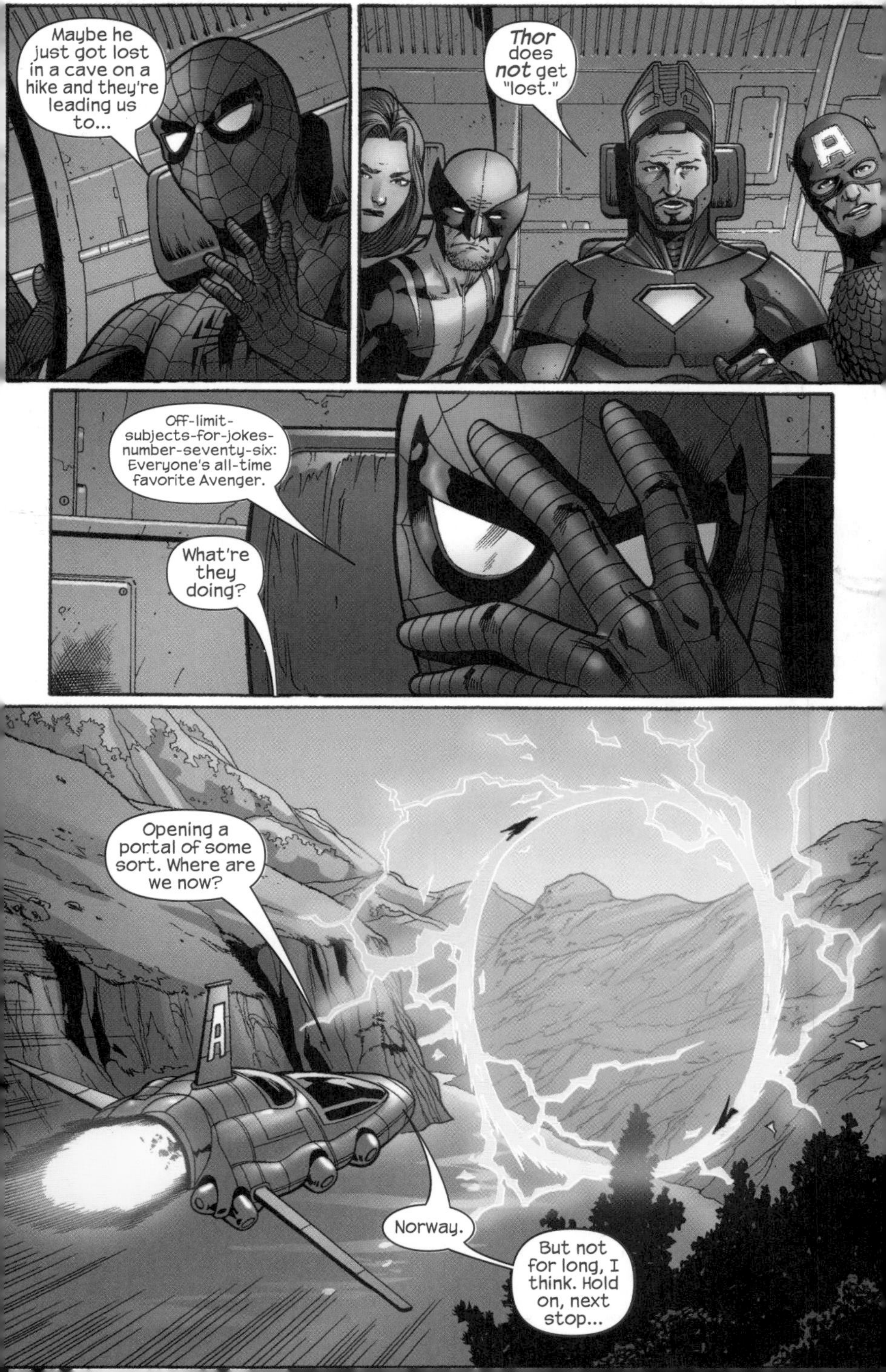
Maybe he just got lost in a cave on a hike and they're leading us to...
Thor does not get "lost."
Off-limit-subjects-for-jokes-number-seventy-six: Everyone's all-time favorite Avenger.
What're they doing?
Opening a portal of some sort. Where are we now?
Norway.
But not for long, I think. Hold on, next stop...

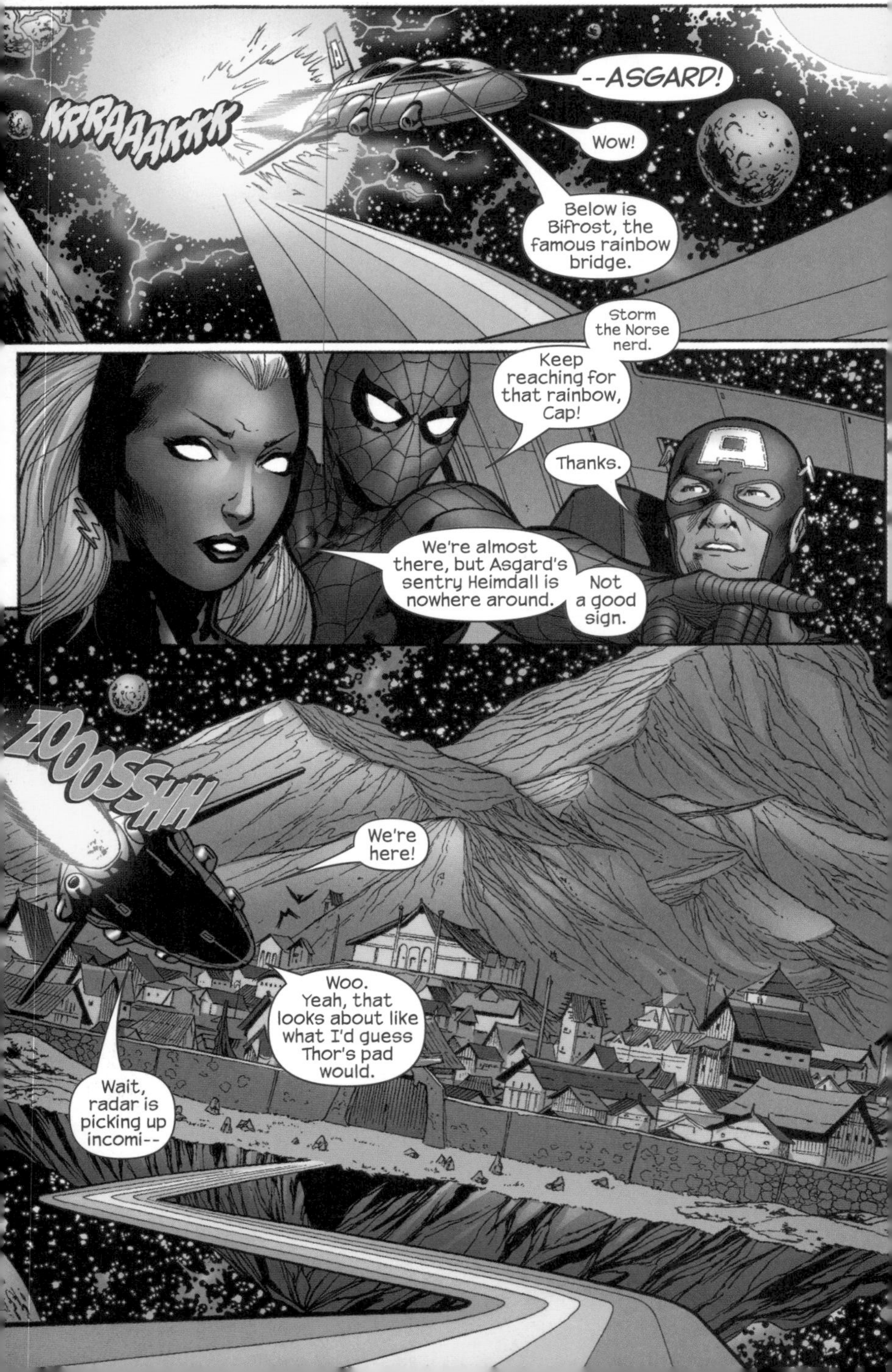
--ASGARD!
KRRAAAKKK
Wow!
Below is Bifrost, the famous rainbow bridge.
Storm the Norse nerd.
Keep reaching for that rainbow, Cap!
Thanks.
We're almost there, but Asgard's sentry Heimdall is nowhere around.
Not a good sign.
ZOOOSSHH
We're here!
Woo. Yeah, that looks about like what I'd guess Thor's pad would.
Wait, radar is picking up incomi--

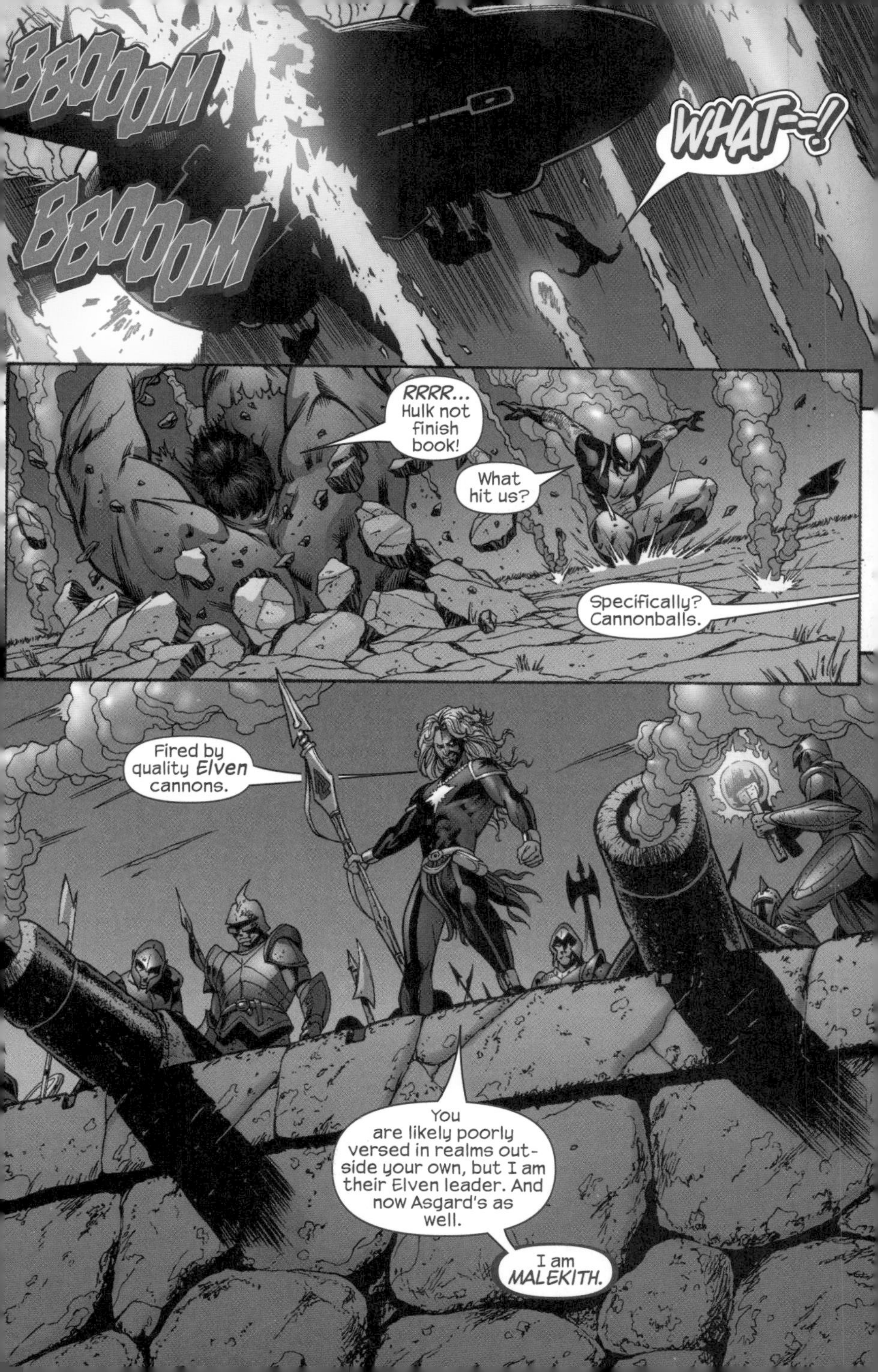
BBOOOOM
BBOOOOM
WHAT--!
RRRR... Hulk not finish book!
What hit us?
Specifically? Cannonballs.
Fired by quality *Elven* cannons.
You are likely poorly versed in realms outside your own, but I am their Elven leader. And now Asgard's as well.
I am *MALEKITH.*

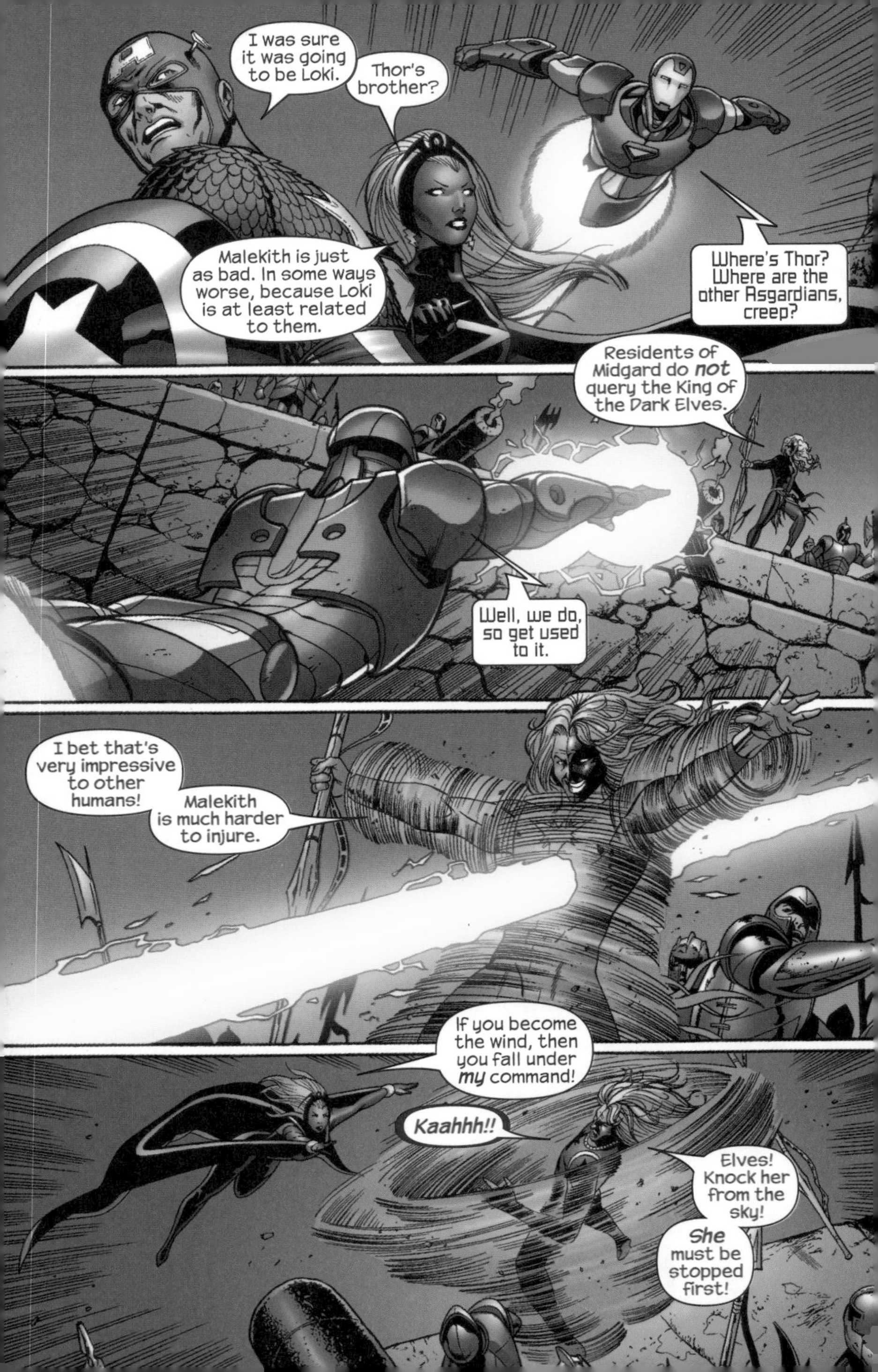

I was sure it was going to be Loki.
Thor's brother?
Malekith is just as bad. In some ways worse, because Loki is at least related to them.
Where's Thor? Where are the other Asgardians, creep?
Residents of Midgard do *not* query the King of the Dark Elves.
Well, we do, so get used to it.
I bet that's very impressive to other humans!
Malekith is much harder to injure.
If you become the wind, then you fall under *my* command!
Kaahhh!!
Elves! Knock her from the sky!
She must be stopped first!

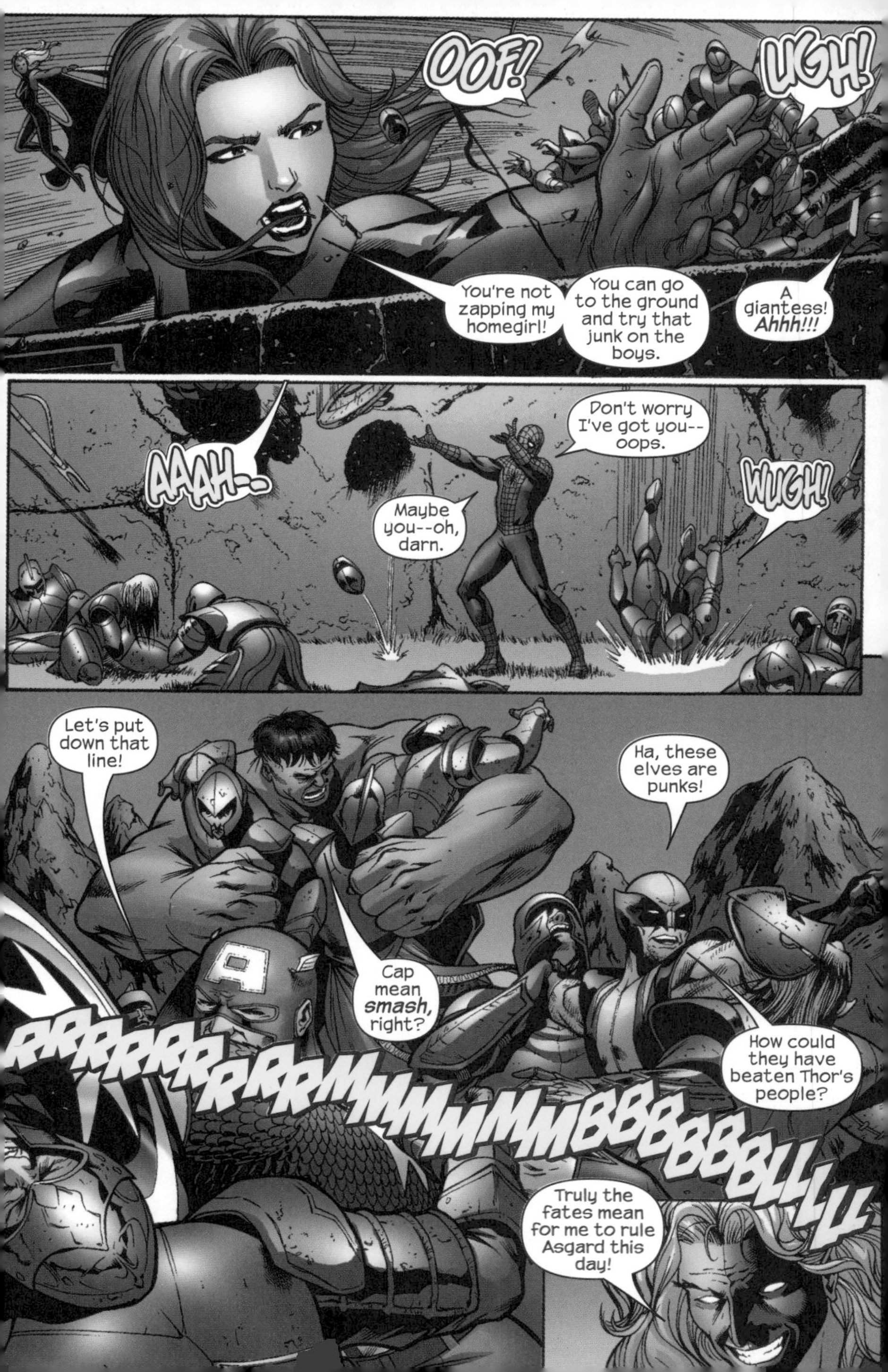
OOF!
UGH!
You're not zapping my homegirl!
You can go to the ground and try that junk on the boys.
A giantess! *Ahhh!!!*
AAAH--
Don't worry I've got you-- oops.
Maybe you--oh, darn.
WUGH!
Let's put down that line!
Ha, these elves are punks!
Cap mean *smash,* right?
RRRRRRRRRMMMMMMMBBBBBBLLLL
How could they have beaten Thor's people?
Truly the fates mean for me to rule Asgard this day!

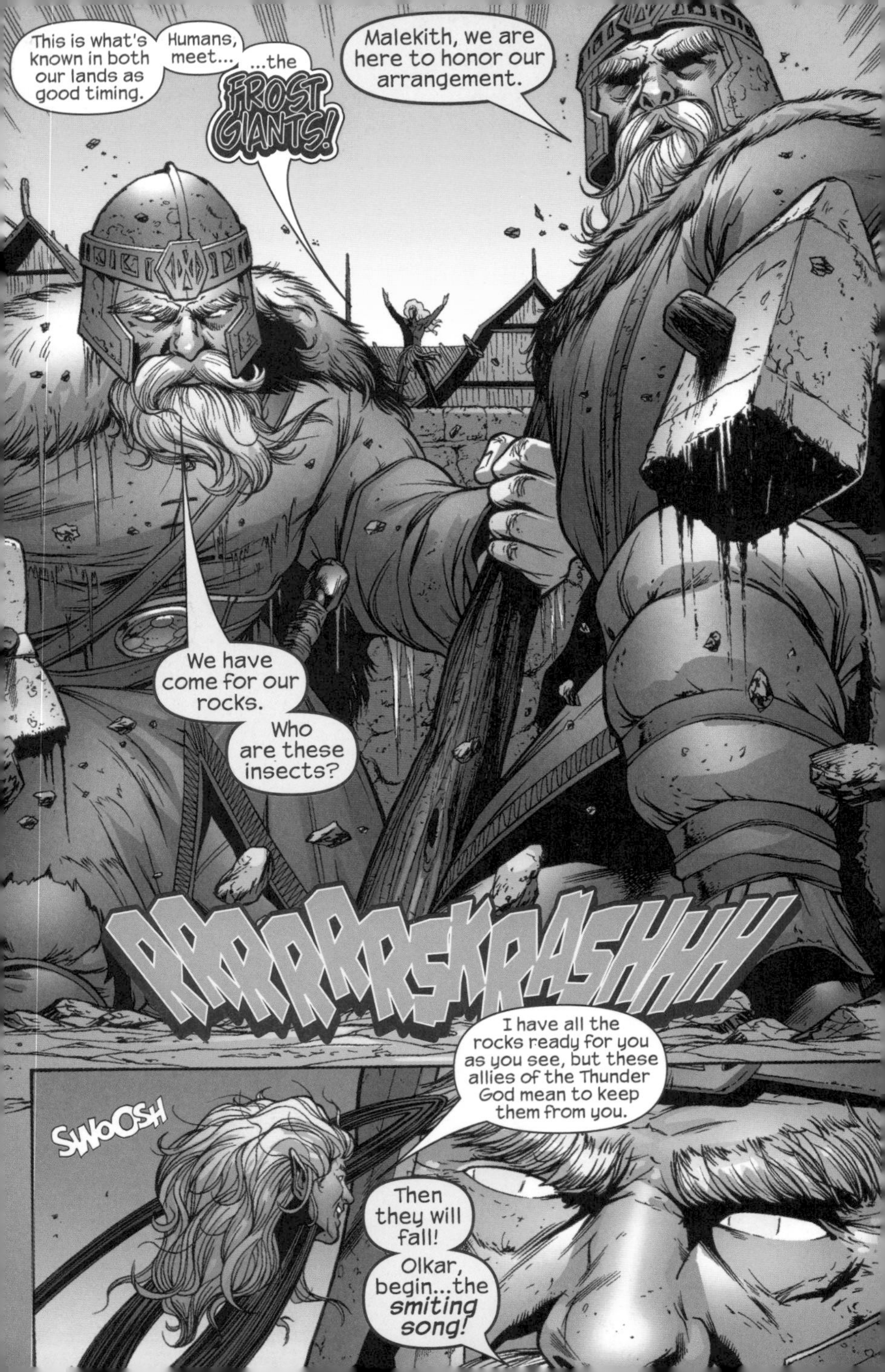
This is what's known in both our lands as good timing.
Humans, meet...
...the FROST GIANTS!
Malekith, we are here to honor our arrangement.
We have come for our rocks.
Who are these insects?
RRRRRRSKRASHHH
I have all the rocks ready for you as you see, but these allies of the Thunder God mean to keep them from you.
SWOOSH
Then they will fall!
Olkar, begin...the *smiting song!*

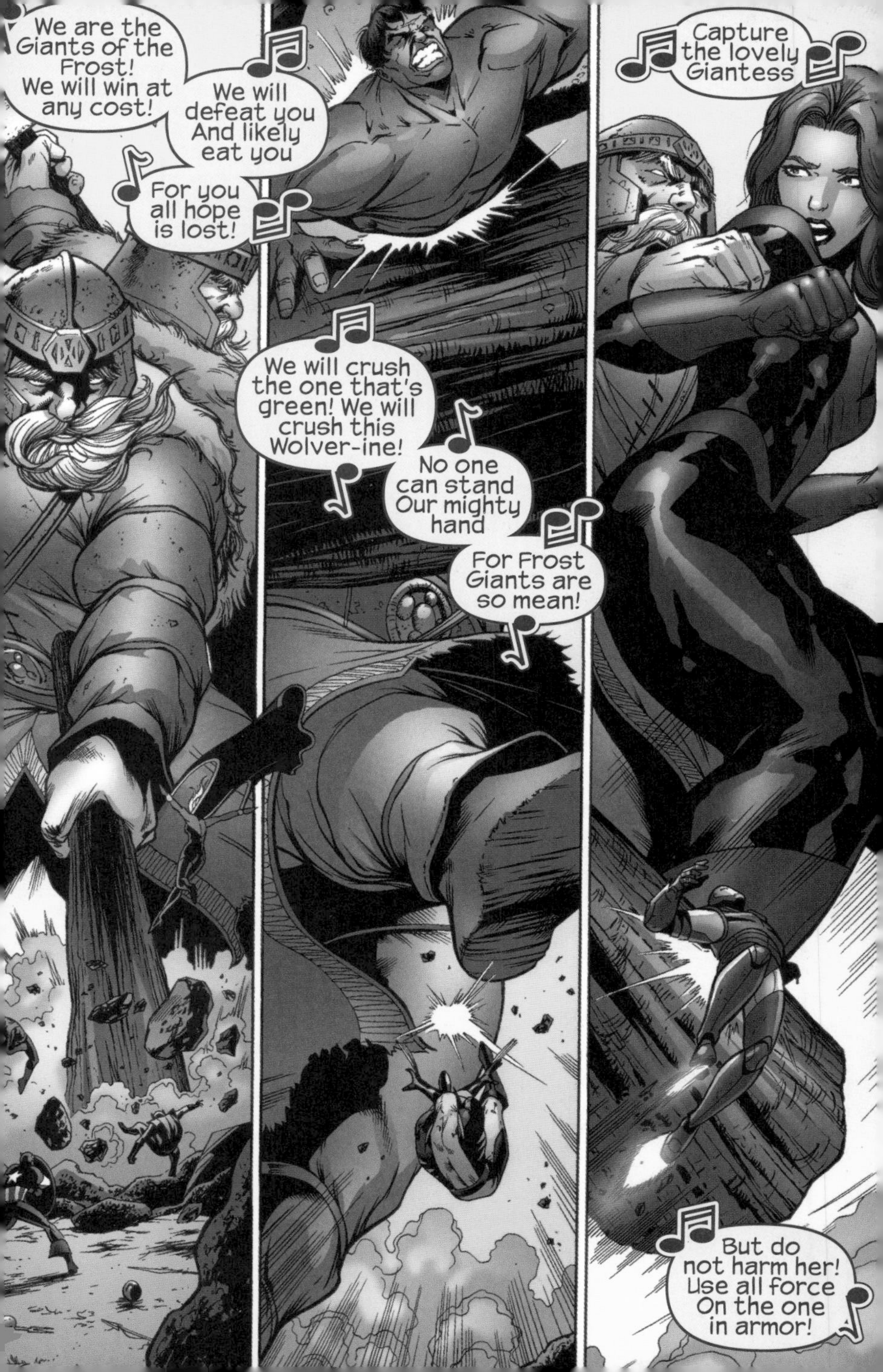
We are the Giants of the Frost! We will win at any cost!
We will defeat you And likely eat you
For you all hope is lost!
We will crush the one that's green! We will crush this Wolver-ine!
No one can stand Our mighty hand
For Frost Giants are so mean!
Capture the lovely Giantess
But do not harm her! Use all force On the one in armor!

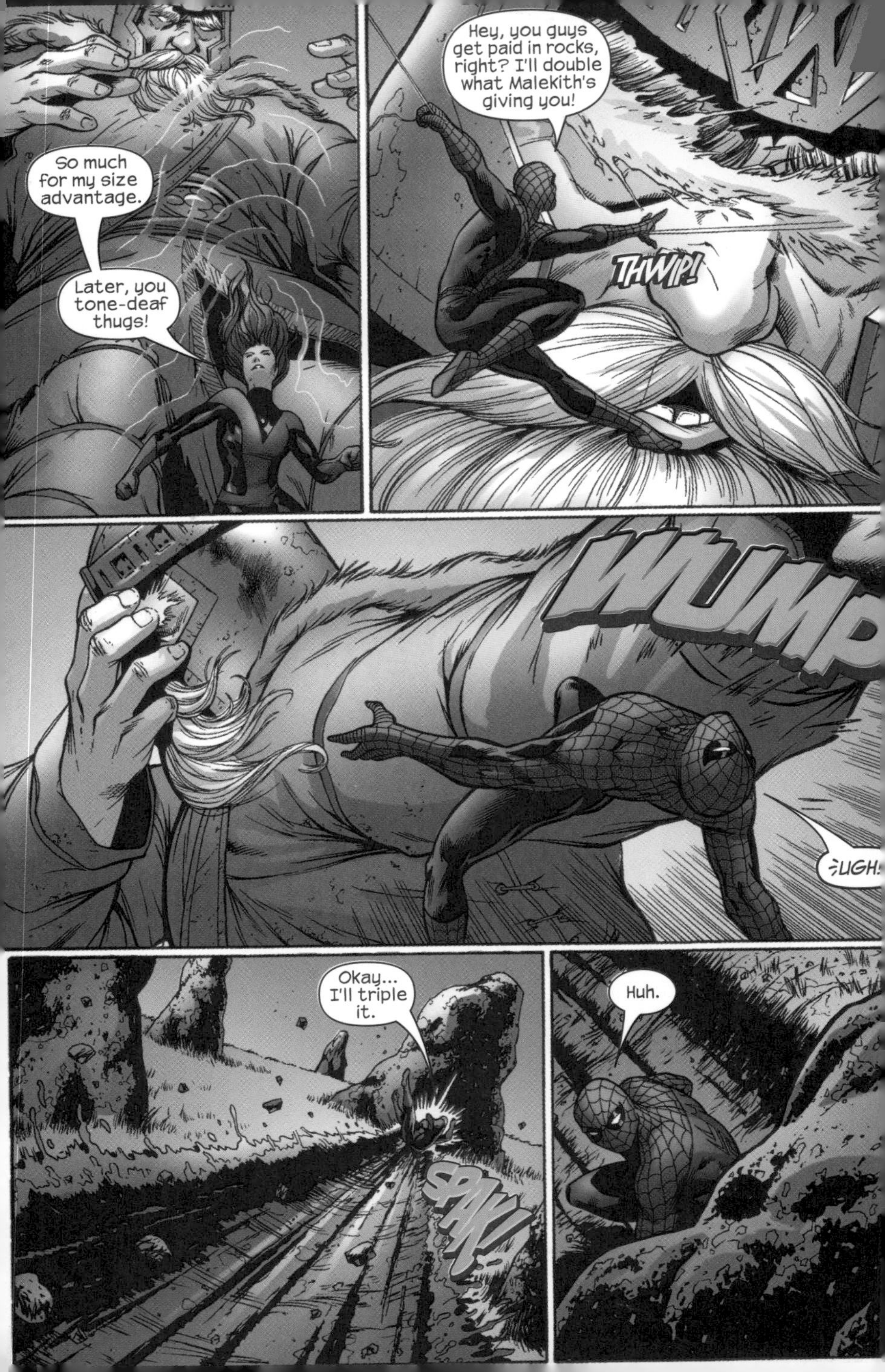
So much for my size advantage.
Later, you tone-deaf thugs!
Hey, you guys get paid in rocks, right? I'll double what Malekith's giving you!
THWIP!
WUMP
UGH!
Okay... I'll triple it.
SPAK!
Huh.

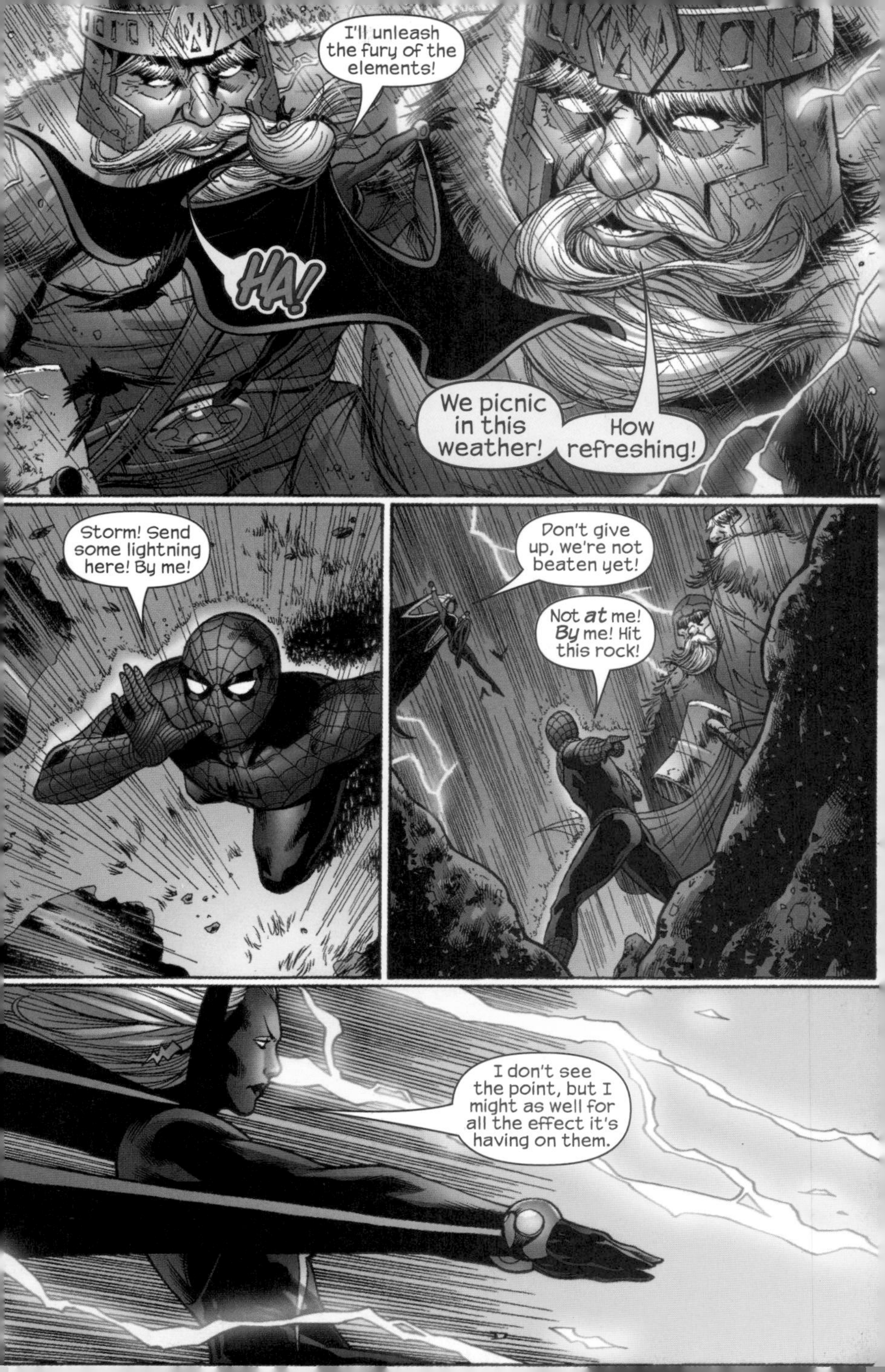

I'll unleash the fury of the elements!
HA!
We picnic in this weather!
How refreshing!
Storm! Send some lightning here! By me!
Don't give up, we're not beaten yet!
Not at me! By me! Hit this rock!
I don't see the point, but I might as well for all the effect it's having on them.

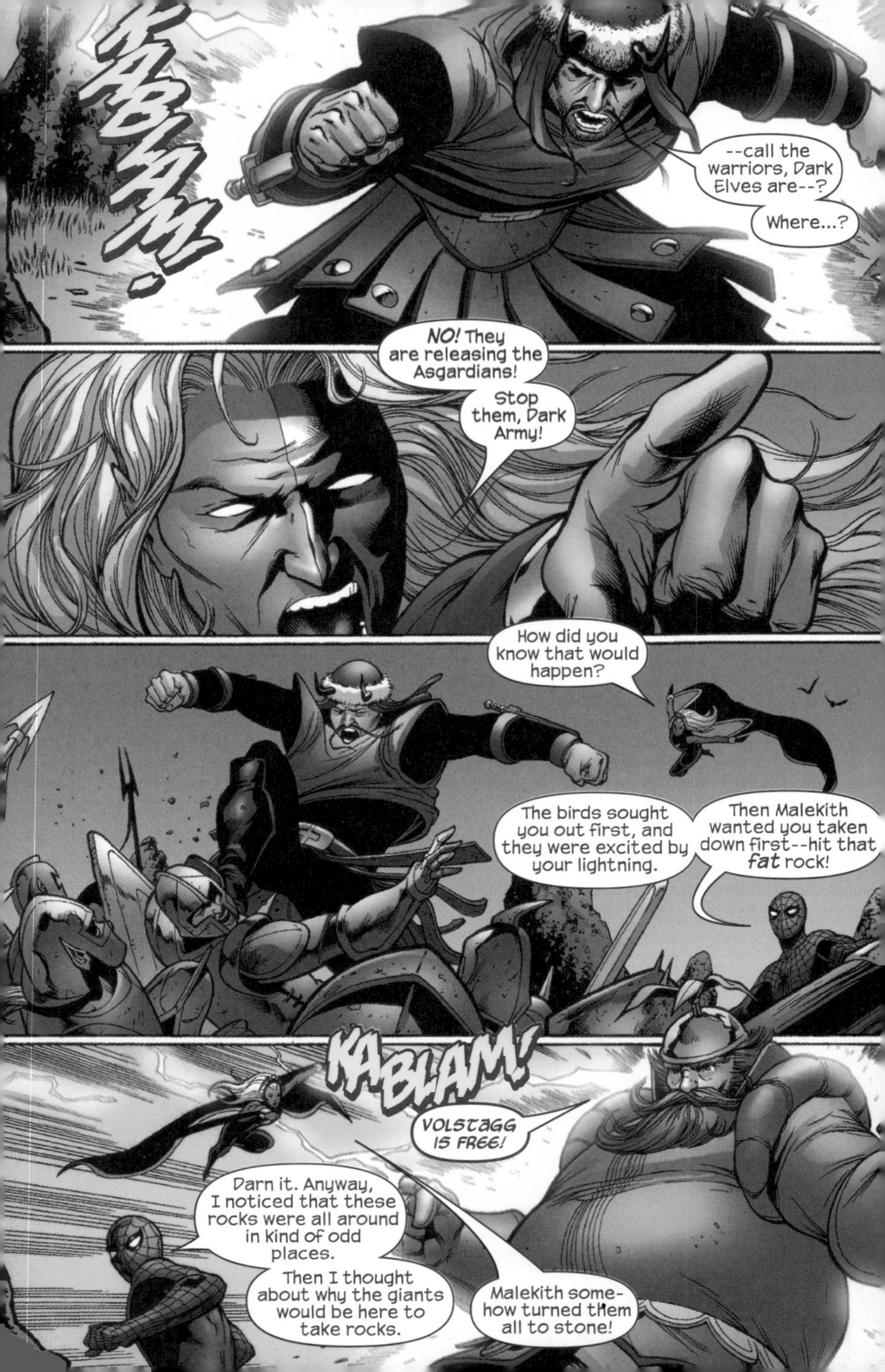
KABLAM!
--call the warriors, Dark Elves are--?
Where...?
NO! They are releasing the Asgardians!
Stop them, Dark Army!
How did you know that would happen?
The birds sought you out first, and they were excited by your lightning.
Then Malekith wanted you taken down first--hit that fat rock!
KA BLAM!
VOLSTAGG IS FREE!
Darn it. Anyway, I noticed that these rocks were all around in kind of odd places.
Then I thought about why the giants would be here to take rocks.
Malekith some-how turned them all to stone!

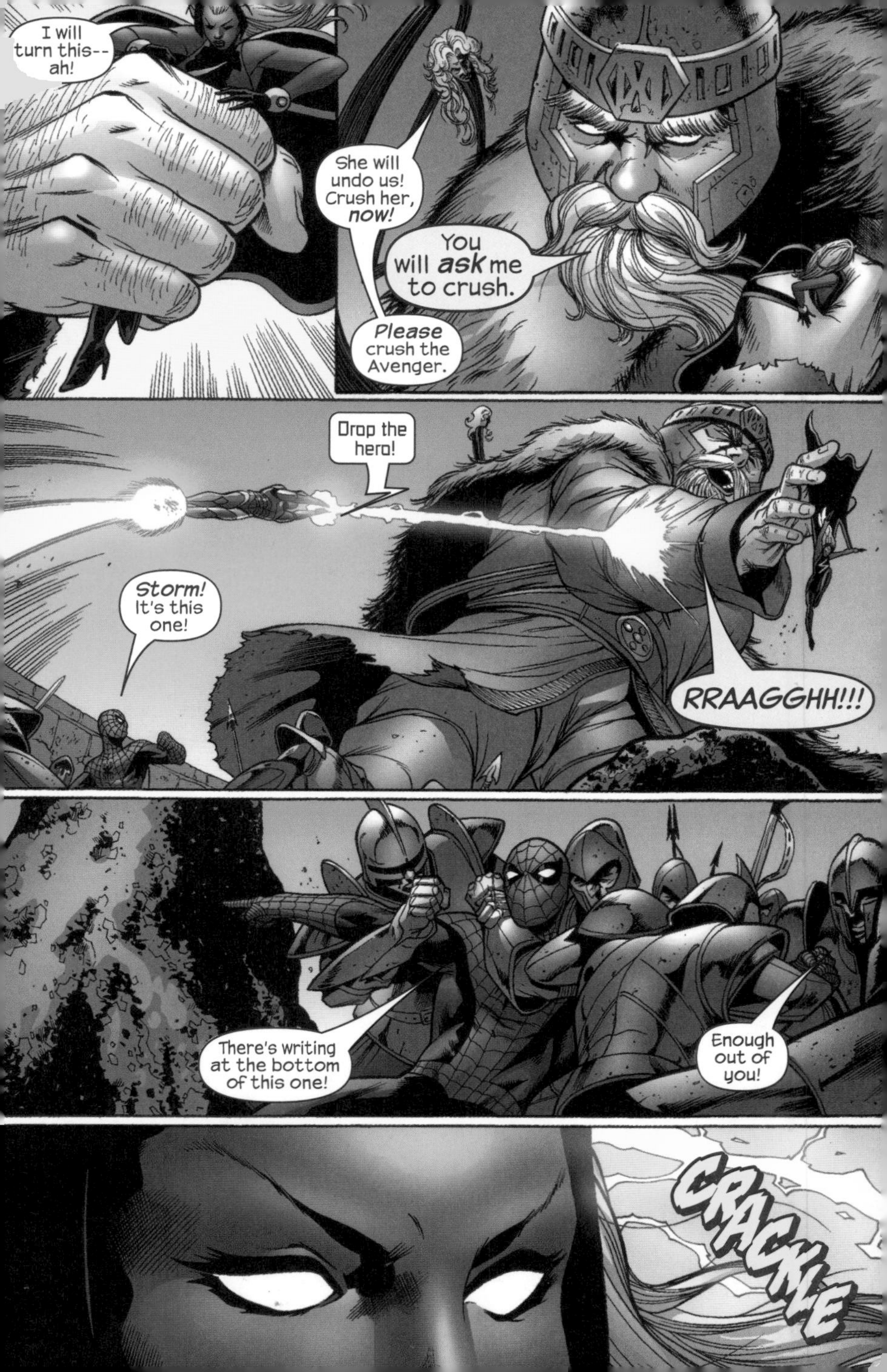
I will turn this--ah!
She will undo us! Crush her, *now!*
You will **ask** me to crush.
Please crush the Avenger.
Drop the hero!
Storm! It's this one!
RRAAGGHH!!!
There's writing at the bottom of this one!
Enough out of you!
CRACKLE

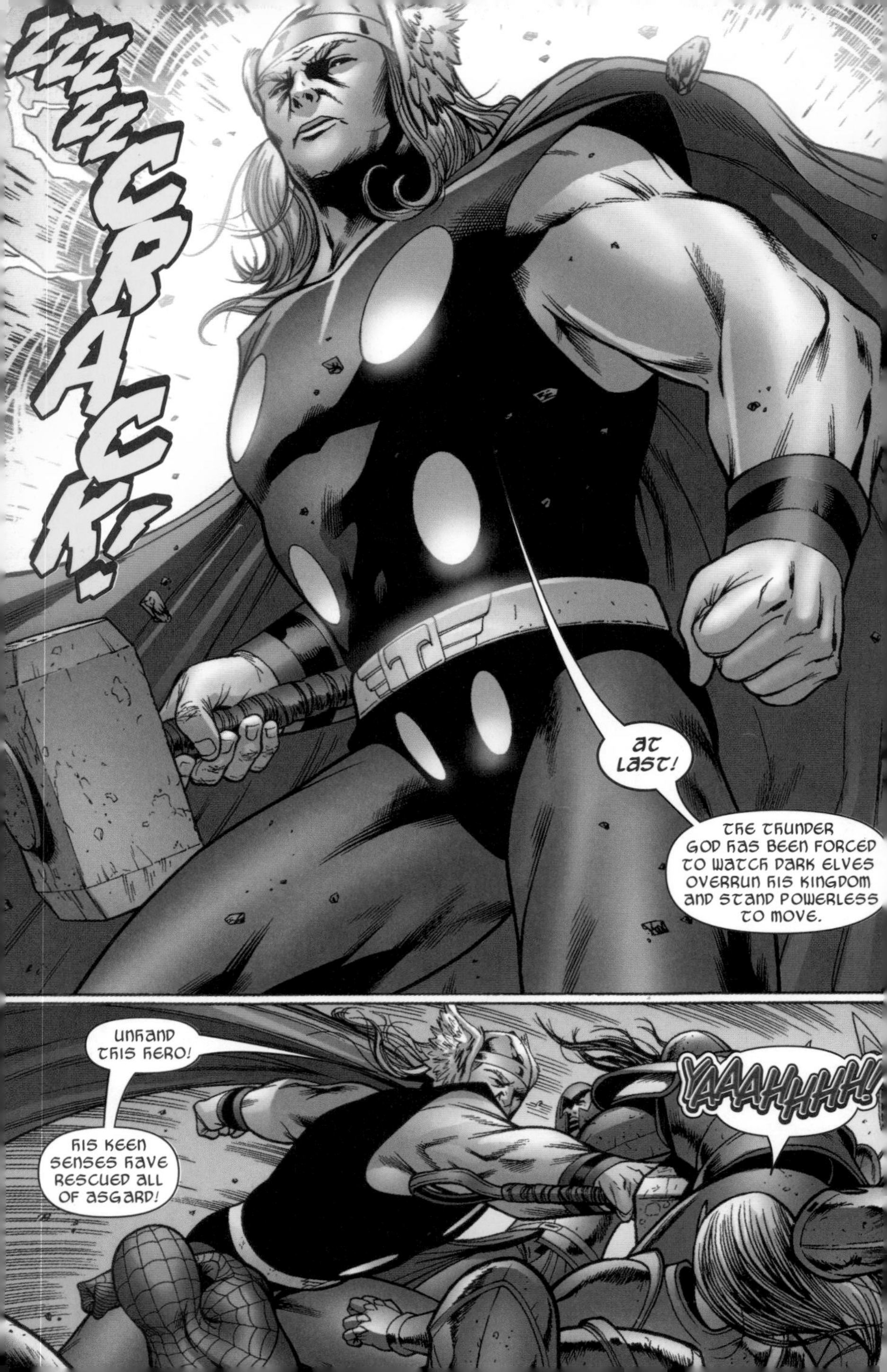
ZZZZZZCRACK!
AT LAST!
THE THUNDER GOD HAS BEEN FORCED TO WATCH DARK ELVES OVERRUN HIS KINGDOM AND STAND POWERLESS TO MOVE.
UNHAND THIS HERO!
HIS KEEN SENSES HAVE RESCUED ALL OF ASGARD!
YAAAHHHH!

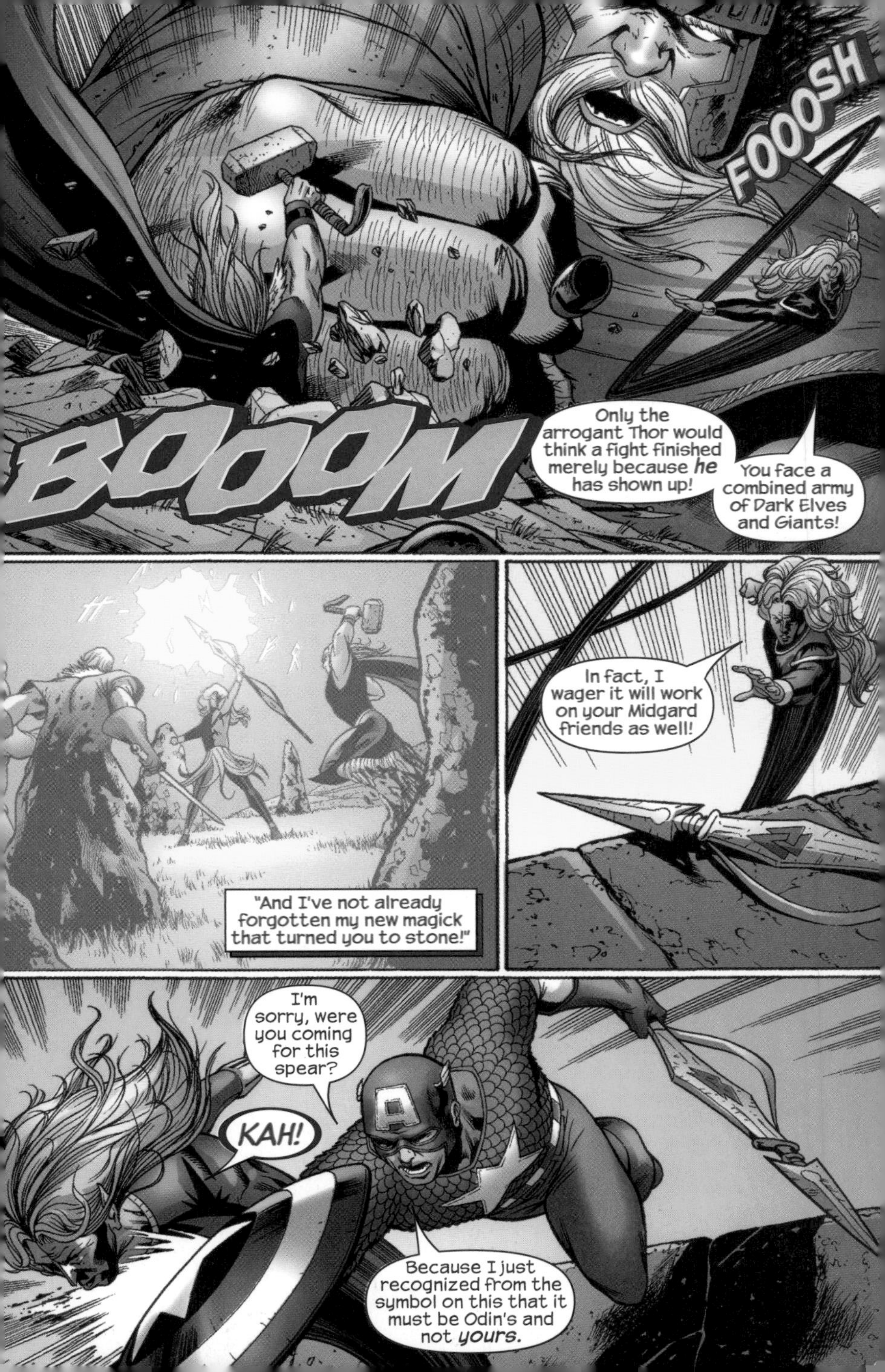
FOOOSH
BOOOM
Only the arrogant Thor would think a fight finished merely because *he* has shown up!
You face a combined army of Dark Elves and Giants!
"And I've not already forgotten my new magick that turned you to stone!"
In fact, I wager it will work on your Midgard friends as well!
I'm sorry, were you coming for this spear?
KAH!
Because I just recognized from the symbol on this that it must be Odin's and not *yours*.

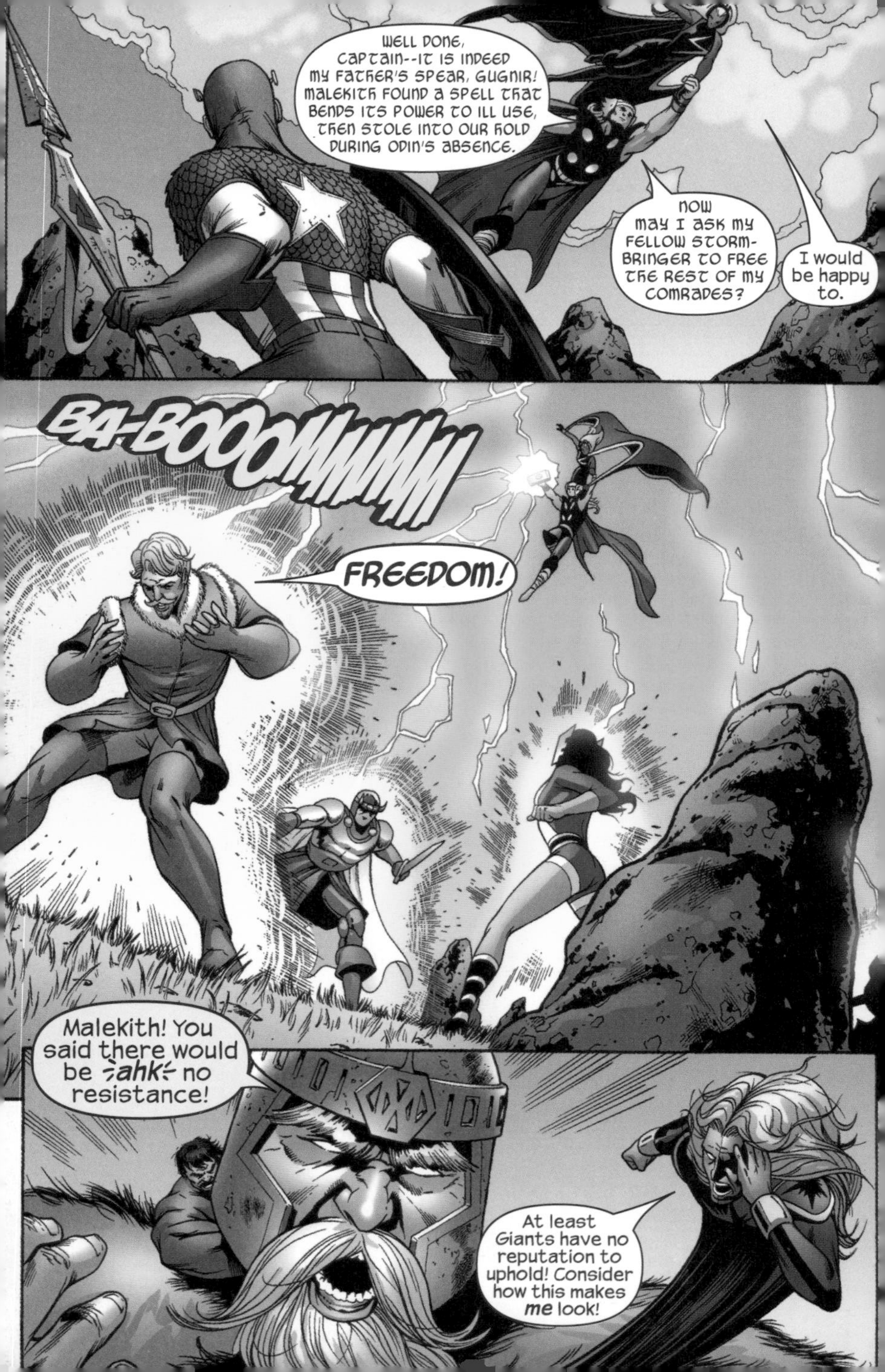
WELL DONE, CAPTAIN--IT IS INDEED MY FATHER'S SPEAR, GUGNIR! MALEKITH FOUND A SPELL THAT BENDS ITS POWER TO ILL USE, THEN STOLE INTO OUR HOLD DURING ODIN'S ABSENCE.
NOW MAY I ASK MY FELLOW STORM-BRINGER TO FREE THE REST OF MY COMRADES?
I would be happy to.
BA-BOOOMMMMM
FREEDOM!
Malekith! You said there would be -ahk- no resistance!
At least Giants have no reputation to uphold! Consider how this makes *me* look!

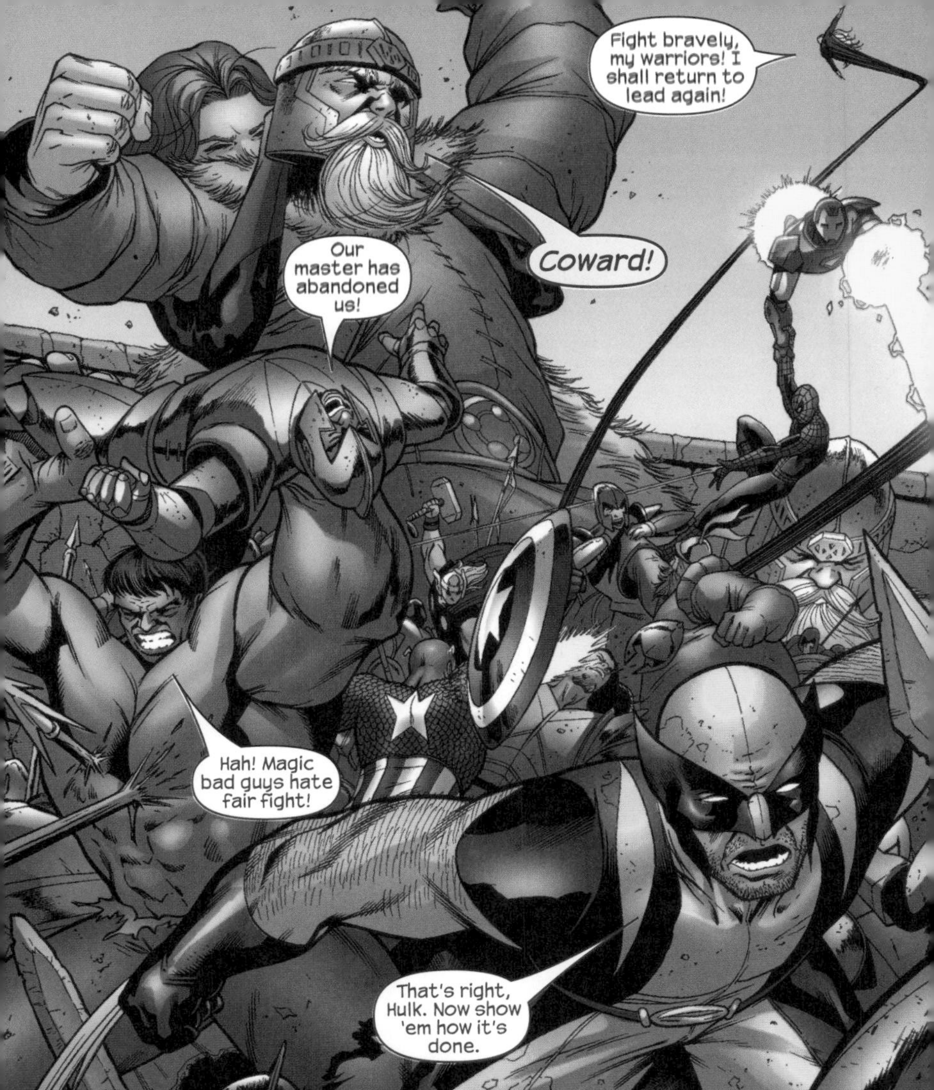
Fight bravely, my warriors! I shall return to lead again!
Coward!
Our master has abandoned us!
Hah! Magic bad guys hate fair fight!
That's right, Hulk. Now show 'em how it's done.

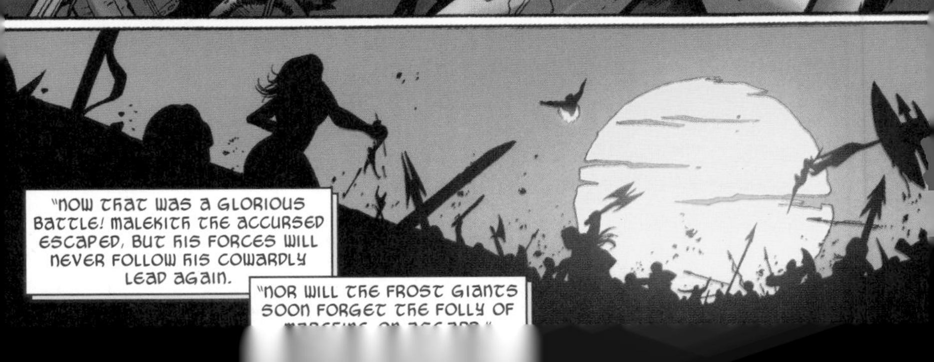
"NOW THAT WAS A GLORIOUS BATTLE! MALEKITH THE ACCURSED ESCAPED, BUT HIS FORCES WILL NEVER FOLLOW HIS COWARDLY LEAD AGAIN.
"NOR WILL THE FROST GIANTS SOON FORGET THE FOLLY OF

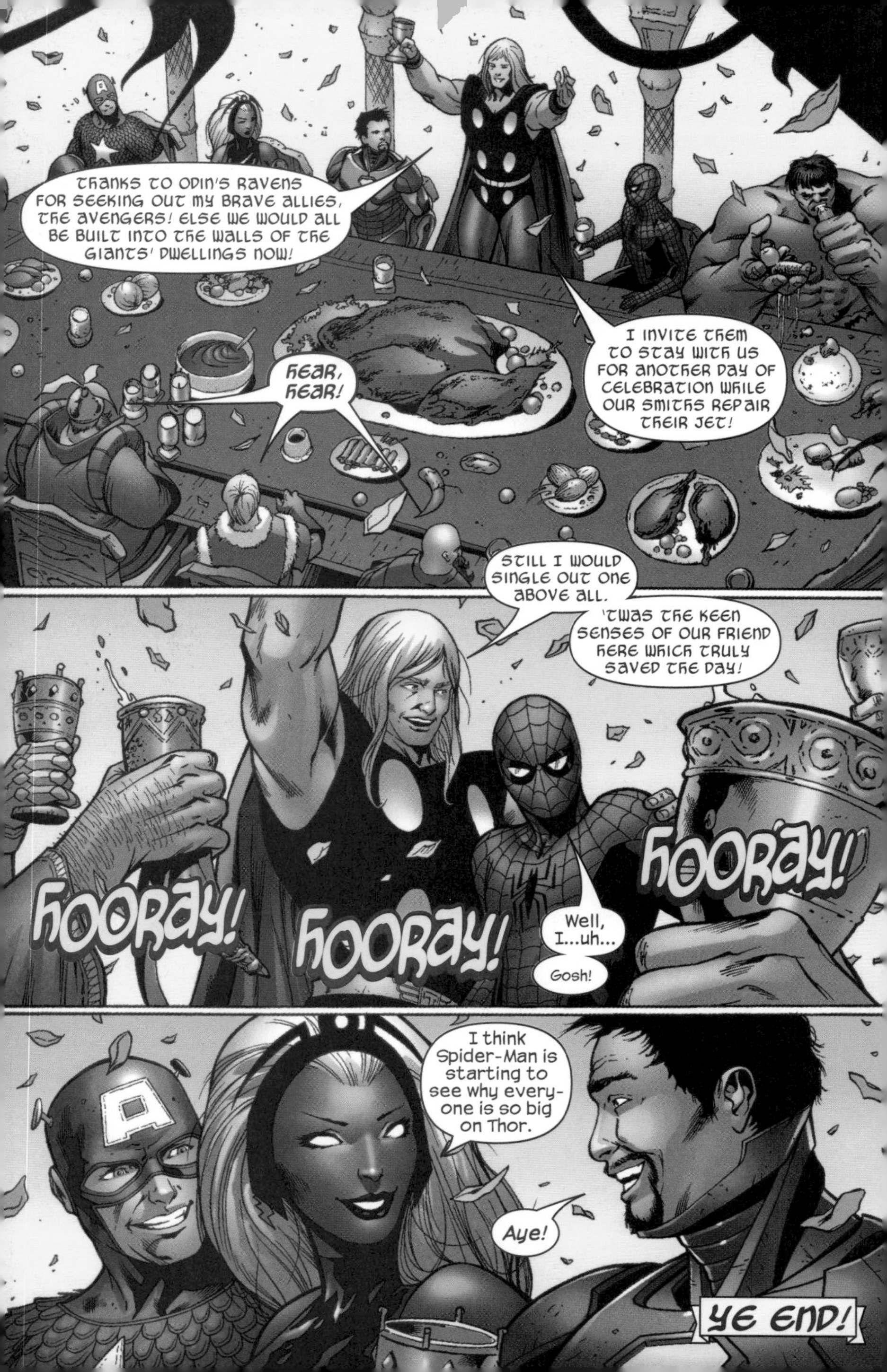
THANKS TO ODIN'S RAVENS FOR SEEKING OUT MY BRAVE ALLIES, THE AVENGERS! ELSE WE WOULD ALL BE BUILT INTO THE WALLS OF THE GIANTS' DWELLINGS NOW!
HEAR, HEAR!
I INVITE THEM TO STAY WITH US FOR ANOTHER DAY OF CELEBRATION WHILE OUR SMITHS REPAIR THEIR JET!
STILL I WOULD SINGLE OUT ONE ABOVE ALL.
'TWAS THE KEEN SENSES OF OUR FRIEND HERE WHICH TRULY SAVED THE DAY!
HOORAY!
HOORAY!
Well, I...uh...
Gosh!
HOORAY!
I think Spider-Man is starting to see why every-one is so big on Thor.
Aye!
YE END!

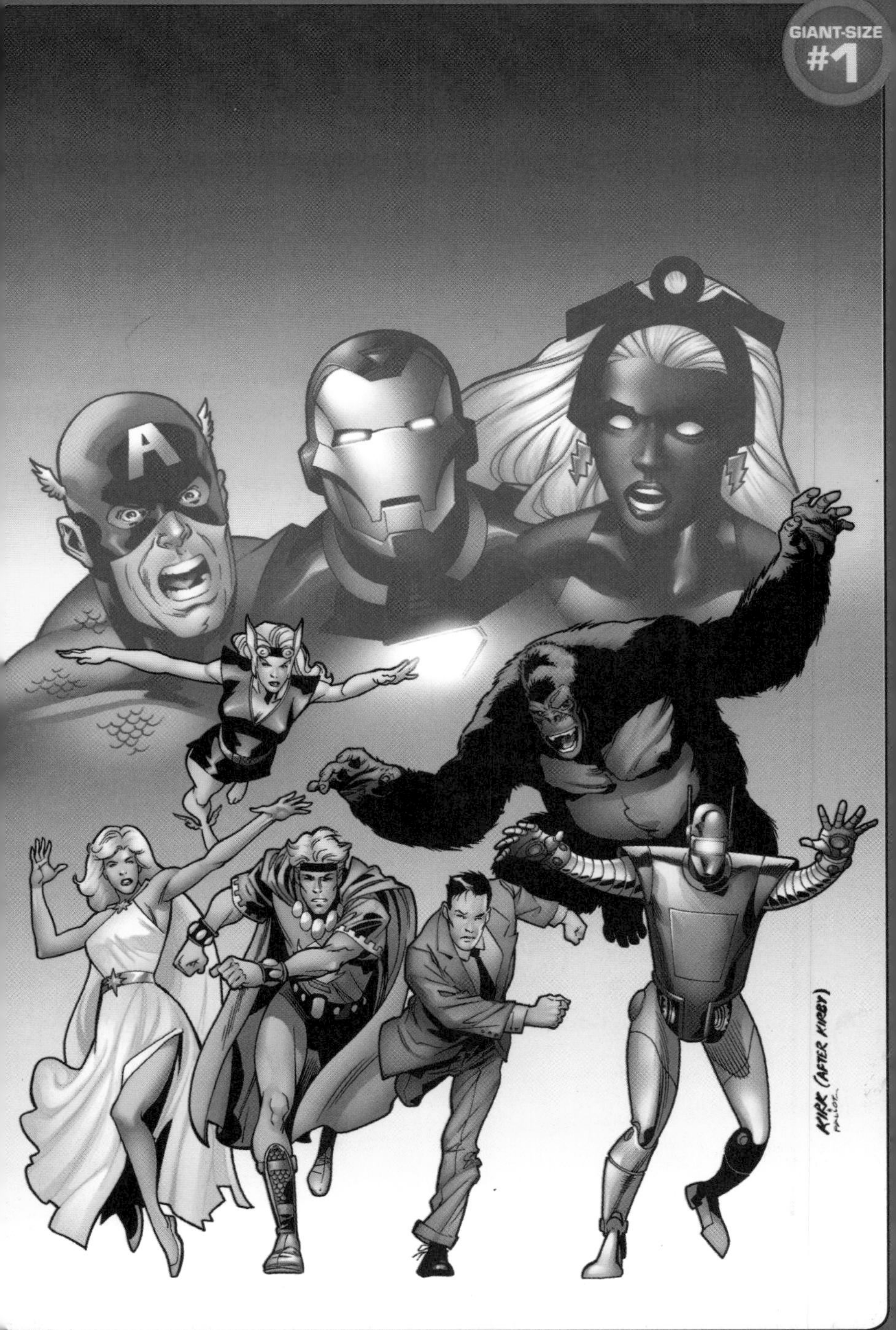
GIANT-SIZE
#1
KIRK (AFTER KIRBY)

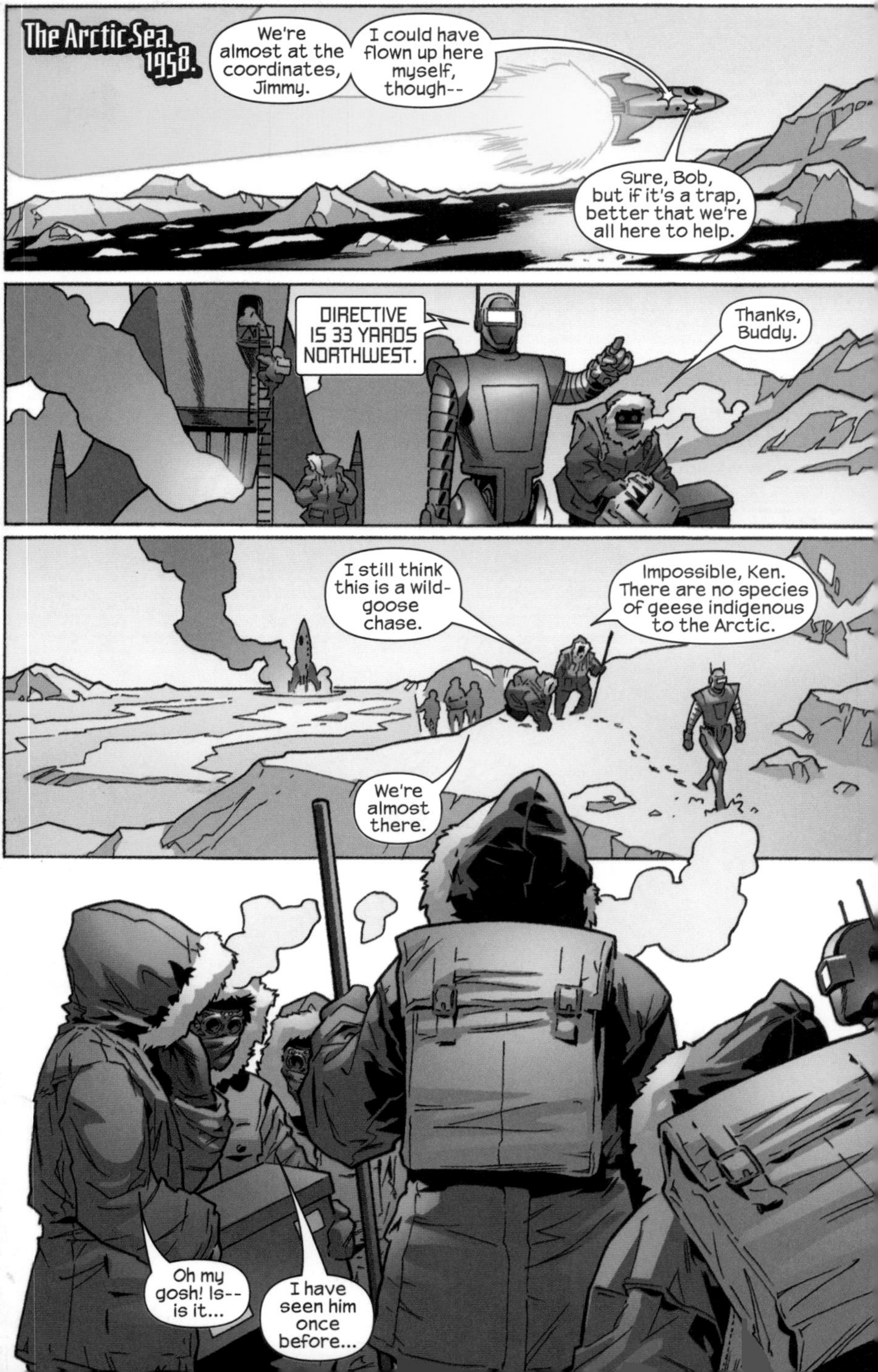
The Arctic Sea. 1958.
We're almost at the coordinates, Jimmy.
I could have flown up here myself, though--
Sure, Bob, but if it's a trap, better that we're all here to help.
DIRECTIVE IS 33 YARDS NORTHWEST.
Thanks, Buddy.
I still think this is a wild-goose chase.
Impossible, Ken. There are no species of geese indigenous to the Arctic.
We're almost there.
Oh my gosh! Is--is it...
I have seen him once before...

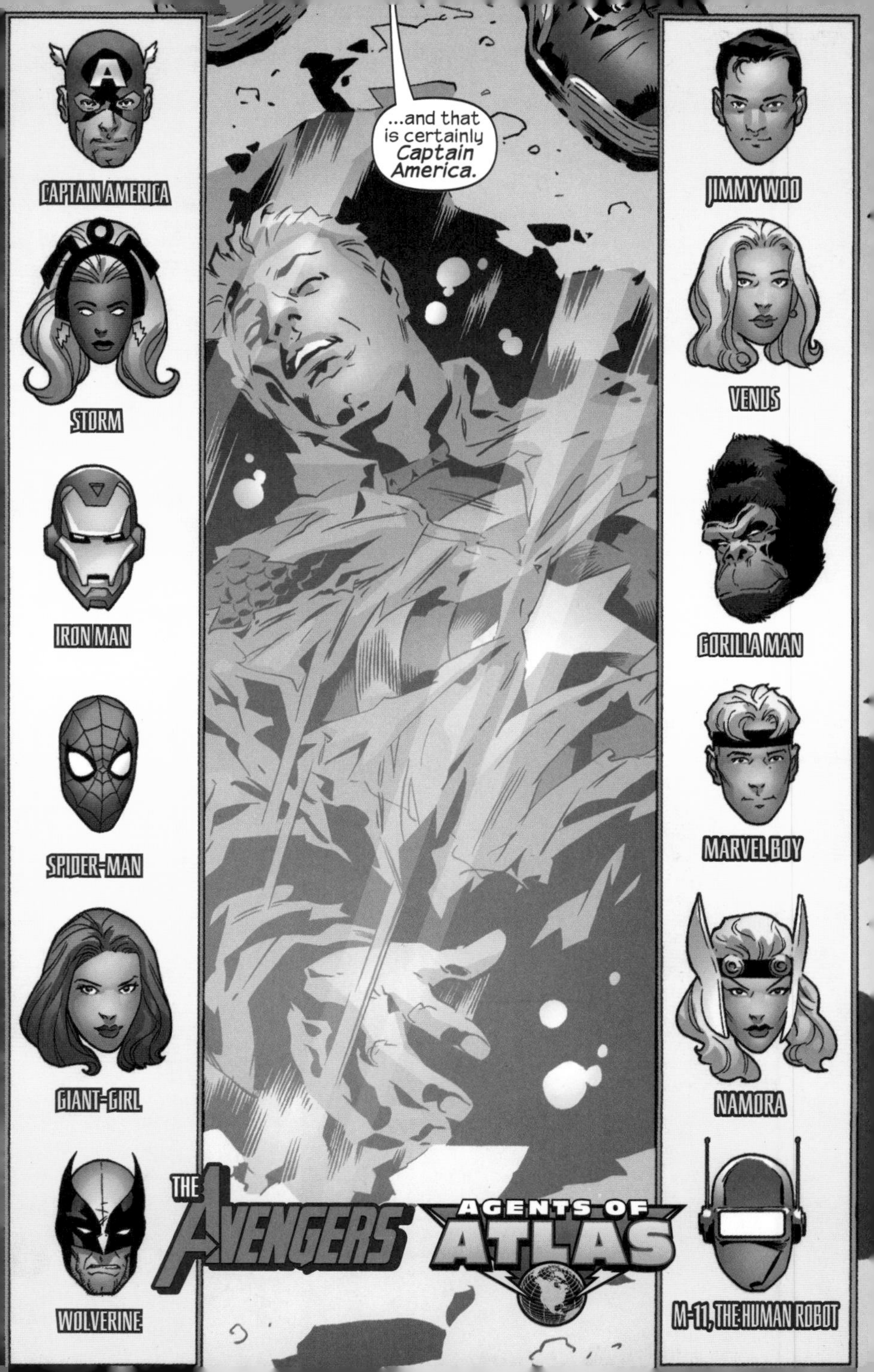

...and that is certainly Captain America.
CAPTAIN AMERICA
STORM
IRON MAN
SPIDER-MAN
GIANT-GIRL
WOLVERINE
JIMMY WOO
VENUS
GORILLA MAN
MARVEL BOY
NAMORA
M-11, THE HUMAN ROBOT
THE AVENGERS
AGENTS OF ATLAS

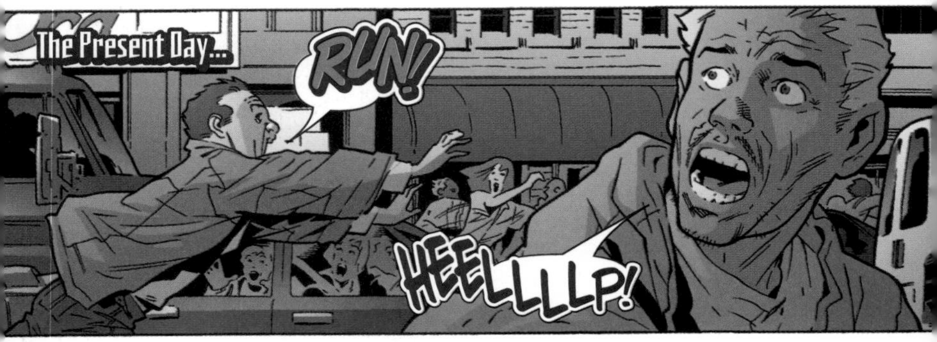
The Present Day...
RUN!
HEELLLLP!

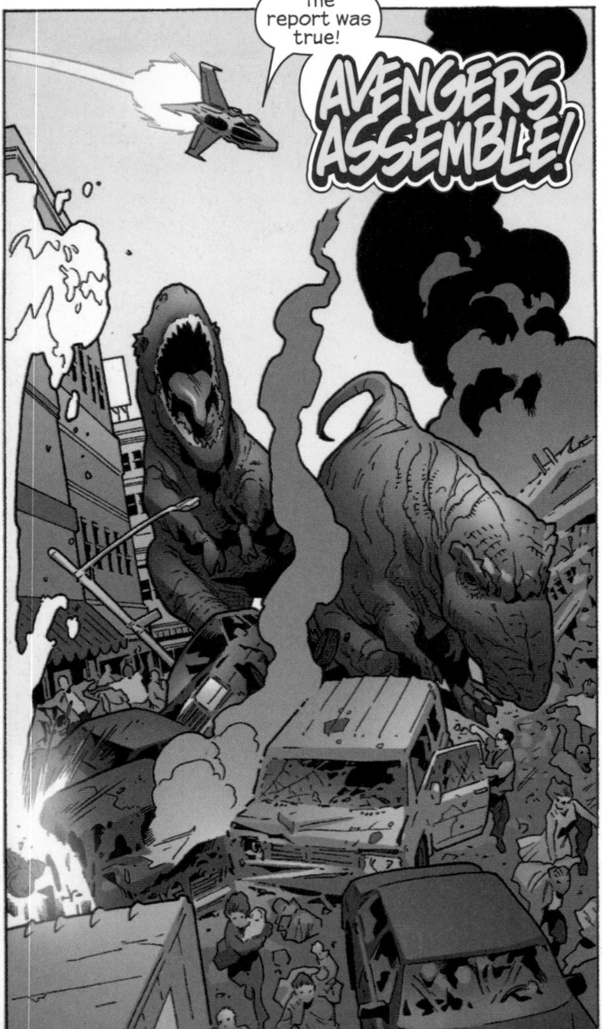
The report was true!
AVENGERS ASSEMBLE!

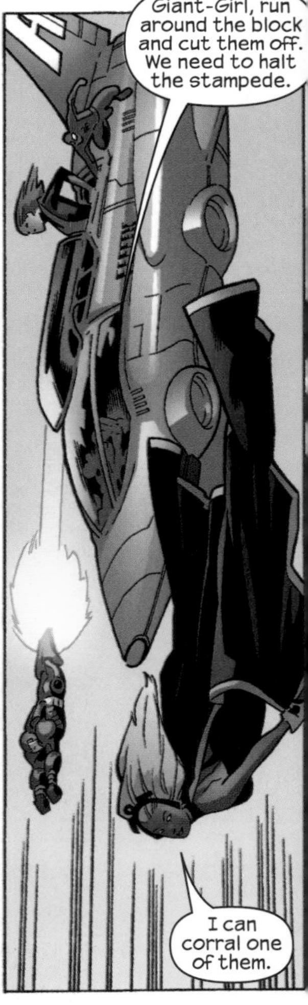
Giant-Girl, run around the block and cut them off. We need to halt the stampede.
I can corral one of them.

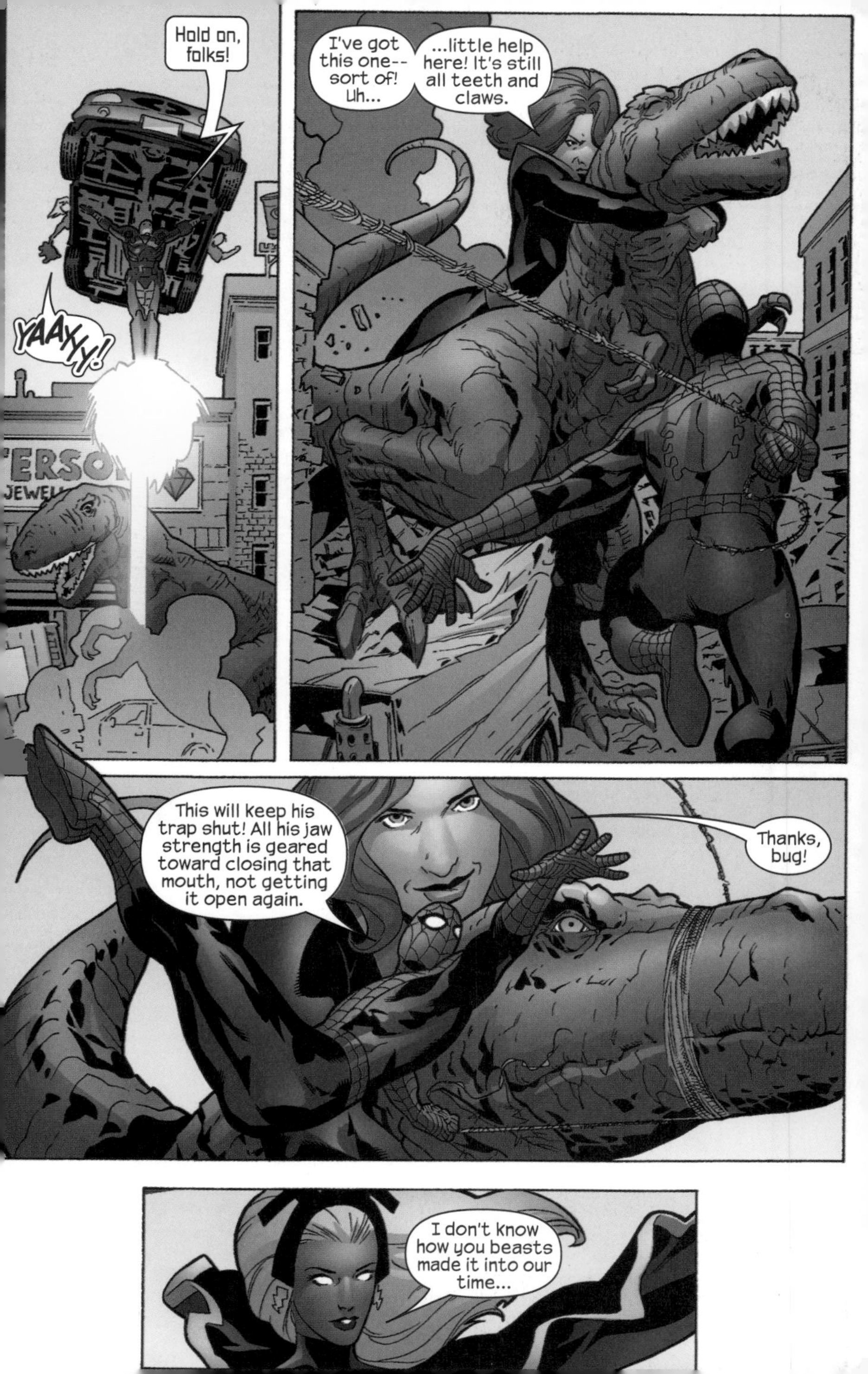
Hold on, folks!
YAAYYY!
I've got this one-- sort of! Uh...
...little help here! It's still all teeth and claws.
This will keep his trap shut! All his jaw strength is geared toward closing that mouth, not getting it open again.
Thanks, bug!
I don't know how you beasts made it into our time...

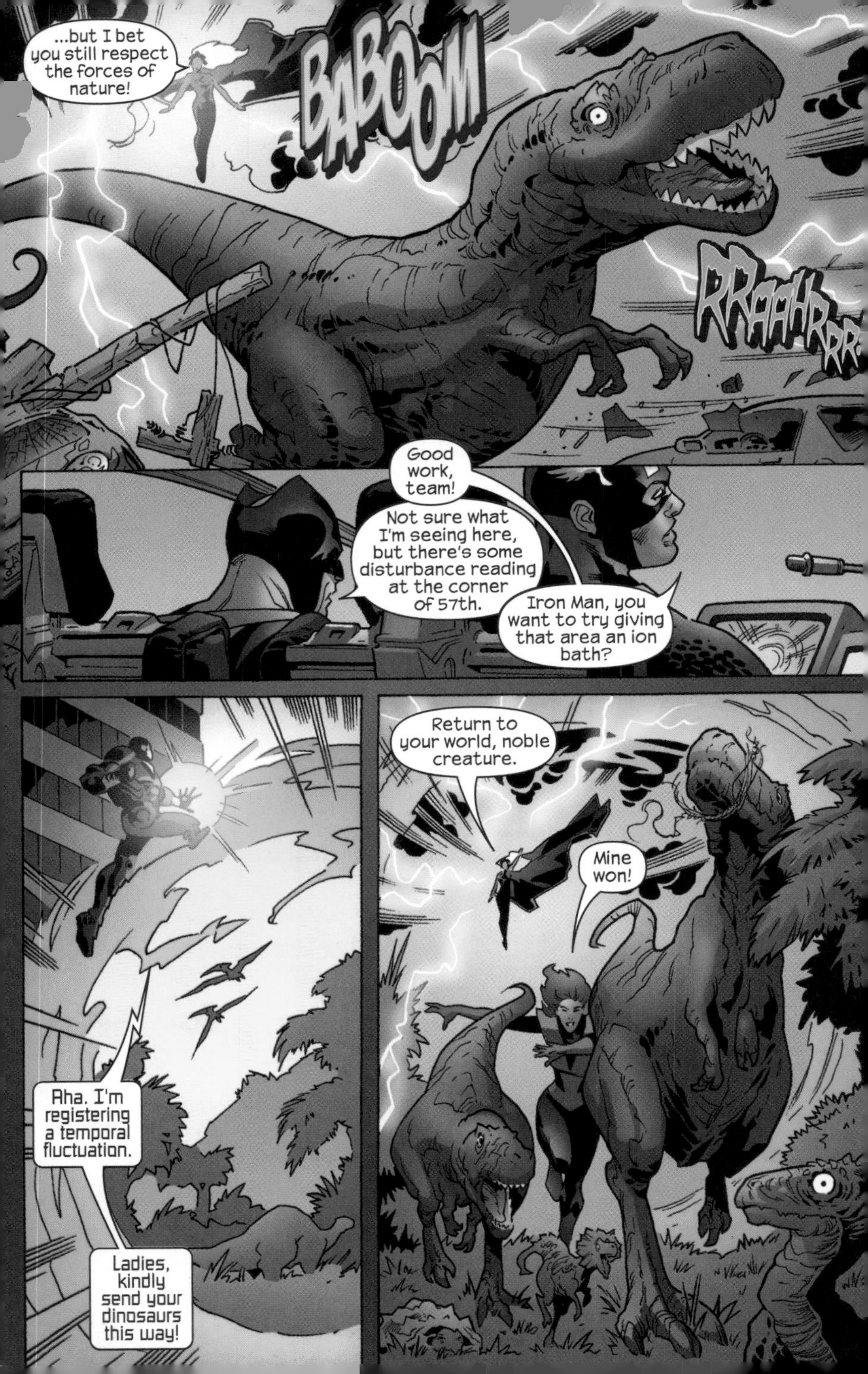
...but I bet you still respect the forces of nature!
BABOOM
RRAAAHRRRR
Good work, team!
Not sure what I'm seeing here, but there's some disturbance reading at the corner of 57th.
Iron Man, you want to try giving that area an ion bath?
Aha. I'm registering a temporal fluctuation.
Ladies, kindly send your dinosaurs this way!
Return to your world, noble creature.
Mine won!

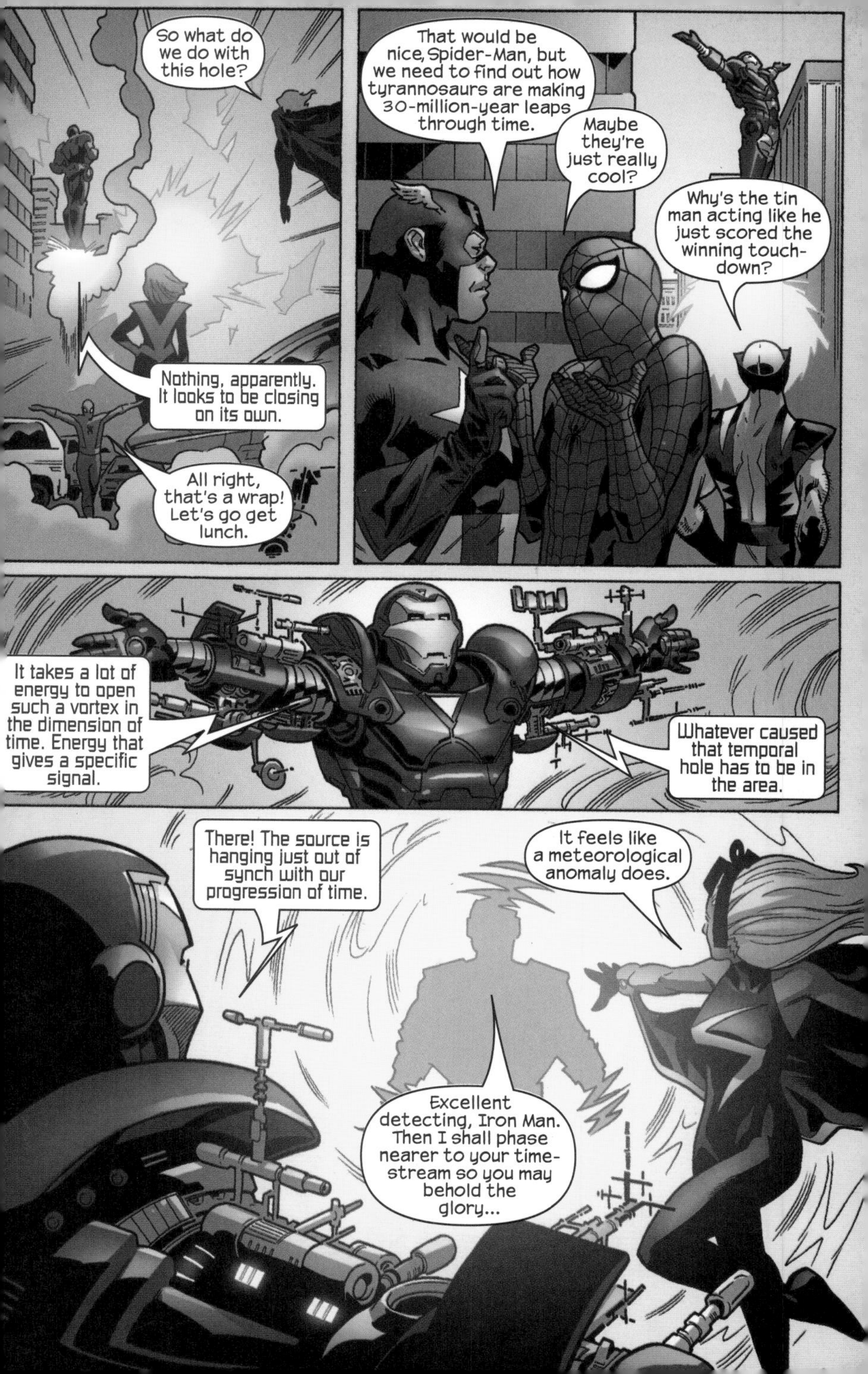
So what do we do with this hole?
Nothing, apparently. It looks to be closing on its own.
All right, that's a wrap! Let's go get lunch.
That would be nice, Spider-Man, but we need to find out how tyrannosaurs are making 30-million-year leaps through time.
Maybe they're just really cool?
Why's the tin man acting like he just scored the winning touch-down?
It takes a lot of energy to open such a vortex in the dimension of time. Energy that gives a specific signal.
Whatever caused that temporal hole has to be in the area.
There! The source is hanging just out of synch with our progression of time.
It feels like a meteorological anomaly does.
Excellent detecting, Iron Man. Then I shall phase nearer to your time-stream so you may behold the glory...

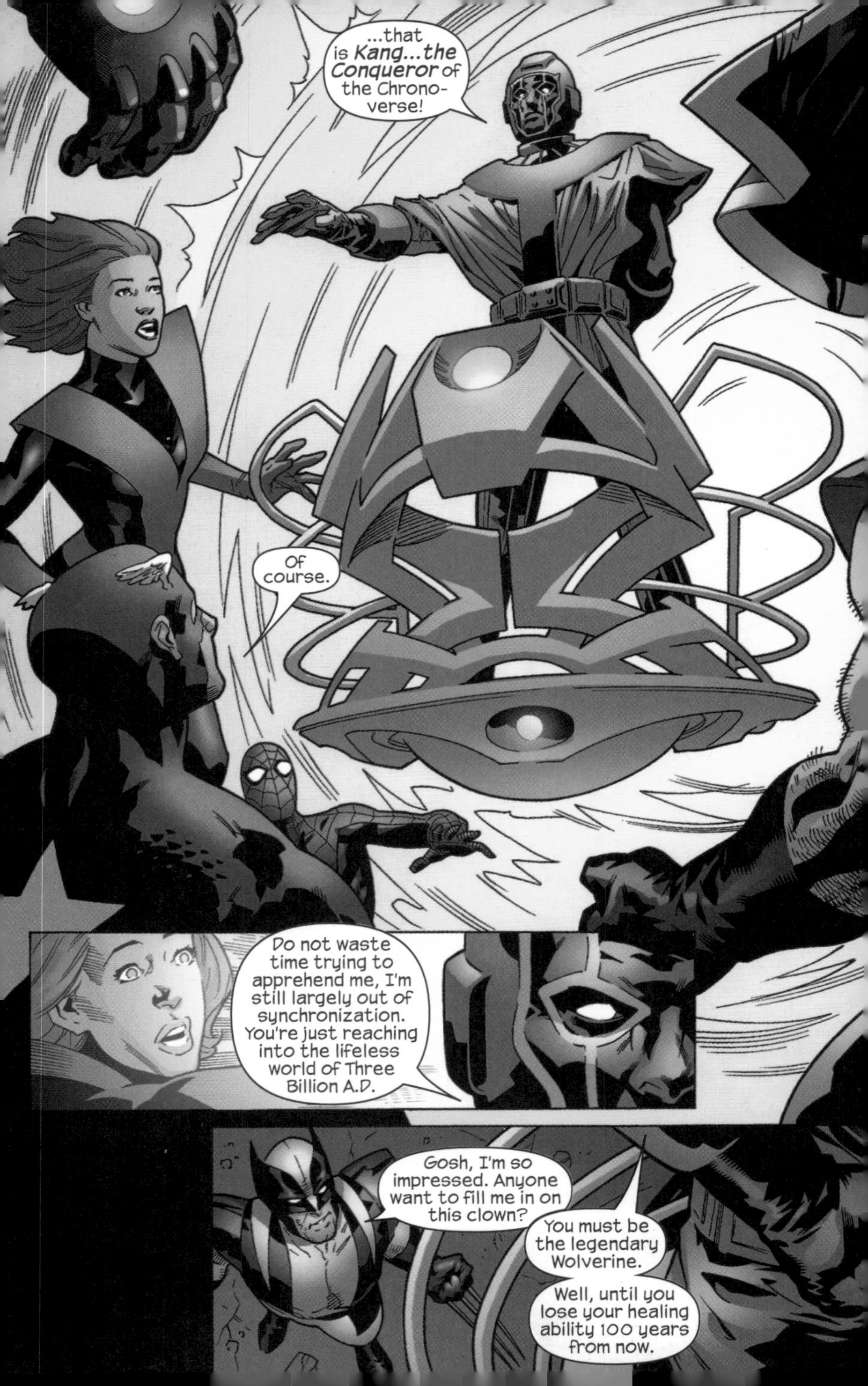
...that is Kang...the Conqueror of the Chrono-verse!
Of course.
Do not waste time trying to apprehend me, I'm still largely out of synchronization. You're just reaching into the lifeless world of Three Billion A.D.
Gosh, I'm so impressed. Anyone want to fill me in on this clown?
You must be the legendary Wolverine.
Well, until you lose your healing ability 100 years from now.

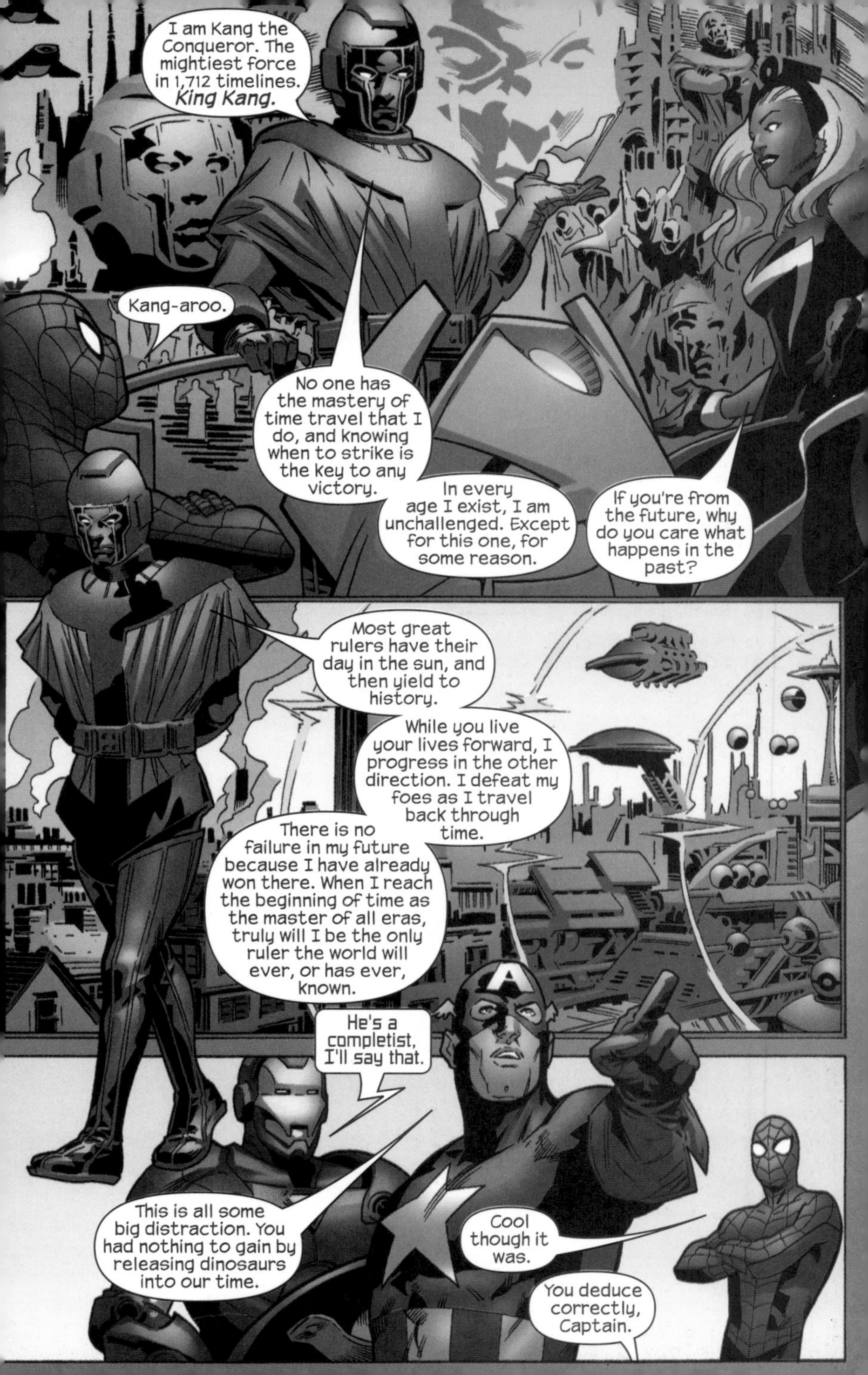
I am Kang the Conqueror. The mightiest force in 1,712 timelines. *King Kang.*
Kang-aroo.
No one has the mastery of time travel that I do, and knowing when to strike is the key to any victory.
In every age I exist, I am unchallenged. Except for this one, for some reason.
If you're from the future, why do you care what happens in the past?
Most great rulers have their day in the sun, and then yield to history.
While you live your lives forward, I progress in the other direction. I defeat my foes as I travel back through time.
There is no failure in my future because I have already won there. When I reach the beginning of time as the master of all eras, truly will I be the only ruler the world will ever, or has ever, known.
He's a completist, I'll say that.
This is all some big distraction. You had nothing to gain by releasing dinosaurs into our time.
Cool though it was.
You deduce correctly, Captain.

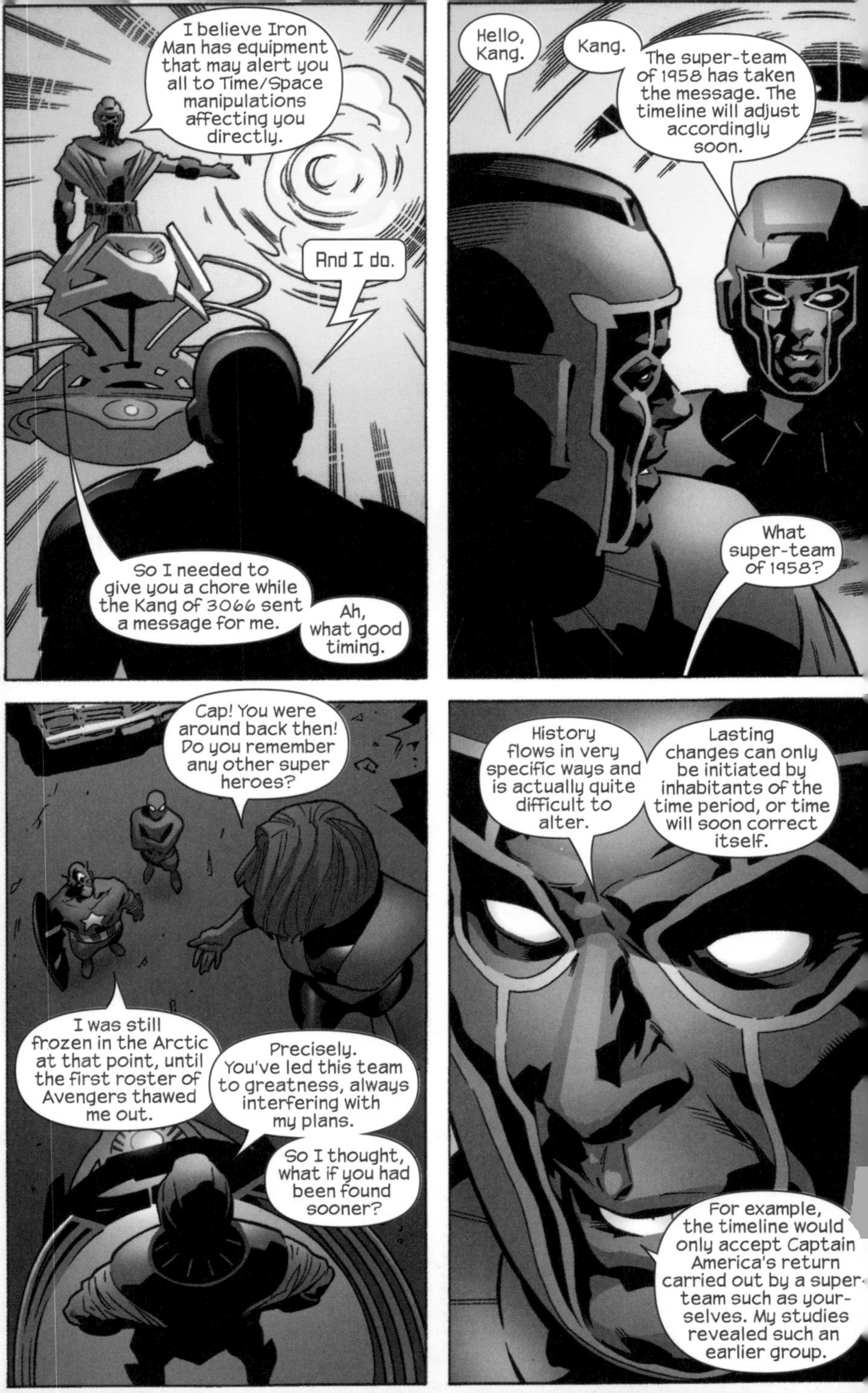
I believe Iron Man has equipment that may alert you all to Time/Space manipulations affecting you directly.
And I do.
So I needed to give you a chore while the Kang of 3066 sent a message for me.
Ah, what good timing.
Hello, Kang.
Kang.
The super-team of 1958 has taken the message. The timeline will adjust accordingly soon.
What super-team of 1958?
Cap! You were around back then! Do you remember any other super heroes?
I was still frozen in the Arctic at that point, until the first roster of Avengers thawed me out.
Precisely. You've led this team to greatness, always interfering with my plans.
So I thought, what if you had been found sooner?
History flows in very specific ways and is actually quite difficult to alter.
Lasting changes can only be initiated by inhabitants of the time period, or time will soon correct itself.
For example, the timeline would only accept Captain America's return carried out by a super-team such as your-selves. My studies revealed such an earlier group.

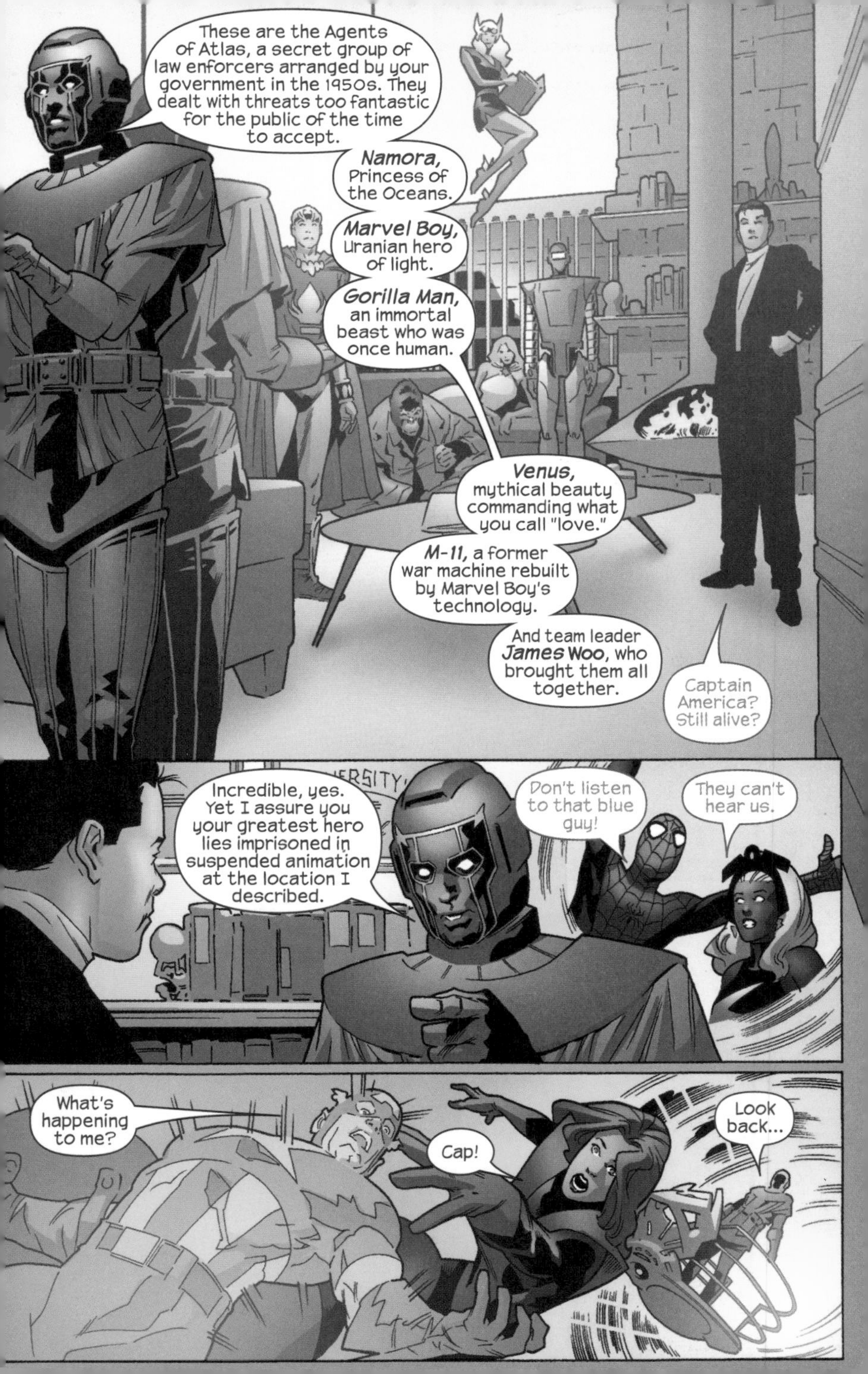
These are the Agents of Atlas, a secret group of law enforcers arranged by your government in the 1950s. They dealt with threats too fantastic for the public of the time to accept.
Namora, Princess of the Oceans.
Marvel Boy, Uranian hero of light.
Gorilla Man, an immortal beast who was once human.
Venus, mythical beauty commanding what you call "love."
M-11, a former war machine rebuilt by Marvel Boy's technology.
And team leader James Woo, who brought them all together.
Captain America? Still alive?
Incredible, yes. Yet I assure you your greatest hero lies imprisoned in suspended animation at the location I described.
Don't listen to that blue guy!
They can't hear us.
What's happening to me?
Cap!
Look back...

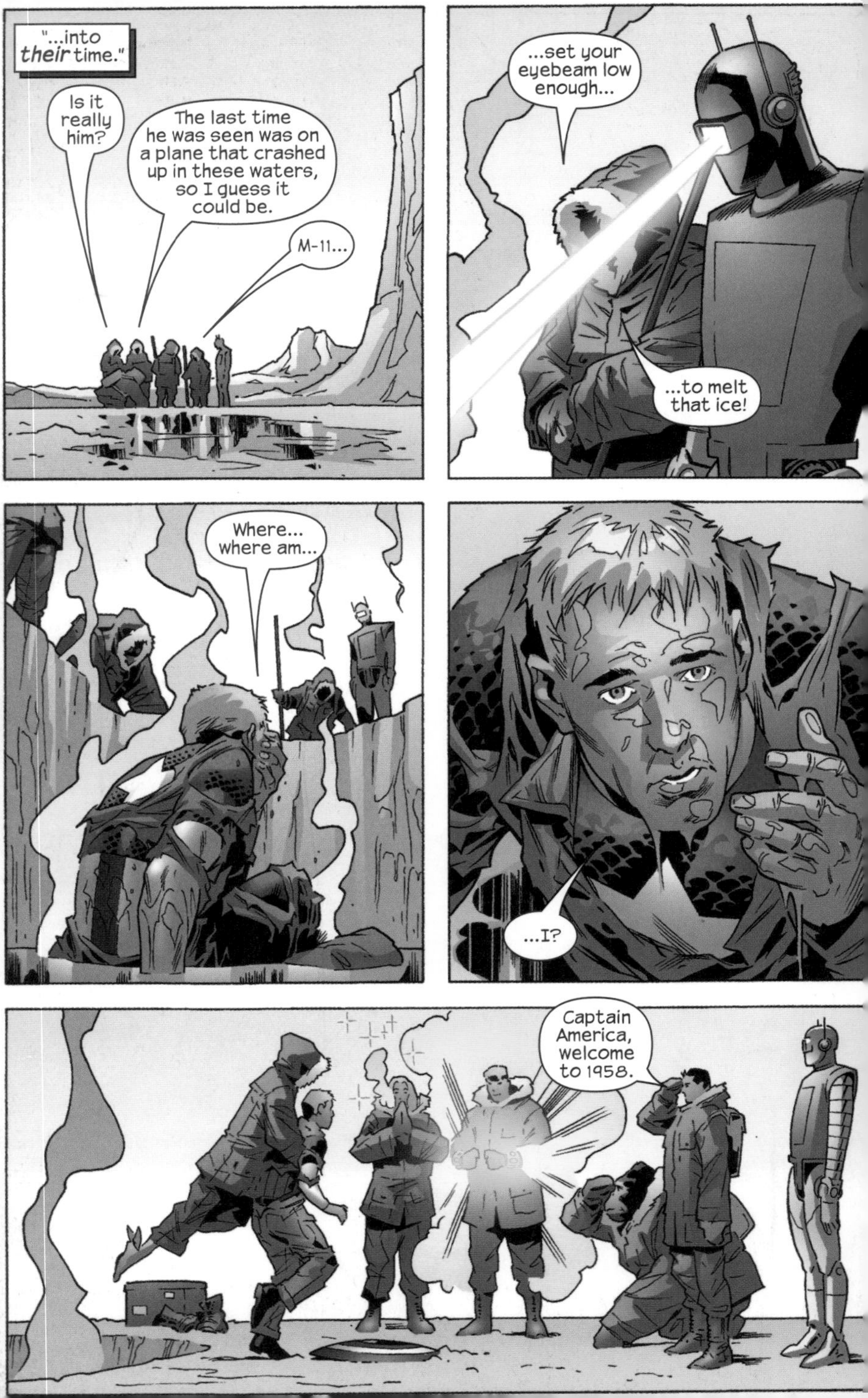
"...into *their* time."
Is it really him?
The last time he was seen was on a plane that crashed up in these waters, so I guess it could be.
M-11...
...set your eyebeam low enough...
...to melt that ice!
Where... where am...
...I?
Captain America, welcome to 1958.

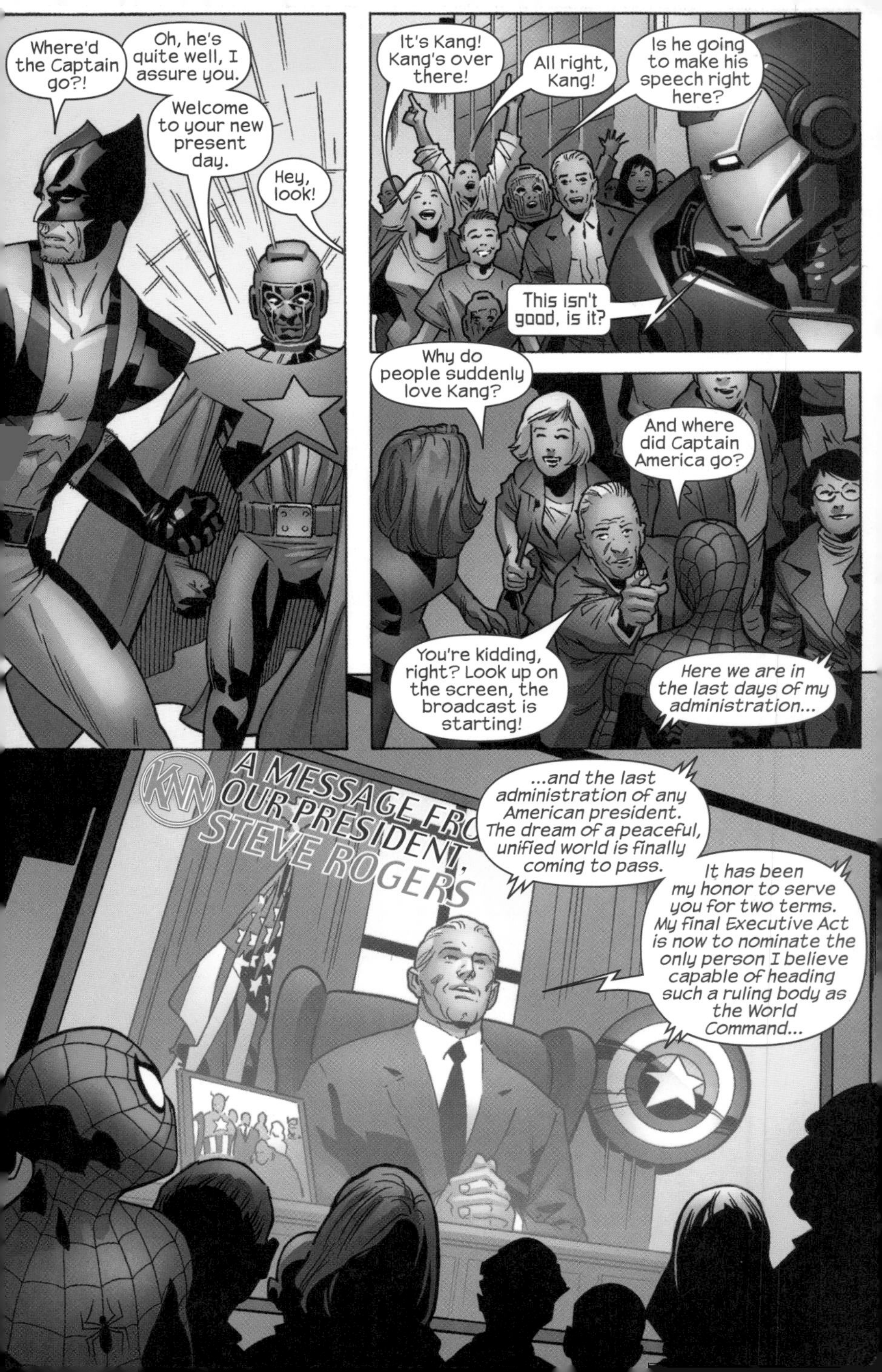
Where'd the Captain go?!
Oh, he's quite well, I assure you.
Welcome to your new present day.
Hey, look!
It's Kang! Kang's over there!
All right, Kang!
Is he going to make his speech right here?
This isn't good, is it?
Why do people suddenly love Kang?
And where did Captain America go?
You're kidding, right? Look up on the screen, the broadcast is starting!
Here we are in the last days of my administration...
A MESSAGE FRO OUR PRESIDENT, STEVE ROGERS
KNN
...and the last administration of any American president. The dream of a peaceful, unified world is finally coming to pass.
It has been my honor to serve you for two terms. My final Executive Act is now to nominate the only person I believe capable of heading such a ruling body as the World Command...

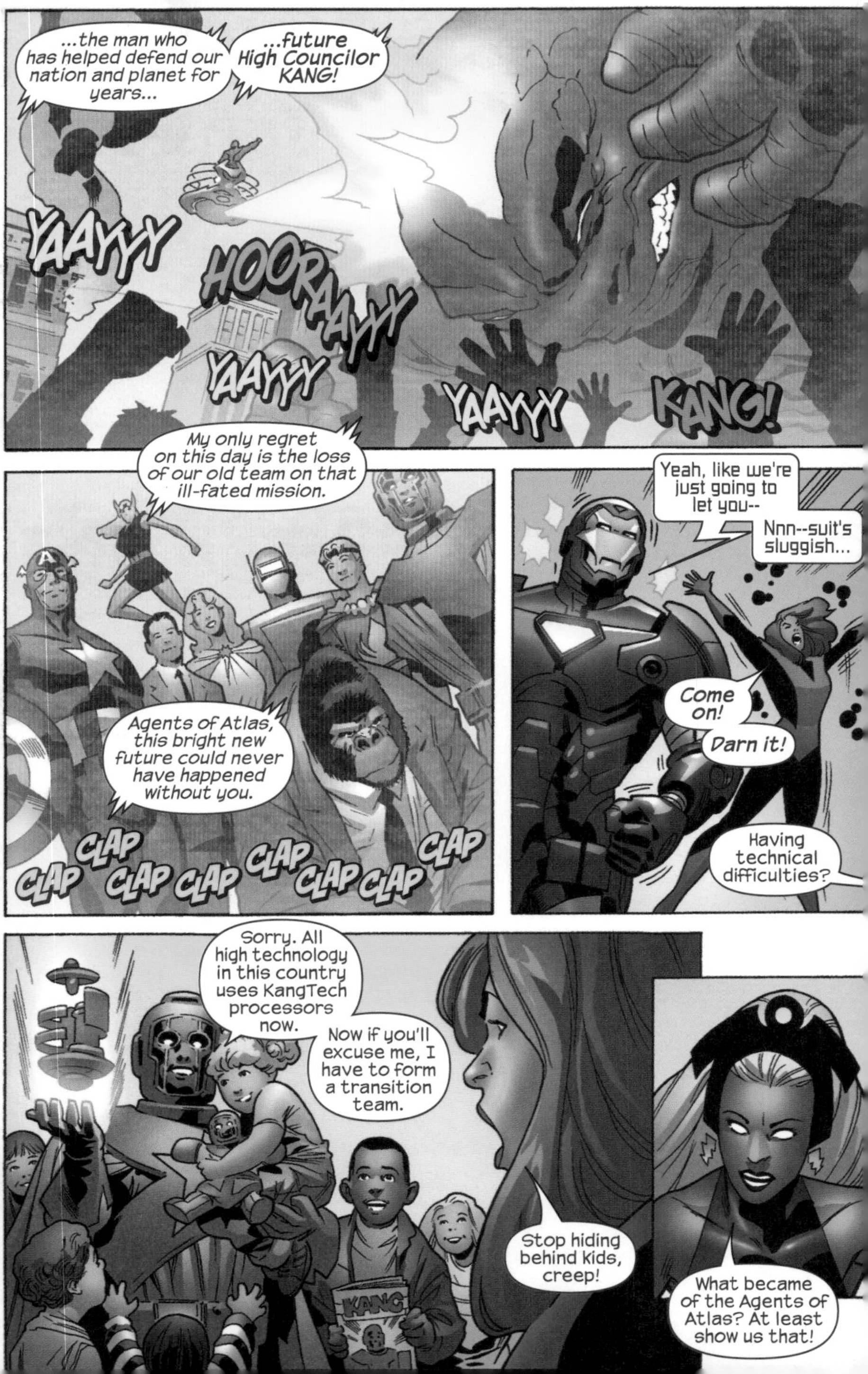

...the man who has helped defend our nation and planet for years...
...future High Councilor KANG!
YAAYYY
HOORAAYYY
YAAYYY
YAAYYY
KANG!
My only regret on this day is the loss of our old team on that ill-fated mission.
Agents of Atlas, this bright new future could never have happened without you.
CLAP CLAP CLAP CLAP CLAP CLAP CLAP CLAP
Yeah, like we're just going to let you--
Nnn--suit's sluggish...
Come on!
Darn it!
Having technical difficulties?
Sorry. All high technology in this country uses KangTech processors now.
Now if you'll excuse me, I have to form a transition team.
KANG
Stop hiding behind kids, creep!
What became of the Agents of Atlas? At least show us that!

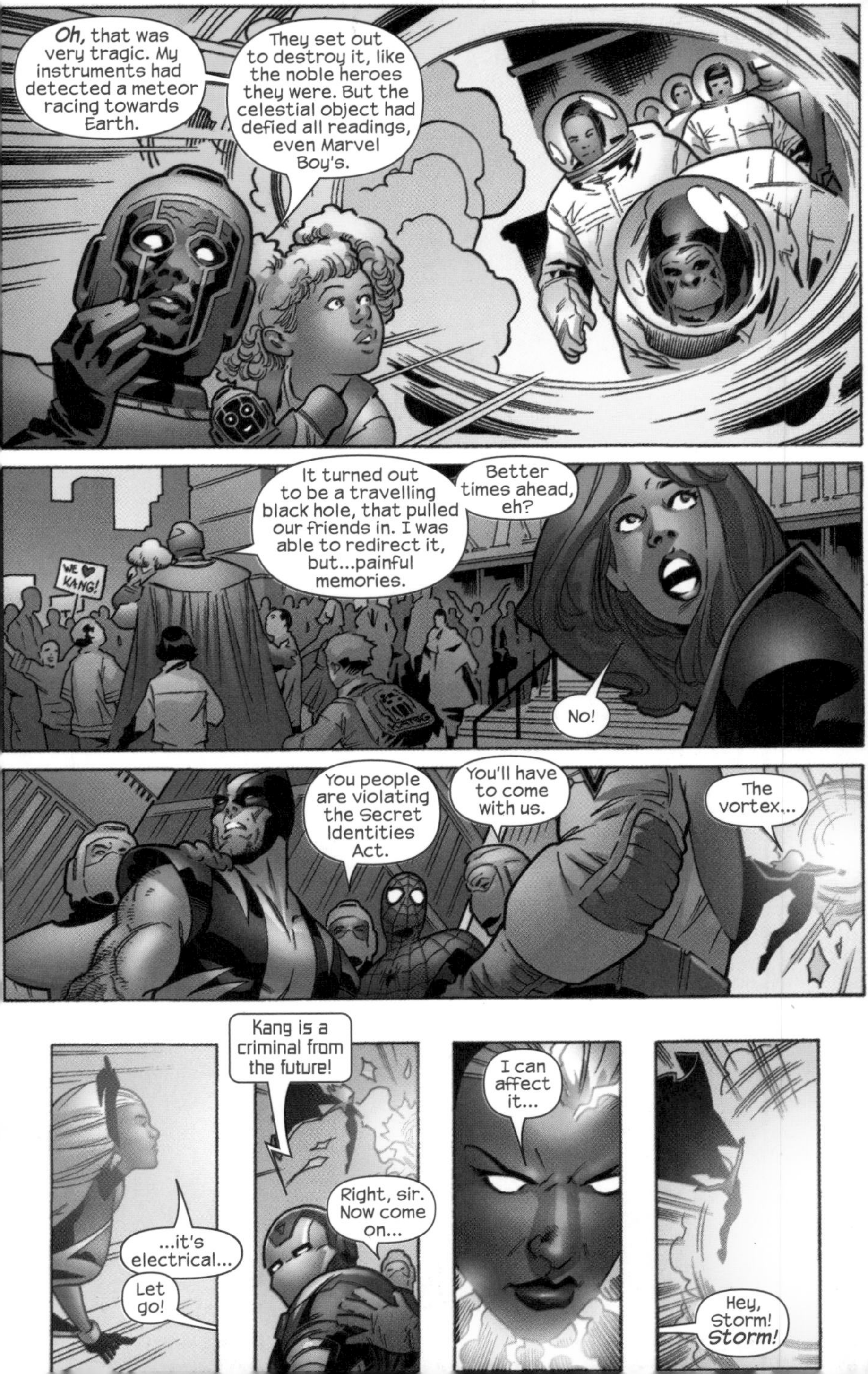
Oh, that was very tragic. My instruments had detected a meteor racing towards Earth.
They set out to destroy it, like the noble heroes they were. But the celestial object had defied all readings, even Marvel Boy's.
It turned out to be a travelling black hole, that pulled our friends in. I was able to redirect it, but...painful memories.
WE ♥ KANG!
Better times ahead, eh?
No!
You people are violating the Secret Identities Act.
You'll have to come with us.
The vortex...
...it's electrical...
Let go!
Kang is a criminal from the future!
Right, sir. Now come on...
I can affect it...
Hey, Storm! Storm!

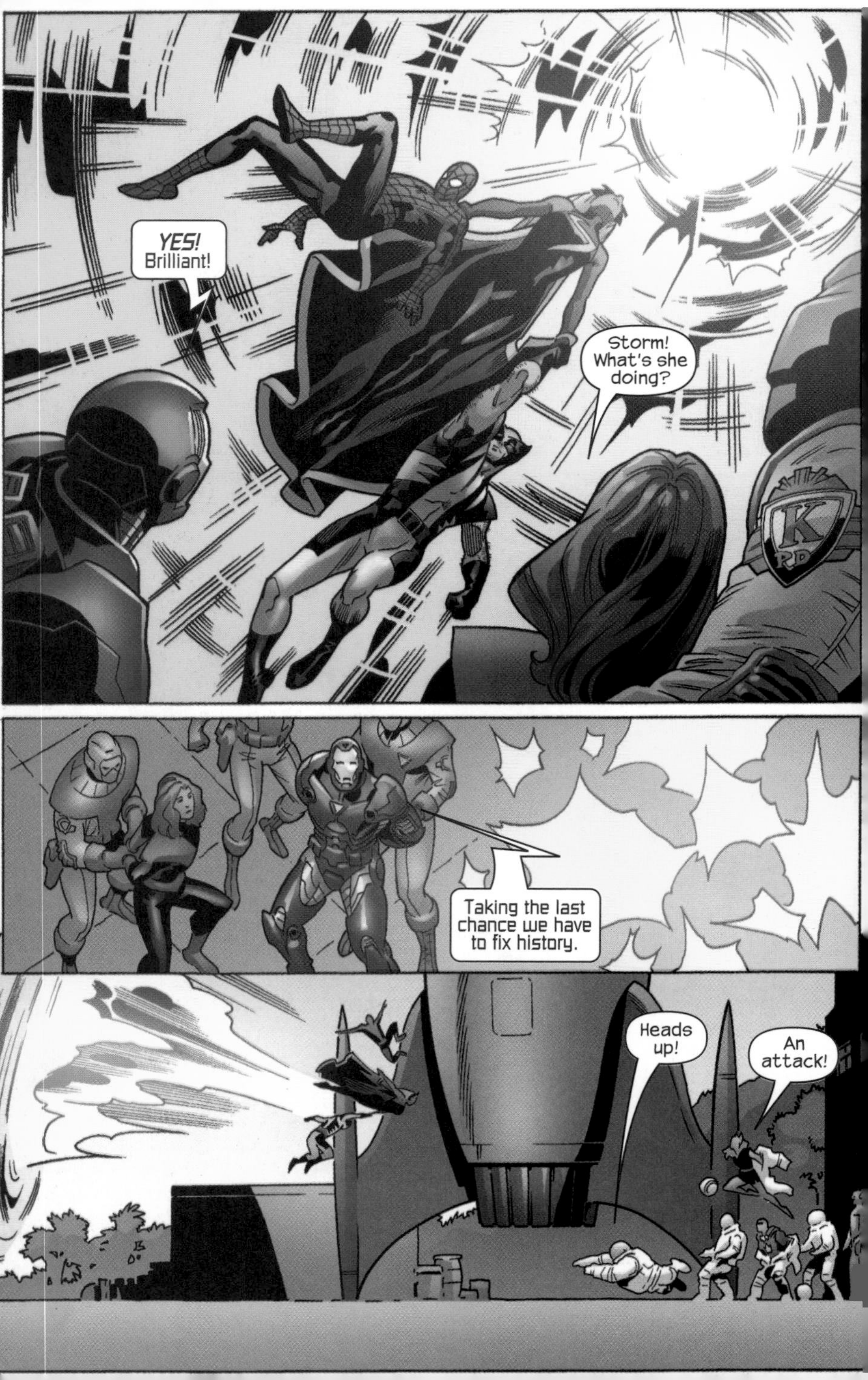
YES! Brilliant!
Storm! What's she doing?
Taking the last chance we have to fix history.
Heads up!
An attack!

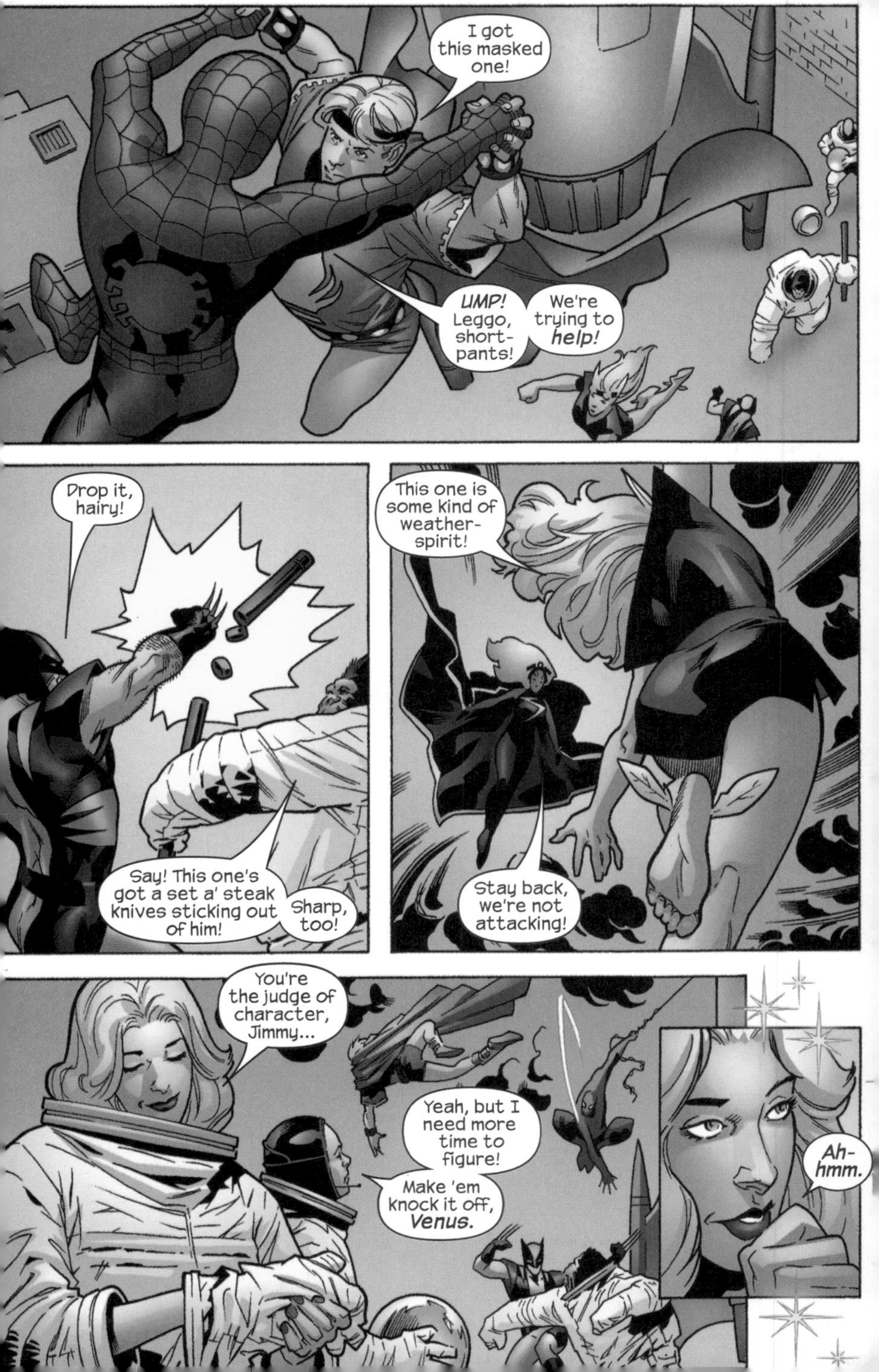

I got this masked one!
UMP! Leggo, short-pants!
We're trying to help!
Drop it, hairy!
Say! This one's got a set a' steak knives sticking out of him!
Sharp, too!
This one is some kind of weather-spirit!
Stay back, we're not attacking!
You're the judge of character, Jimmy...
Yeah, but I need more time to figure!
Make 'em knock it off, Venus.
Ah-hmm.

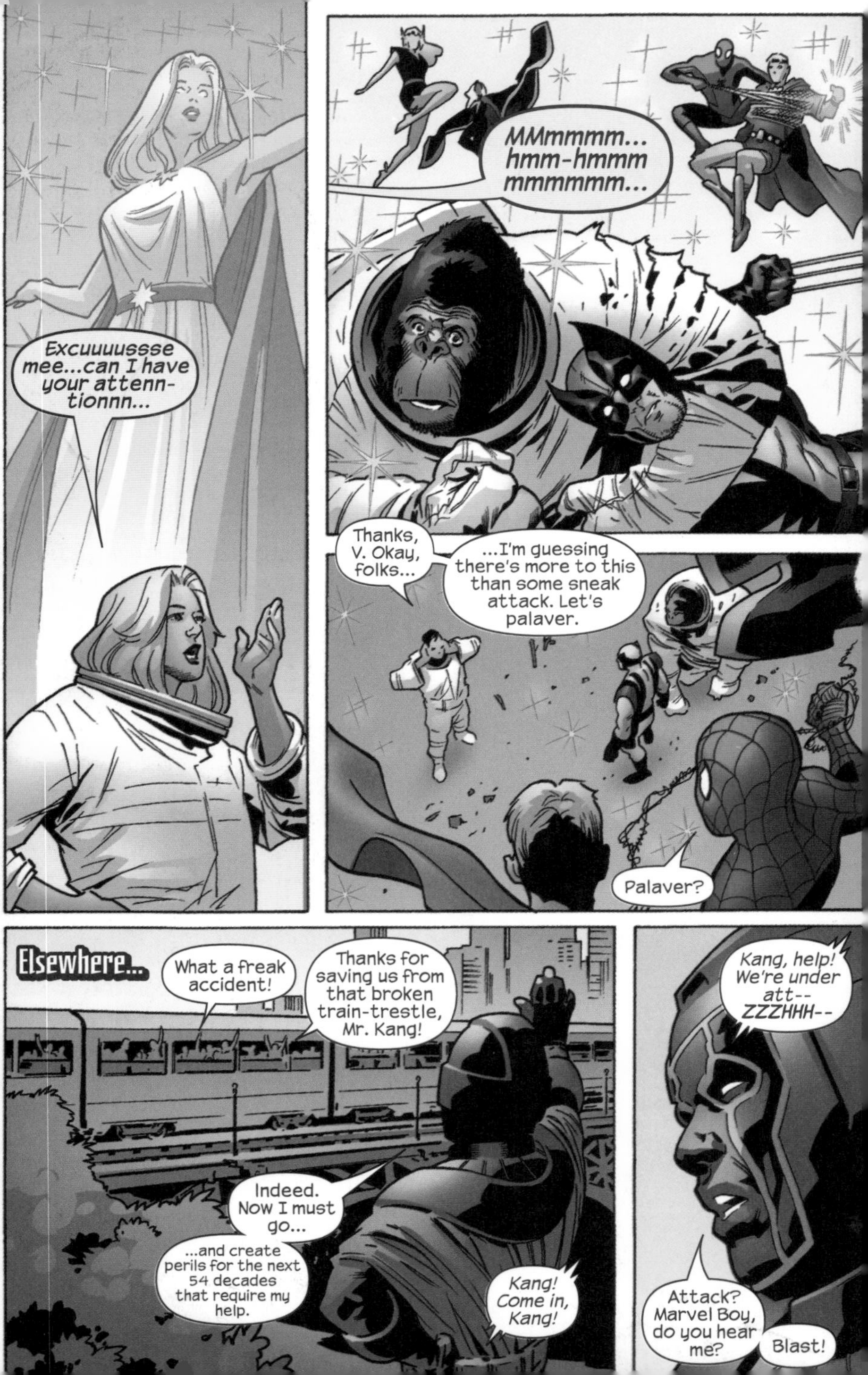
Excuuuussse mee...can I have your attenn-tionnn...
MMmmmm... hmm-hmmm mmmmmm...
Thanks, V. Okay, folks...
...I'm guessing there's more to this than some sneak attack. Let's palaver.
Palaver?
Elsewhere...
What a freak accident!
Thanks for saving us from that broken train-trestle, Mr. Kang!
Indeed. Now I must go...
...and create perils for the next 54 decades that require my help.
Kang! Come in, Kang!
Kang, help! We're under att-- ZZZHHH--
Attack? Marvel Boy, do you hear me?
Blast!

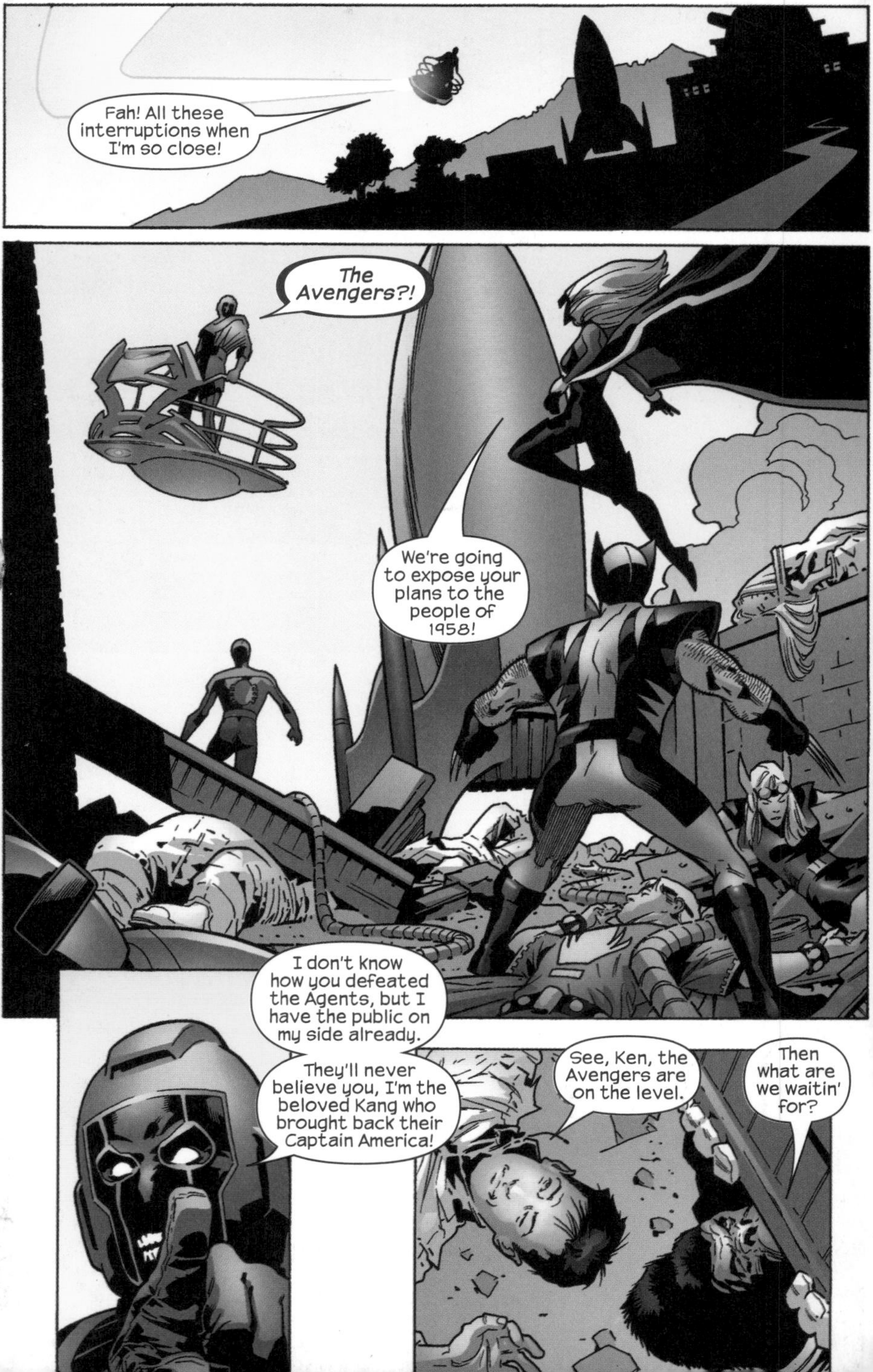
Fah! All these interruptions when I'm so close!
The Avengers?!
We're going to expose your plans to the people of 1958!
I don't know how you defeated the Agents, but I have the public on my side already.
They'll never believe you, I'm the beloved Kang who brought back their Captain America!
See, Ken, the Avengers are on the level.
Then what are we waitin' for?

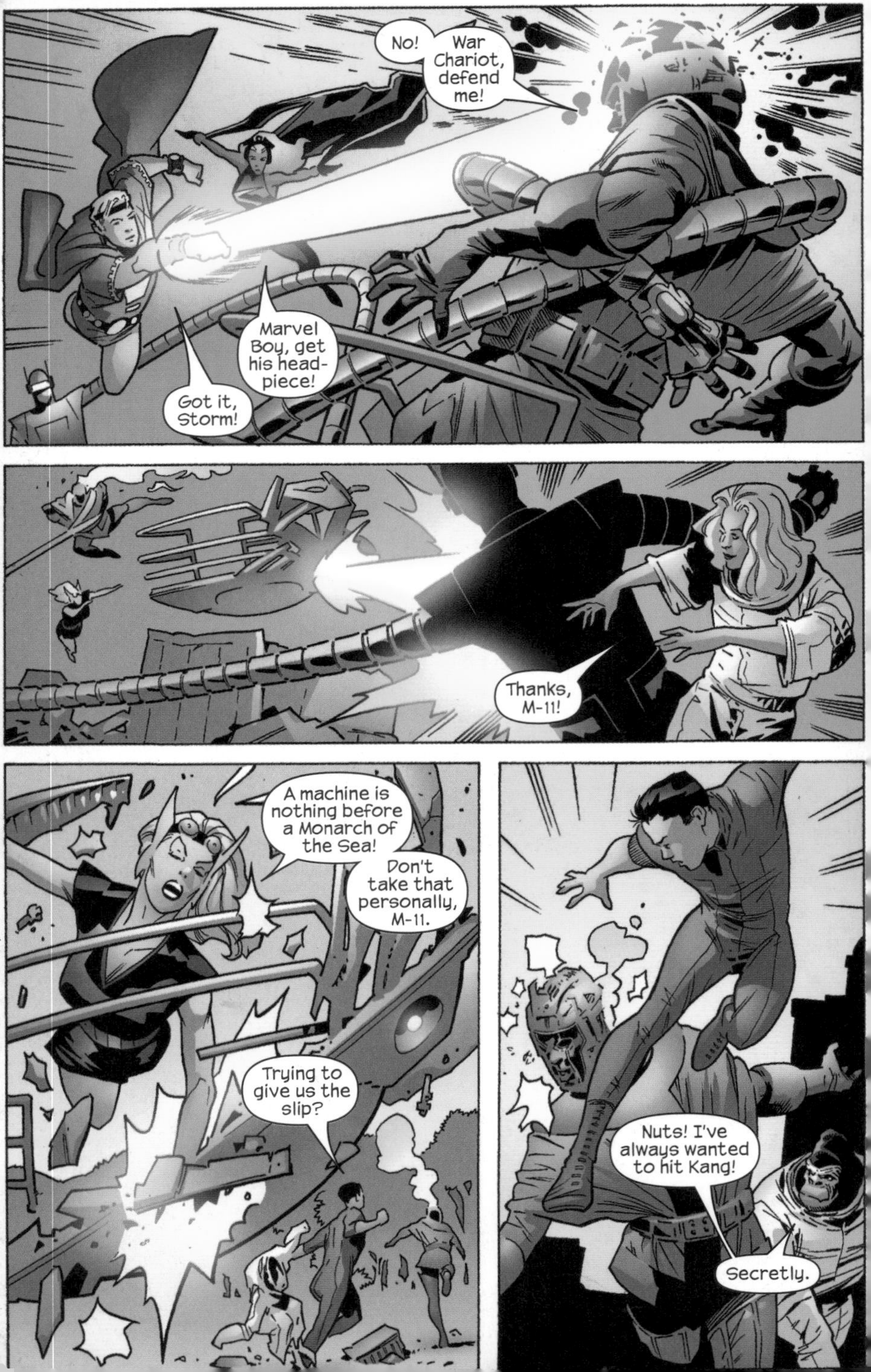

No!
War Chariot, defend me!
Marvel Boy, get his head-piece!
Got it, Storm!
Thanks, M-11!
A machine is nothing before a Monarch of the Sea!
Don't take that personally, M-11.
Trying to give us the slip?
Nuts! I've always wanted to hit Kang!
Secretly.

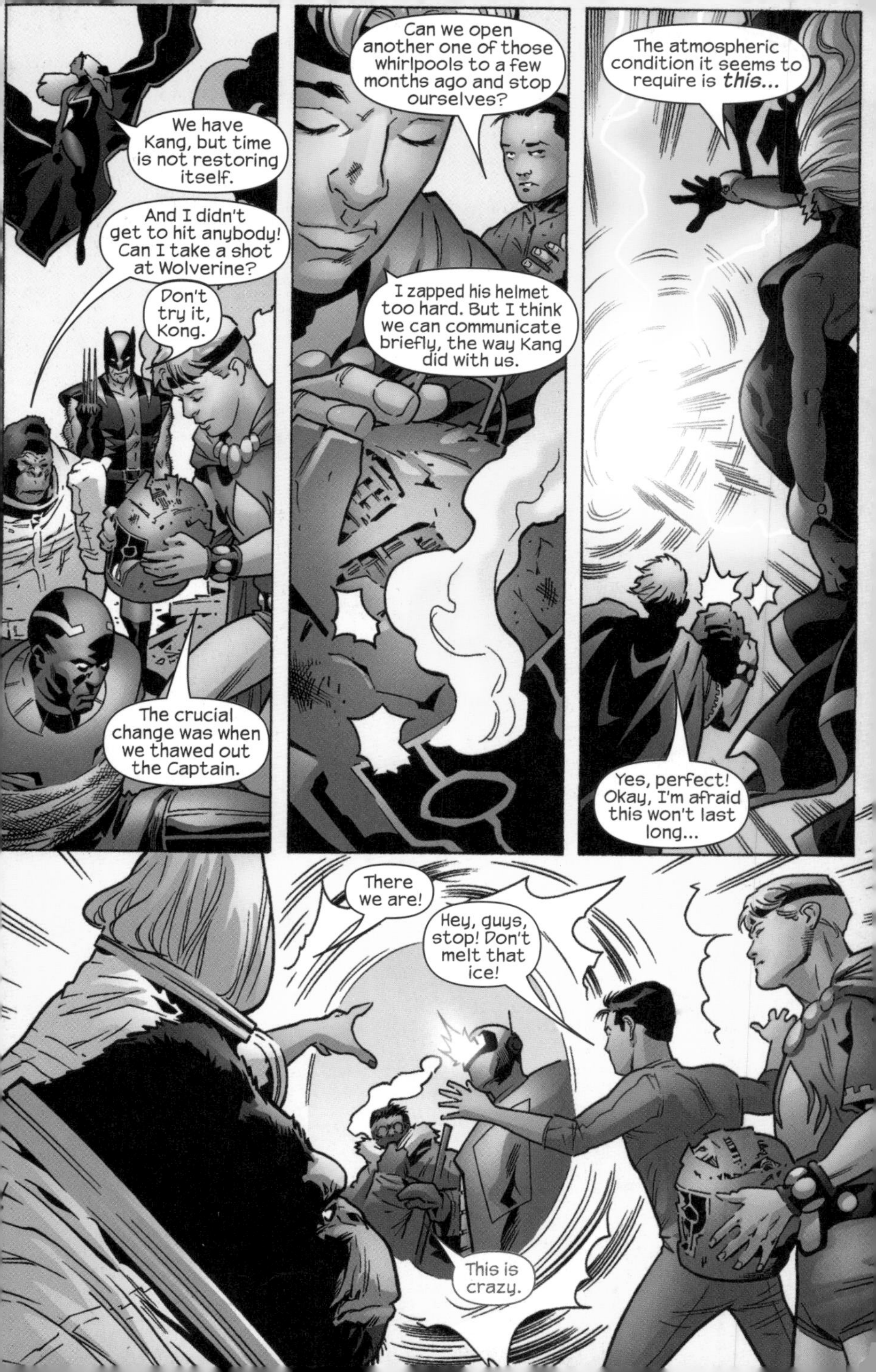
We have Kang, but time is not restoring itself.
And I didn't get to hit anybody! Can I take a shot at Wolverine?
Don't try it, Kong.
The crucial change was when we thawed out the Captain.
Can we open another one of those whirlpools to a few months ago and stop ourselves?
I zapped his helmet too hard. But I think we can communicate briefly, the way Kang did with us.
The atmospheric condition it seems to require is *this...*
Yes, perfect! Okay, I'm afraid this won't last long...
There we are!
Hey, guys, stop! Don't melt that ice!
This is crazy.

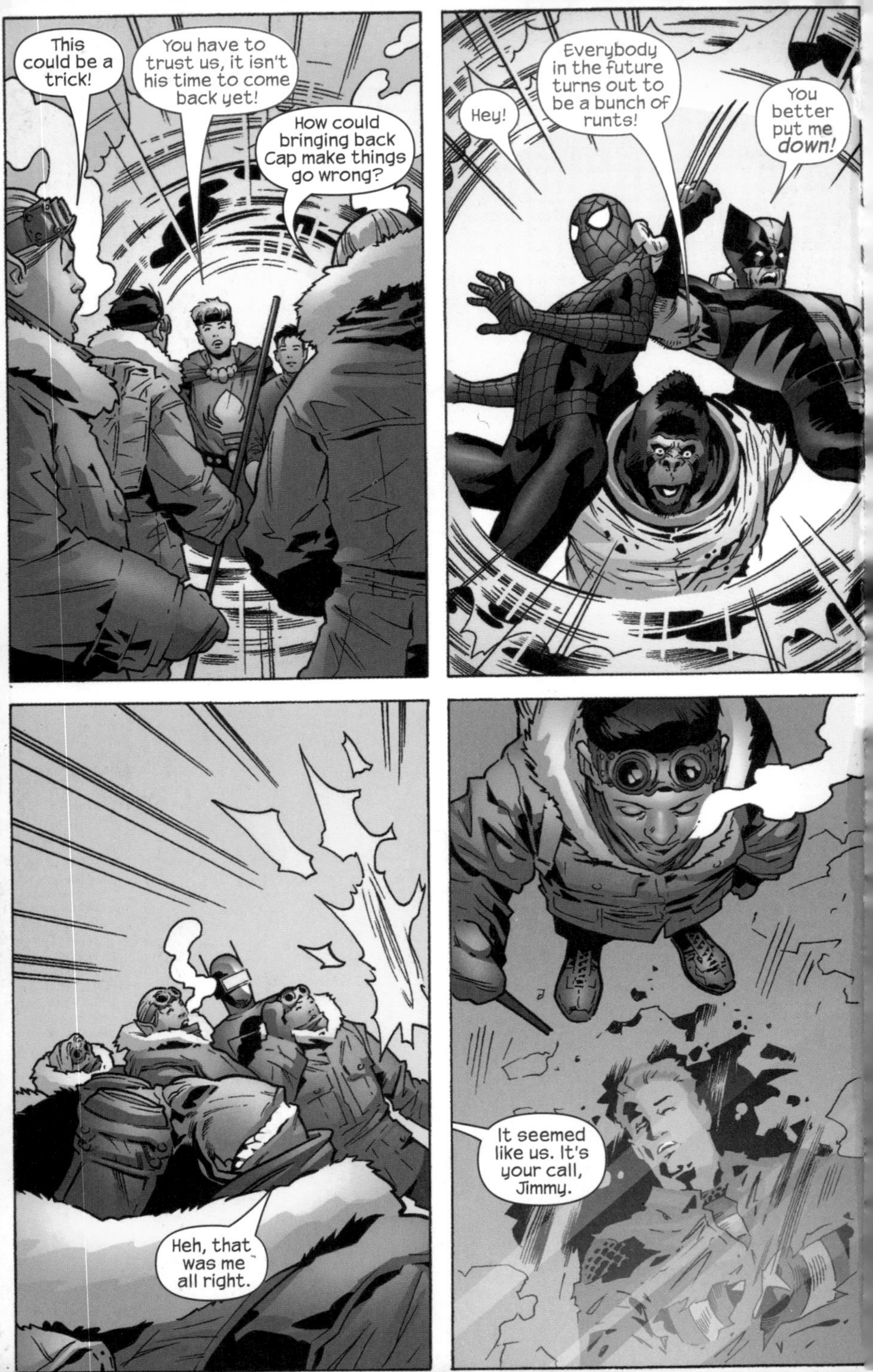
This could be a trick!
You have to trust us, it isn't his time to come back yet!
How could bringing back Cap make things go wrong?
Hey!
Everybody in the future turns out to be a bunch of runts!
You better put me *down!*
Heh, that was me all right.
It seemed like us. It's your call, Jimmy.

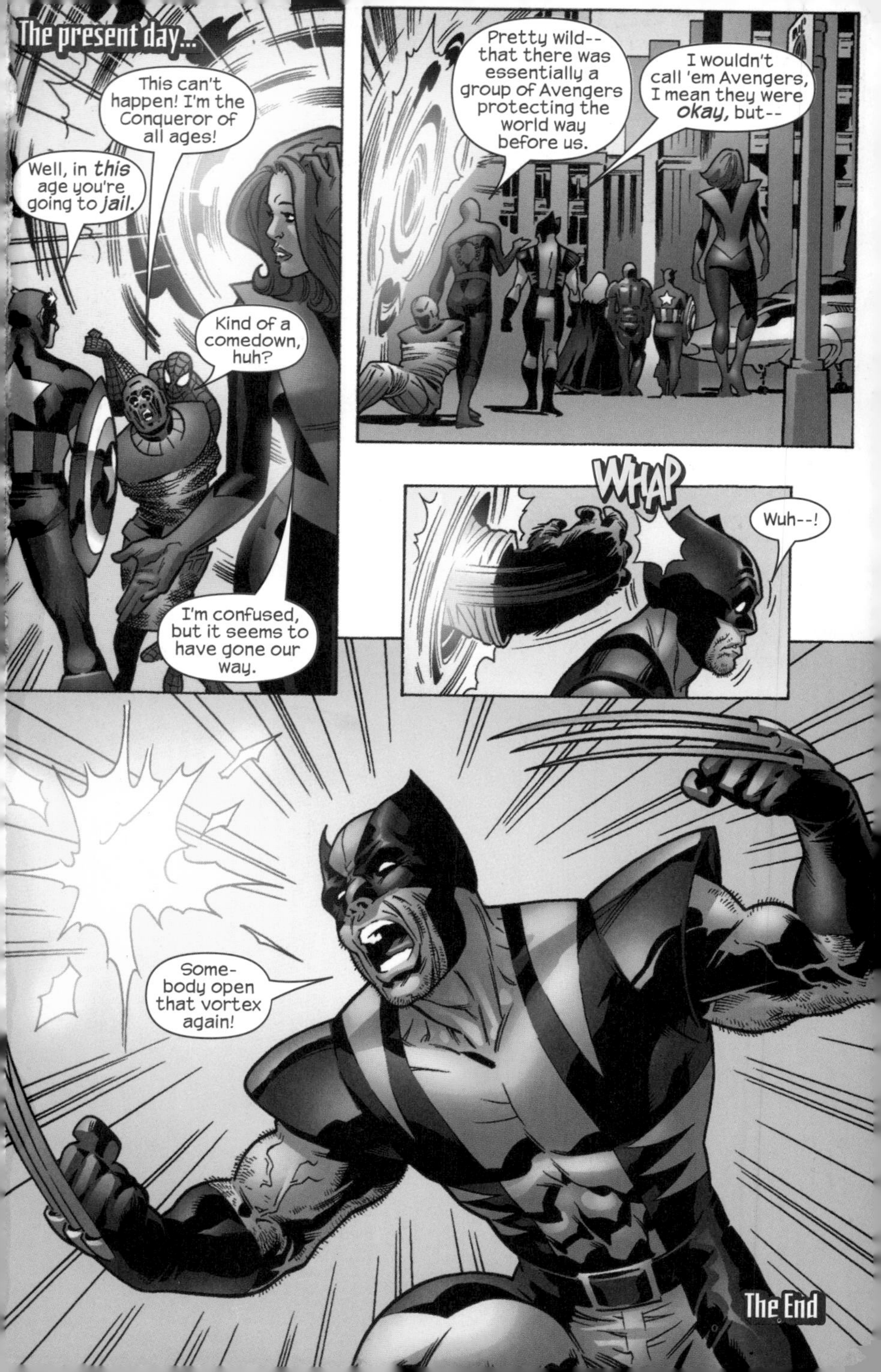
The present day...
This can't happen! I'm the Conqueror of all ages!
Well, in this age you're going to jail.
Kind of a comedown, huh?
I'm confused, but it seems to have gone our way.
Pretty wild-- that there was essentially a group of Avengers protecting the world way before us.
I wouldn't call 'em Avengers, I mean they were okay, but--
WHAP
Wuh--!
Some-body open that vortex again!
The End